Property of the Purdue Fort
Wayne LGBTQ Resource
Center

Donated by
James Velez

W9-DGH-740

THE DEVIL INSIDE

BY RANDY BOYD

WEST BEACH BOOKS

THE DEVIL INSIDE is a West Beach Book

West Beach Books
PO 68406
Indianapolis IN 46268
www.westbeachbooks.com

THE DEVIL INSIDE. Copyright © 2002 by Randy Boyd. All rights reserved. No part of this book may be used or reproduced in any manner whatsoever without written permission except in the case of brief quotations embodied in critical articles or reviews. For information, address West Beach Books, PO Box 68406, Indianapolis, IN 46268.

This novel is strictly and entirely a work of fiction. All references to real people, events, establishments, organizations or locales are purely and solely intended to give the novel a sense of reality and authenticity. All other names, characters, incidents, organizations or locales are strictly the product of the author's imagination, as are those fictionalized events and incidents that involve real persons and entities. Of the fictional characters, any resemblance to actual persons, living or dead, is entirely and purely coincidental.

Designed by Alan Bell

Publisher's Cataloging-in-Publication
(Provided by Quality Books, Inc.)

Boyd, Randy.
 The devil inside : the suspense thriller / by Randy
Boyd. - 1st ed.
 p. cm.
 LCCN 2002100826
 ISBN 1-931875-01-4
 1. African American gays—Fiction. 2. Hispanic
American gays—Fiction. 3. Asian American gays—
Fiction. 4. Santa Barbara (Calif.)—Fiction.
 I. Title

 PS3552.O8786D48 2002 813'.54
 QBI33-358

ISBN 1-931875-01-4
ISBN may vary on eBook editions

First Paperback Edition: April 2002

For Max

PROPERTY OF
THE Q CENTER
PURDUE FORT WAYNE
WALB STUDENT UNION
RM 215
260-481-6167

PROPERTY OF
THE O CENTER
PURDUE FORT WAYNE
WALB STUDENT UNION
RM 215
260-481-6167

BY RANDY BOYD

In the very near future ...

ONE

The morning fog was in full effect, the air gray and thick with moisture. Everything that made Santa Barbara the stuff of picture postcards and movie star hideaways was hidden from view. The mountains hugging the coastline barely peeked through the heavy mist, and only then in hazy, sporadic clumps. A few miles offshore, the Channel Islands were invisible to the naked eye. Only those previously aware of their existence would even know they were out there, lonely and uninhabited. The high-priced homes nestled on the Riviera—the name given to the hills overlooking the city—were also buried deep within the vapors. This morning the multi-million-dollar view was worth nothing.

The harbor was quiet; the only sounds that of docked boats creaking in a faint wind. The beaches were deserted save an occasional jogger and the rush of white waves upon the darkened sand. The surf wasn't calm, but it wasn't exactly violent either. In the coves and caves along the shore, the Pacific slapped against the rocks with mock anger, as if to say: you know I can hit you much harder than this.

The fog would disappear. It always did. Sooner or later, the lay-

ers would peel away, slowly revealing the sleepy coastal town at the southern tip of the central California coast.

By mid-morning, a few layers had already evaporated, replaced by a hint of sunlight hovering over the only part of town already stirring: a huge parking lot just this side of a large swatch of beach. The lot was cordoned off with temporary fences. Inside, Santa Barbara Gay Pride at the Beach was beginning to come alive.

"I refuse to believe it," said a woman who was taking tickets at the entrance to the daylong festival. She had long blonde hair and was topless except for a black leather bra. "Three hundred sixty-four days of the best weather Goddess has to offer and what do we get today? *Soup.*"

"Afternoon burn-off," Kordell said without looking up from his post at the adjacent gate. "You should know that by now."

"If it doesn't," warned the woman, "the Holy Rollers will claim the fog is some kind of sign, like that big quake the morning of LA Pride a while back."

Kordell chuckled and continued taking the little yellow admission tickets from the small line of festivalgoers. Signing up for morning shift had been a bit of a copout, he knew. It was, after all, the easiest shift of the day. But volunteering was volunteering, what the hell. Ironic that this part of him—the volunteering part—first surfaced during that pathetic cesspool otherwise known as his last relationship.

He glanced up, half-expecting to see Tommy and his "body by 'roids" heading toward the gate.

Deep breath. Fuggedaboutit.

No way would Toxic Tommy miss a weekend of partying and playing in LA. So many dicks to suck in WeHo, so little time.

"Okay, Kord," said another woman's manly voice. It was Sal in her sky-blue North Carolina Tar Heels basketball uniform. "It's getting crowded. Your turn to see and be seen." She ran a comb through her short black hair. "Just let me do a quick touchup on the 'do."

"The next crew isn't here yet," Kordell said, noticing that the lines were backing up for the first time all morning. "Give me a few."

"I think homegirl's creeping on me," said Sal. "I saw some kind of freaky movement behind the curtain in our booth. I was like, *damn, yo, 'sup wit' dat?*"

"*Homegirl* wouldn't know how to creep on you if she read a gay boy's guide to tricking." Kordell got a kick out of Sal using the lingo some of her teenage nieces and nephews learned at school. In truth, Salina Del Rio was from a middle-class Latino family and received her BA at Cal Poly, San Luis Obispo the same day as Kordell. They had been best friends since sophomore year, the year they both worked in financial aid and were the only two students in an office made up of middle-aged women. Midway through second semester, Kordell and Sal were having lunch at Burger King when Sal opened up about her newfound lust for one of their co-workers, Jenna, who was black, fifteen years older, and straight, as far as Sal knew. Sal was the first person to ever come out to Kordell. A half hour later, after working up enough nerve, Kordell returned the favor: Sal became the first person Kordell ever came out to. Over a decade later, their friendship was still going strong, like that bunny in the battery commercials. And after a few soap opera-like detours, including Jenna's divorce from her husband, Sal and Jenna were partners—in life and at the women's health clinic they ran together.

"Let's go find your black ass a new boyfriend," Sal said to Kordell. "You've been single—and cranky—too damned long."

"Like I really need another cock addict right now." Kordell waved through the gate two Asian men brandishing press passes.

"You do," Sal insisted. "Just one who's only addicted to *yours*, not whoever's posting messages any given night on cruisingforsex. com."

"Men are dogs," said Kordell. "And that's giving dogs a very bad rap."

"Fine," said Sal. "Then don't look for the exception. Or exceptions."

"I won't be anytime this millennium."

Sal turned to the line and set her sights on each man passing through the gate. "Listen up," she began, "who's single, anybody single? How about you? Excuse me; are you single? Live in the area? Got a job? Not a ho? Won't creep on your man? How many AOL screen names do you have?"

Some men laughed; others averted their eyes. As for Kordell, he simply made an effort to suppress his embarrassment and pretend that he had no idea who this crazy Latina was.

"*Baby!*" Arthur cried out. He was eyeing a brown-haired, college-aged boy who was out of earshot, licking latte foam off his upper lip. "Dibs," Arthur added, then started singing like the blue-eyed soul man that he was: "Gotta get you home with me tonight."

"Give it up, honey." Sal shot her empty ice cream cone into the trash like a basketball, then reached in her sock for a pack of smokes. "Homegirl's only into old money from the hills."

"Besides," Kordell shot a look of disdain toward Sal and her can-cer sticks, "I think I saw that kid with Richard what's-his-name the other night."

"That's why I'm outta this Pony Express stop as soon as I get a job in LA." Arthur tugged his shirt over his huge belly. "Everybody's already done everybody and everybody knows about it."

Kordell, Sal and Arthur had been walking around the festival grounds for over an hour, greeting their friends and watching as the crowd grew larger and the temperature climbed into the seventies. They had been to every Santa Barbara Gay Pride and always man-aged to find time to become a trio for at least part of the day. They were in line now for iced coffees from the booth run by the Mission, the gay/alternative coffeehouse that Arthur managed.

"As soon as I get my drink, okay?" Sal said, noticing Kordell's dirty looks and pre-empting his request to smoke elsewhere. "Just remember, tell my girlfriend I had a cigarette and I'll spill your secrets to your next boyfriend."

"Yeah," said Kordell, "it'll sound real pretty coming out of a hole in your throat."

Sal gave him the finger—a good-humored "fuck you"—and after they received their coffees, she joined two of her lesbian friends who were smoking near the Mission tent.

Kordell and Arthur decided to sit atop an empty picnic table in the cordoned-off area meant to represent an outdoor coffeehouse, and unwittingly, they found themselves facing the outside of the fes-

tival grounds and another cordoned-off section: that of the religious right, here to save the fags from eternal damnation. Yellow police tape separated the Holy Rollers from the rest of the gay world—fitting since *they* were the crime—and the all-male convocation held signs encouraging the homos and dykes to give up their wicked ways.

GIVE IN TO THE LORD, NOT SINFUL SEX, DRUGS AND DEEP HOUSE MUSIC.

FEEL ALONE AND EMPTY AFTER A NIGHT AT THE BATHS? GOD IS TELLING YOU SOMETHING.

"You ever stop to wonder" —Kordell crunched a piece of ice until it melted into his tongue— "if maybe they're right?"

"All the time," said Arthur. "Usually when I'm praying with rosary beads and watching a vintage tape of the *Pat Robertson Show.*"

"I'm serious."

Arthur did a double take. "You? Mr. Gay Pride? Mr. Head of the Santa Barbara Gay Business Alliance?"

"You're confusing me with the Kordell Christie of ten years ago, back when all of this was new and fresh. Remember how we got hyped up for Pride for weeks beforehand, if not months?"

"And I quote" —Arthur went into his imitation of Kordell— "I'll have to be near death on my sickbed for me to miss a Gay Pride."

Kordell shook his head nostalgically. "That was when it was amazing just to see several hundred thousand sweaty, chiseled torsos be-bopping down Santa Monica holding hands and being sexual in public."

"LA Pride is only a few weeks away, honey," said Arthur.

"As usual, you miss my point."

"Then get to it already."

"What do we have to be proud of?" asked Kordell. "Circuit parties? Bareback websites? X? K? Tina? A bunch of gay characters on network television?"

"You leave my party favors out of this—just kidding." Arthur sipped on his coffee, then said, "Gay life is not just what white muscle boys do between steroid shakes. What about our fierce lesbian celebrities having babies in the public eye? And guys fighting to stay in the military—although, besides the porno-type scenarios, God

knows why. What about all the political razzle-dazzle, queers hold-ing office and stuff? And—*duh?*—most important of all, we *are* help-ing more and more gay kids to grow up feeling okay about them-selves."

"The other night …" Kordell shifted his ass on the table.

"Yeah?"

"The other night I needed it."

"Needed what?" asked Arthur.

"What do you mean: *what?* What every man needs: to shoot his wad on something besides his stomach or the good sheets."

"Ooo, do tell."

"I went down to Ventura," said Kordell.

"How is the old Adult *Depot Your Sperm Right Here?*"

"I was seventeen the first time I went there," said Kordell. "I used to see all these old men and think that that was the sole defini-tion of fagdom. And I *vowed* on everything I believed in that I was-n't gonna be like them when I grew up, hanging out in bookstores, lurking around for strange, raw meat."

"Preferably of the young variety."

"Not me, not Kordell Christie. I went there for temporary relief. *I* was gonna meet Mr. Right and have a healthy, monogamous rela-tionship—no cum-stained bookstores in my future." He sighed. "Now I'm one of them. I'm an old man hanging out in bookstores, lurking around for strange, raw meat."

"Thirty-six is not old, Kordell—uh, I know: that's not your point."

"But—"

"You've got more going for you than any gay man I know: homeowner, business owner, courted by the bluebloods in this 'burb to run for city council, *had the gall* to turn 'em down. Dude, get real, you da man, man!"

Kordell took a shallow breath. "There's this old, *old* black guy that goes to the Adult Depot. He's got to be in his seventies, hunched-over back, walks with a limp, wrinkled, glasses. Now mind you, I haven't been there much, but every time I go, he's there. I mean, who's gonna let this guy suck them off?"

"Or anything, for that matter."

"But he's there," said Kordell, "prowling around, completely unashamed and indiscreet. I wanna think to myself: fate willing, if I live that long, I will *not* be like him at that age. But I know better now than to utter those kinds of proclamations again."

"He's just a pervert like you." Arthur tried for levity. "Not all gay men are sex-obsessed."

"Yeah, right. Gay men don't wanna get laid by a different piece of flesh every night. Gay men aren't like animals going through the jungle of life, looking to squirt their seed in as many holes, literally or figuratively, as they can. Gay men aren't *men*."

Just then, Sal came up, the smoke still emanating from her skin and clothes. "This latest Kordell Christie rant is brought to you by..."

"Toxic Tommy," said Arthur. "First Pride postmortem."

"It's not Tommy." Kordell stood up. "It's not anybody."

He walked ahead. Before long, his friends joined him and they made their way through the festival grounds. Sal and Arthur did their best to lighten the mood with silly jokes, juicy gossip and, of course, man-watching. It worked. Kordell even found himself smiling as they watched a game of beach volleyball at the festival's edge.

"I think we're going to get a lot of breeders again this year," Sal said as she observed a crowd milling near the main stage. "That surfer slash grunge slash hip hop slash acid rock group, Big Bobby's whatchamacallit from Ventura, gonna bring 'em in just like last year."

"I've never understood the nasally wigga music craze," Kordell said, still focused on the game.

"Whoa," said Arthur. "Please tell me *he* isn't a Big Bobby breeder fan."

"Where?" Kordell turned around.

Arthur nodded toward the middle of the festival grounds. "White tank, tan shorts, brown muscles. Thank God he's showing off even though it's cloudy."

Right away, Kordell knew that Arthur was referring to the broad-shouldered man with the ruddy complexion near the main stage. He was just this side of six feet, but those massive shoulders and his solid, athletic frame made him appear taller, as did his long

brown legs and meaty calves. His hair was jet-black and cut quite short, almost too short, which only served to highlight his pronounced cheekbones and smooth, square-jawed face.

"Hubba, hubba," came from Sal. "He's all that and *six* bags of chips."

"I picked the wrong lifetime to weigh 300 pounds," said Arthur. "I can't tell if he's Latino or Indian or both."

"Maybe he's a chub chaser," said Sal.

"Right," said Arthur. "And did I tell you: I'm going to father Jodie Foster's next baby."

Sal turned to Kordell, who had yet to chime in. "And what does the West African judge give the homeboy?"

Kordell said nothing. His face was solemn, his eyes fixated on the man.

"*Hello?*" said Sal. "We need a score from the West African judge before someone else can take the ice."

Still silence from Kordell.

"I think K is in a K-hole," said Arthur.

"I know him," said Kordell.

"Get out," said Arthur.

"Details," said Sal.

"Is he single?" asked Arthur. "I'll pay you all the money I owe you, plus interest, if you tell me he's a member of Girth and Mirth. Or that you've seen him in a chubby chaser chat room on AOL."

"Think I've seen him before, too," said Sal. "Maybe at the bar or the Mission."

"Doubt it," said Kordell, not taking his eyes off the man.

"I'd remember a bod and face like that," said Sal. "*Mijo,* you think just cause I'm a lez—"

"So did you guys go out," asked Arthur. "Is he single? Is he into white meat?"

"He's straight," Kordell said flatly.

"Get out," cried Arthur. "In that tight tank top in this overcast weather? *Here?*"

"I said he's straight."

"The concert's not for a couple of hours," said Sal. "He's family."

"He's straight, dammit, let it go!" Kordell saw that his friends were taken aback by his harsh tone. He shrugged awkwardly, trying but failing to retract his missive. "He's a ladies' man. Must be here for the band."

Unable to force an apology out, he walked away, hoping his friends would forget his outburst and the broad shouldered man with the ruddy complexion near the main stage. Sal and Arthur stayed behind and stood speechless, having never seen this kind of reaction to *any* man from their friend of over a dozen years.

Santa Barbara had one gay nightclub, and tonight, Liquid was packed beyond capacity. The bodies around the bar were ten deep. The balcony upstairs, already a fire marshal's nightmare, looked ready to collapse from the weight of way too many people. A repetitive house song blasted over the speakers, making conversation nearly impossible. Sal and Jenna were huddled together in a corner table near the exit, sipping margaritas but not looking too happy to be here. Kordell and Arthur were on the dance floor with three more male friends, forming their own private dance circle as best they could.

Kordell's mood had lightened since the afternoon. In fact, he had almost convinced himself that everything was all right in his world, that today's surprise festival guest didn't have to mean anything at all. Don't jump to conclusions, he told himself. You never know what happens to people.

He danced on, determined to excavate the high he'd known from Prides past. Gay life in Santa Barbara had come a long way since he moved here five years ago. Gay Pride itself was getting bigger and better. At thirty-six, Kordell had also come a long way. His company was in the black and he was rid of Toxic Tommy. So what if men acted like animals and relationships didn't last. So what if he couldn't lose the pesky ten pounds he'd put on the last couple of years, pounds that made him self-conscious whenever he was deep inside the superficial gay world of perfect gym bodies ready for underwear ads or porno box covers. Tonight, for better or worse, he was going to act as if he had all kinds of pride—black pride, gay pride, survival pride—and then, just maybe, he'd actually feel it.

He lifted his arms over his head and let out a "wohoo!" His friends responded with their own rally cries, and they danced on as song after song merged into one long ritual of sound and movement.

Then Kordell saw him again. *Him.* From the festival. From Oxnard, Kordell's hometown thirty-five miles to the south. He was at the opposite end of the long corridor that made up the club. He had on the same white tank top and was taking a swig of a bottle of beer. Was he alone? It was impossible to tell with the sea of bodies surrounding him. Kordell stood motionless amidst the gyrating bodies on the dance floor. Without realizing it, his feet began moving forward.

It took a full ten minutes to reach his destination. When he did, the man was facing away from Kordell. The white tank top made his already dark skin seem even more reddish-brown. Arthur had been right to question whether the man was Latino or Native American. He was both, though mostly Latino.

Will he recognize me?

Kordell uttered the man's name in a normal voice and it was quickly lost in the music. He tried again. No luck. He was going to have to shout a lot louder.

"*Mario!*"

It worked. Mario did a 180. Kordell held his breath. There was alarm on Mario's face, then confusion, then dubiousness.

"Kordell?" came from Mario. "Kordell Christ? Christie?"

"Right," Kordell said. It came out sounding like: *guilty.*

"Whoa." Mario stumbled backward. "Homie! What's up?"

His tone was friendly; Kordell began breathing again.

"How you doing, Mario?"

Mario hesitated, as if the question momentarily confused him.

"Cool," he said, eventually remembering to answer rhetorically.

"You all right?" asked Kordell.

"Huh? Oh, sure." He held up his bottle of beer. "First one tonight—all day, matter of fact. A dude bought it for me. Wassup with you? It's been, like, fifteen, twenty years."

"At least," Kordell said and they both laughed. "How you doing? What you doing up here?"

"Huh?" asked Mario.

"How you doing? What you doing up here?"

"Can't hear you."

Kordell came to within an inch of Mario's ear.

"What are you doing here?"

Mario paused, searching for an answer. "Pretty cool place, huh?" he said, coming so close, his tongue grazed the inside of Kordell's ear.

"It'll do." Kordell recoiled. There was an awkward pause, then Kordell said: "Sorry about your brother."

"He didn't do it," Mario said instantly, then pointed to his chest with his thumb. "I know."

Kordell nodded out of sympathy. His sister had said that Mario's twin brother Javier had recently been arrested for trying to meet a minor over the Internet.

"I'm serious," Mario said of his brother. "He's innocent. Twin instinct. We're working on the bail. He'll get out in … in … like … real soon anyway." Mario's mind ventured somewhere else for a moment, his eyes staring into a black hole of thought. Then he added: "Javy. My brother. Javy's my brother. My twin."

"I know," said Kordell, but Mario didn't seem to hear or care.

Kordell was bewildered by this version of the man standing before him. Mario Cervantes was never this scattered growing up. True, they were all young and stupid back then, but Super Mario, as they had called him, was a kid truly worthy of the title "super." He aced the books and was a graceful stud on the athletic field. And with the girls. His family was proud of him. His teachers and coaches were proud of him. The whole neighborhood knew and liked Super Mario.

He was five years younger than Kordell, and when Kordell was around twelve, Mario and Javy used to come over to Kordell's house after school because both Cervantes parents worked late. Kordell's older sister Mimi got paid to watch them until six o'clock, but she was usually in her bedroom with Tall Greg Warren, her basketball-playing boyfriend. Even after Kordell went off to college in San Luis, he often heard about Mario's newsworthy exploits on the Oxnard High sports teams: all-state running back, pitcher of three no-hitters,

even a season on the track team that was conference champs. Kordell had also heard that Mario had attended a JC for a while and played sports there. Of course, much of this was secondhand information. While Kordell's parents still lived in the house of his childhood, the Cervantes family moved out of the old neighborhood long ago. And abruptly, if Kordell remembered correctly.

"So, man, you gay?" Mario shouted in his face.

"What?" asked Kordell, even though he'd heard the question. "Oh, well, um, yes."

Mario raised his beer bottle as if to salute Kordell, then took a swig. Was it a gesture of solidarity? Or was he saluting Kordell's honesty? Or giving Kordell his approval? Kordell smiled, but just as quickly, the smile evaporated. He wanted to ask Mario if he was gay, but didn't have the guts.

Okay, so maybe he is gay. Or bi. Or straight but here with gay friends. Gay-friendly. Maybe he's just gay-friendly.

"What's wrong, man?" asked Mario.

"What?"

Mario's lips went for Kordell's ear again, lightly brushing against them as he repeated: "Wrong. Something up with you?"

"Nothing," Kordell said a little too quickly. They stood for a moment in silence. Mario took another swig of his beer, then began moving his head to the music. Kordell stood there, not knowing what to do next, until he finally he shouted in Mario's ear: "When did you know?"

Even as he said it, Kordell himself wasn't sure what he was asking. When did you know about me? When did you know you were gay? Are you gay? Why are you gay? What happened to all those little Latinas you used to impress with your skateboard tricks?

"Say what?" asked Mario.

"I said when did you know?"

"Know what?"

"You know. *Know.*"

"Man, it's crazy trying to have a conversation in here," Mario said, quelling the Q&A. Kordell was deflated until Mario added: "Wanna get outta here?"

Kordell was floored. Happy, but floored.

Seconds later they were walking down State Street, the busy thoroughfare filled with bars and clubs for the straight crowd. It was Saturday night. Traffic on the two-lane road was at a standstill and the sidewalks were equally jammed with packs of young people in search of other packs of young people. Kordell and Mario walked in a vacuum, paying little attention to the bodies passing them. Mario was walking swiftly, to where Kordell had no idea.

"I was saying in there," Kordell went on, "when did you know?"

"When did I know?" Mario repeated, as if dumbfounded.

"Yeah," Kordell insisted.

"When did I know what?" asked Mario.

Kordell scoffed, stalled, then balked. "That there was a bar up here called Liquid? And that you would come to it?"

Mario remained mute for half a block. "I don't know," he said eventually, causing Kordell to stop in his tracks and regard his childhood friend, who simply kept walking.

A black and white mutt sniffed its way around an overflowing trash can lodged in the sand. Mario, who had been throwing rocks into the ocean, suddenly took aim at the little dog and hurled a small piece of sea shale toward it.

"Go back to where you came from," Mario said angrily. The rock hit the trash can and scared the pooch, causing it to scamper away in search of a friendlier patch of sand.

It wasn't hurting anyone, Kordell wanted to say, but checked it. He didn't understand Mario's mood or why they were suddenly at the beach.

While walking farther down State Street, they had talked about the old neighborhood, their old neighbors—everything but where they were heading. Kordell had wanted to ask but never got around to it. They had ended up on a small sliver of beach just below a cliff. They both sat on a large boulder, Kordell staring at the ocean and Mario hurling rocks into the night.

"I never liked dogs." Mario threw another missile at the mutt, who had turned back and was eyeing them. The rock fell short, but

that was enough for the dog, who gave up and disappeared down the beach. "Remember that German Shepherd who chewed up my brother's leg when I was six? Fucking dogs."

"But you sure liked the ladies back then," said Kordell.

"What?" Mario picked up another rock. "Oh ... humph." His answer was somewhere between cocky and cynical.

"So you came up here all alone today?"

"Yeah ... well, no. I was with ... someone. But he left." Mario cocked his arm, ready to heave the rock. "I ditched him."

"Which was it?"

"Huh?"

"He left you or you ditched him?"

Mario looked at Kordell with bewilderment, then dropped the rock.

"I wish I knew," he said, searching the ground for an answer.

Kordell paused, trying but failing to process Mario's peculiar answers. "You seeing anyone?"

"I was. Split up with her a while ago."

Her. "Her?"

Confusion swept over Mario's face, his eyes and brows twitching, his full lips quivering. Kordell didn't know what to say, so he tried diverting the spotlight:

"I think I could be bi in the right circumstance. Like with my lesbo friend Sal. She wanted me to father a kid for her, but I was too chicken. She ended up getting another guy, but now, with all the crap in gay culture, sometimes I think it wouldn't be so bad being a straight family man." Kordell rambled on, more to the sea than to Mario. When he finally shut up long enough for Mario to get a word in, there was only silence. Kordell glanced Mario's way and realized that Mario was walking on the beach. Did he realize the waves were washing over his sneakers? Kordell hurried to catch up with him and said: "You want me to leave you alone or something?"

"Frustrated, man. Ain't you ever been frustrated?" Mario kept walking, jaw clenched, eyes teary, rage simmering. "Where you just wanna ... hit something or somebody ... or do something?"

"You sure you're not *on* something?" Kordell asked, surprised by his own impatience.

"Hell, no. I haven't done that shit since college." Mario stopped. His voice was reflective, as if he were reassuring himself as much as Kordell. "Even then I never did the hard stuff. That's been fucking years." He started walking again, punching the palm of his left hand with his fist. "I wanna hit some *thing.*"

"Then you've come to the right man." Kordell reached out to grab Mario, but stopped short of touching him. *Can't touch this.*

Mario halted, shrugged and laughed. Then he stuffed his hands in his pockets. "What, you want me to hit you?" he asked sheepishly, almost sounding like a New Yorker. "You get off on that?"

"As if," Kordell scoffed. "No. I'm talking about my business, the place that I own."

"Oh." Mario let out a small, confused laugh, looked away to the darkened sea, then back to Kordell, as unsure and unsteady as he'd been all night.

An 80 miles-per-hour fastball shot out of the pitching machine like a cannon, flying past Mario before he had a chance to react.

"Yo!" he shouted, turning back to Kordell, who was on the other side of the batter's cage. "This shit is fast—whoa—" he shouted again as another baseball flew past his big beefy ass and hit the backstop.

Kordell laughed. "We can switch to one of the softball cages if you like."

"Hell, no," Mario said. Another ball sped past him. "Shit." He turned toward the pitching machine. "I can do this. You saw me play for the Yellowjackets." He swung at the next pitch, missing it. "Or maybe you didn't cause you were older." Another swing and a miss. "But just—" He hit the next pitch, getting a good cut on the ball and sending it flying into the protective net. "Fuckin' A!" he shouted. "Homer for Oxnard High School!"

Kordell watched with relief and delight as Mario hit the next twenty balls all over the batting cage, following up each swat with some baseball-announcer proclamation, like: "The boy is going pro, ladies and gentleman, straight to the Dodgers' starting lineup!"

It didn't take long for Kordell to add his own commentary—ego-boosting remarks that Mario seemed to relish. Eventually, Kordell took a turn, and because he owned the place and used the cages often, he swatted the ball with the ease of Sammy Sosa at batting practice. Mario was impressed, so much so that they began a friendly competition to see who could get the best cuts on the ball, each of them razzing the other when he didn't measure up. They hit balls for over an hour, thinking of nothing and no one else. They were two guys having fun doing "guy stuff," the stuff of Kordell's dreams.

"Talk about the perfect gig," said Mario when they finally took a break. They were both breathing heavily and covered in a thin layer of sweat. "You couldn't own a better, more fun joint."

"You haven't seen the inside yet," Kordell said, indicating the white adobe building behind them.

Inside Batter Up, they turned into two grown-up kids who were allowed to have their run of the arcade for the night. They played air hockey till their knuckles were sore. They shot baskets in the carnival-style hoop game. They took turns at Boxorama, the electronic punching bag, and played foosball, ping pong and the latest video games. Neither cared who won, but neither wanted to be the one who lost. Their competitive banter made them laugh till their bellies ached. The case of beer from the private fridge in Kordell's office made them silly. They'd never done anything together while growing up—Mario was too young to run with Kordell's crowd and vice versa—but now, in their thirties, their five-year age difference meant squat.

They even engaged in a little physical banter, especially when there was a spark of controversy concerning whatever game they were playing. Much to Kordell's surprise, Mario even leaned on him a couple of times while they played video games. But as much as Kordell treasured that kind of physical male bonding—indeed, craved it—he felt uneasy touching and being touched by Mario, so much so that he would make a point of diplomatically untangling himself from the intimacy.

He told himself it was because he didn't know Mario's story and

didn't want to make him uncomfortable. But even as Kordell came up with these muted justifications, he knew they were bald-faced lies. Still, he tried not to put himself on trial and made a concentrated effort to enjoy the moment, the night, the way he was getting along so well with this childhood friend who had appeared out of the blue. Indeed, it was the best time he'd had with another guy since ... since ... he couldn't even remember the last time he'd had so much fun.

He also noticed something about Mario that he hadn't remembered from back in the day. Mario was masculine to be sure, but there was a side to him that Kordell didn't see in a lot of straight guys. It only came out when Mario was joking around or doing his silly little victory dance (hands in the air, "raising the roof," knees clapping like a seal). Those brief glimpses of another side of Mario caught Kordell off-guard, affording him little chance to process them. But certain words did linger in Kordell's mind. Goofy. Soft. Sensitive. Mario could be all three, and far from being a turn-off, it made him all the more human. And adorable. And a more *complete* man. A man who, now that they were relaxing and having fun, seemed light years away from the edgy, confused weirdo of a few hours ago.

Kordell even thought about something Sal had said much earlier in the day, a phrase she had used after Kordell had ranted about how "all men are dogs and that was giving dogs a very bad rap." Sal had used the word "exception," as in there has to be an exception to every rule.

Fool's gold, Kordell thought of Sal's optimism as he watched Mario fire the air hockey puck his way. But if there were exceptions in life, what an unparalleled exception Mario would be. And if Mario were the exception to all the rules that govern men's actions, maybe, just maybe, they could also overcome the gigantic obstacle from the past that lay ahead, smack dab in the middle of the road.

Kordell teetered on the edge of a cliff. Graceful hawks soared overhead, six or eight of them in a circle, their wings expanded but not flapping. Their eyes were humongous and he could make out their pupils quite clearly. They were cartoon-like—the eyes—bulging, oversized, exaggerated.

Or were they vultures?

He woke abruptly, his line of sight even with his old-fashioned roll top desk, which was cluttered with a mountain of paperwork and several boxes of Girl Scout cookies. He was on his brown leather couch in his office at Batter Up. He must have passed out in the wee hours of the morning, after Mario had beaten him six times in a row at air hockey.

Mario.

If Kordell had slept on the lone couch, where had Mario slept? Did he even stay? How drunk did they get?

Kordell stood—his joints more stiff than anticipated—and staggered to the doorframe to collect himself. He tried to recall how the night had ended but failed. He thought to call Mario's name but didn't.

Outside his office was a long narrow hallway, his buffer from all the bleeps, buzzes and sirens when he needed to do office work. He made his way down the corridor, trying to create moisture in his dry contact lenses by blinking. From the arcade, a child's voice cried out: "Level twelve, I know this!"

Fredito. Sal's boy. Eight years old. He didn't have a key to the place, but as much as he was at Batter Up, he may as well have been co-owner. Kordell must have not bothered to lock up last night; he and Mario's night of male bonding had been much too fun to worry about adult tasks like security. He imagined Fredito planted in front of Monkey Warriors, his favorite video game. The kid must have been racking up all kinds of points, too; the giant mutant apes were howling in anger over their fallen comrades.

"Come on, suckers," Fredito shouted. "Come to *papi* so he can destroy you!"

"You go, boy," said another voice: Mario's. Kordell smiled and wondered if they knew one another, then chided himself for such a ridiculous notion. Just because they're both Latinos. He paused to rub his eyes but checked himself, knowing that would cause more havoc with his contacts. He thought about retreating to his office for some wetting solution, but frankly, he was too giddy at the prospect of seeing Mario playing video games with Fredito.

"You gotta put your whole body into it," Mario was saying now.

Kordell reached the arcade and expected to see Mario standing next to Fredito. Instead, he only saw Mario's broad brown shoulders silhouetted in front of the Monkey Warriors screen. His legs were spread wider than what seemed normal or comfortable. His baggy tan shorts were down to his ankles, revealing white briefs that covered his ass and were in stark contrast to his dark brown skin.

"I can do it myself," said Fredito. He was on the other side of Mario, in front of the console. Kordell couldn't see Mario's arms. Were they around the boy? The boy's waist? No, not the waist ... the ... his ...

He's molesting him, Kordell's mind told him before he had a chance to edit.

He tried to rewind his thoughts and rewrite the scene. In a flash, he looked around the room for Sal. Mario wouldn't do anything with Sal there.

Clear this up right away, feel like a fool for thinking such a thing.

But Sal wasn't there. No one else was there.

Oh my God, what is Mario doing? What have I done?

You know what he's doing. You know what you've done.

Monkey Warriors was mute now, so were Mario and Fredito. They were staring at Kordell, all three of them frozen, waiting for a reaction, a spoken word, anything—

They heard an older Latina's voice as she came through the front door, speaking in broken English: "It's okay? Here okay?"

It was Carlota, Sal's mother, Fredito's grandmother. Kordell had met her the last time she had been visiting from El Salvador. Sal had had to do a lot of translating. Mama Carlo was in her seventies and spoke *poquito* English.

She crossed the threshold of Batter Up. The scene—Mario's shorts around his ankles, his hulking arms enveloping her grandbaby—quickly registered in her face. If she could have died right then and there, she would have. The pain in her eyes was that salient. But other instincts took over. She dropped the big black purse she was carrying and screamed.

"¡Déja de abusarlo! Déja de abusarlo!"

She hurried over to her grandson and dragged him away from
Mario. The boy's game tokens fell from his hands, hitting the floor
like bouncing bullets. Fredito began crying and speaking to her in
what little Spanish he knew. Mario stood there stunned, repeating
something that was lost in the commotion.

"Mama Carlo!" Kordell shouted. *"Por favor,* please wait!" He
knew less Spanish than Fredito. He raced toward her, wanting to stop
her before she got carried away. He had to sort this out before ...
before what?

Fredito resisted his grandmother's attempt to drag him to the
door, but she was winning, even though they were about the same
size. Still screaming anguished words in Spanish, she reached the
door just as Kordell reached her.

"Grandma, *por favor.* It's me, Kordell. Sal's best—"

She slapped at his chest and face with her free hand, forcing
Kordell to cover himself to deflect the blows.

"¿Que pasa, que pasa?" said a stocky, light-skinned Latino who
ran up from the parking lot. Kordell didn't recognize him, but Mama
Carlo did.

"¡Fredito estaba siendo abusado!" She pointed toward Kordell
and Mario, then grabbed her chest. A strained muscle? A broken
heart? A heart attack? The man grabbed Kordell by his shirt and was
about the beat the shit out of him or kill him or both, but Mama
Carlo wailed: *"¡El carro, el carro!"*

Kordell knew *el carro* meant car. The man spit out fiery words
in Spanish, pointed to the ground below, then shook his fist violently in Kordell's face, apparently ordering Kordell to stay put. Then he
wrapped both Mama Carlo and Fredito in his big hairy arms and literally carried them to an old white Cadillac.

Fucking Mario, why? Why? Kordell braced himself against the
door. *Mario, how could you? How could I?*

You deserve it, nigger.

Kordell swung around. The arcade was empty. He panned the
room, eyes darting every which way. Toward the air hockey tables.
Toward the basketball goals. Toward the little pizza café.

Mario was gone.

The restroom? *Why?*

The back door? *Oh, God.*

Kordell swung back around to the parking lot. Fredito was in the front seat crying "*¡Tío Guero!*" and trying to open the passenger door while Mama Carlo was in the back seat moving about hysterically. Kordell knew enough Spanish to know that *tío* meant uncle. The uncle's butt was sticking out of the backseat. He was trying to calm Mama Carlo, no doubt so he could return to the arcade to try, convict and execute Kordell. And Mario.

No time to think. Nothing else to do. He had to get to Mario. Mario couldn't be a molester. This was impossible. Had to be impossible.

Oh, God, please don't let this be possible.

Uncle Guero closed the back door of the Cadillac and was now struggling to keep a wailing Fredito in the front seat.

No other choice. At least no other sane choice. Kordell bolted through the arcade, down the narrow hallway to his office and out the back door of Batter Up. The same back door through which Mario had escaped only moments ago.

TWO

Kordell crept around the backside of a huge white service truck, straining to get a view of the rancher's market on the other side. Short, bronzed Latinos stood on top of a loading dock, handing over bags of oranges, strawberries and fresh vegetables to white housewives and lanky health-conscious men who forked over cash in return. Typical morning at the business adjacent to Batter Up. No frantic accusers or hysterical lynch mob, just shoppers who had no idea that, right next door, a tornado had just landed.

Where the hell was Mario?

In the opposite direction: the train tracks, leading south and outta town. What a damned good idea right about now. Kordell hurried toward them, staggering from the chain of events more than the uneven, woodsy terrain. Now that he had a sec, was there any doubt Mario must have headed this way? The area was secluded except for the train that came through several times a day, rumbling through a forest of tall oak trees.

Kordell walked parallel to the tracks. Still no sign of Mario. He thought about calling out Mario's name but didn't, couldn't, was still

fucking speechless from what had happened. Or might have happened.

In the distance he saw a sequoia-like figure of a man wobbling away from a thicket on the other side of the tracks. It was Mario. Kordell was faced with a dilemma: call out his name or race to him without a word. He chose stealth and doubled his speed, following Mario, who was southbound. In his mind, he called Mario's name several times, shouts of desperation echoing in his head. Was he saying it aloud to himself?

Another sound coming through the trees overtook his senses. A more familiar sound. An everyday sound. Louder and louder. The train. It was coming from the north. If Mario was as dazed and confused as he seemed last night, he might not realize that he was stagger-walking inches away from the train tracks. If he had just scarred little Fredito for life, he might not care.

"Mario!" Kordell yelled. "Mario, get away from the track! A train!"

No reaction from Mario, who was stumbling, swaying.

"Mario!" Kordell yelled, but a warning horn roared, drowning out all other sound. The train sped toward Kordell, then past him, hurling by a few feet away. Up ahead, on the other side of the track, Mario kept walking right next to the rails, as if preparing to die. "Mario, forgive me!" Kordell's words were one long cry in vain. The cars of the train were all he could see now, whizzing by with bone-crushing speed. The steel bullet reached the point where Mario had been standing and kept on going, as if nothing or no one could stop it. Kordell sprinted alongside the churning locomotive, which outran him and kept on going with no intention of halting. He came to a stop where he estimated Mario had been walking and waited for the train to pass completely and reveal a bloody corpse.

The last cars flew by. The train was gone just as quickly as it had came. On the other side of the track, Mario's body lay motionless in the dirt. In one piece. No blood. No scattered body parts. No severed head.

"Mario, are you okay?" Kordell hurried to him and knelt down, afraid to touch him. "Are you hurt? Can you hear?"

Mario was out cold. Or dead. Kordell extended his hand. Mario's cheek was feverishly hot.

"Let go of me!" Mario's body buckled upward. His eyes were shut tight, his arms flailing in battle. "Get the fuck off me! Don't fucking touch me! Ever!"

"Mario, I'm sorry." Kordell was torn between restraining Mario's arms and shielding himself. He tried to do both. "I'm sorry, I'm sorry, Mario, stop!"

"Fucking kill! Fucking kill!"

"Are you talking to me? Mario, I didn't mean—I'm sorry—"

"Everyone! Every little!" Mario shouted. "Fucking kill!"

"Mario!" Kordell cried desperately, but Mario passed out, half of his opened mouth resting in the dirt below.

When Mario came to, he was quite calm.

"How long have I been out?" he asked, still lying on the ground.

Kordell shrugged. He had been sitting in the dirt, waiting patiently like a nun caring for the sick. "Can you move? Or talk?"

"I think so." Mario propped himself up by the elbows and rubbed his eyes.

"What just happened?" asked Kordell.

No answer.

"You and I both just stepped into a vat of deep shit," said Kordell.

"I know."

"You do?" Kordell asked, just to make sure.

"That kid thinks I molested him. Or his grandmother does." Mario tried to sit up but felt a twinge in his back and grimaced.

Kordell reached out to help steady Mario and eased him back into a horizontal position. "I don't even know if you should be moved right now."

"It didn't hit me," Mario said of the train. "I heard it coming. I was just a little … confused at the time." He started to pass out again, his skull heading toward a softball-sized rock on the ground. Kordell grabbed the back of Mario's head for support.

Kordell, can I see your dick?

Vertigo raced through Kordell's body. For a moment everything was hazy blue and in suspended slow motion. Then, just as quickly, the blur passed and he was back by Mario's side next to the train tracks.

"Are you strong enough to move over there?" Kordell indicated a fallen tree trunk farther away from the tracks. Mario nodded and Kordell helped him up.

"So how did you leave things with Fredito's nana and uncle?" Mario asked once they were both sitting on the tree trunk.

"I didn't," said Kordell. "How do you know Fredito's name and that those are his relatives?"

"He told me his name when I woke up this morning on the air hockey table and saw him playing Monkey Warriors. I heard the relatives when all the confusion started. I speak Spanish."

"Then why didn't you stay and speak your way out of this—I mean—explain what—why did you just run off? Shit, Mario, I don't … you and I … what the fuck?"

"You want the truth?" asked Mario.

Kordell let out a shaky, nervous breath. "Nothing but."

Mario looked toward the ground. "Something's happening to me. Since last night, maybe longer."

"Are you saying you have no idea—"

"I don't know what I'm saying." Mario ran a hand over his face.

"Mario, I gotta ask you this and" —another unsteady breath from Kordell— "please tell me the truth. I won't judge you. I promise I'll help. In every single way I can, I swear on my life."

"You're asking me if I molested Fredito." Mario held his head in his hands.

Kordell paused, not sure if he was ready for this.

"Not judge me?" Mario stood up abruptly. "Nobody can help me. I can't help … you can't escape. There's no escape!"

"Escape from what?" Kordell stood up.

Mario swung around with anger in his eyes. "Why? What's your agenda?" His eyes rolled toward the back of his head. He had to steady himself to keep from falling.

"To get to the bottom of this," said Kordell. "And sort out this mess, this misunderstanding, if that's what it is."

"And if it isn't?" asked Mario.

Kordell paused. "I wanna help you."

"Help me?" Mario scoffed, as if the notion were entirely ridiculous. "Every little ... this world ... every single one of us ..." His anger turned to confusion. He let out a muffled cry. "Every little ... homo ..."

He trailed off, his fury spent, replaced by devastation. He sat back down on the log, deflated.

"Mario, I promise I'll help."

"Why? Because you think I'm innocent?"

There was so much Kordell could have said at that moment, like: *it's possible I did this to you.* But he didn't want to add to the confusion and uncertainty. At least that was the spin he could live with for now.

"Because I remember a kid named Super Mario," he said aloud, "a kid who was intelligent, bright, fun and athletic. I want to know what happened to him."

"If I promise to tell you the truth—*my* truth—do you promise to believe me?"

"Yes," said Kordell. "And I'll help you no matter what."

"Why? We aren't even friends, haven't seen each other in years."

"Do you have to question that right now?" asked Kordell. "Frankly, do you have a choice?"

Mario looked toward the morning sky and Kordell took the moment to sit on the log. Then Mario spoke:

"I don't know."

The phrase hung in the air while Kordell eyed Mario, unsure what to make of it.

"I don't know what I was doing when you and the grandmother walked in," Mario said. "I'm fucked up in the head and I don't know why. But I do know I would never, *ever* do anything to a kid, *any* kid."

"Mario, the circumstantial—"

"My shorts? They were still down from last night." Mario saw the confusion in Kordell's face and went on: "Last night ... when I was beating you at air hockey."

Kordell shook his head.

"Remember, dude? I took off my belt and starting cracking it like a whip."

Kordell's mind conjured up a vague scene of Mario, big black belt in hand, joking about how he was whipping Kordell's ass in all the games they were playing. But was this merely the power of suggestion?

"These are way too baggy, homie." Mario grabbed at the waistband of his shorts. "Last night, they fell down and you wrestled the belt away and threw it behind the pinball machines, making fun of me 'cause I had to hold my pants up."

Kordell pictured himself hurling a snake-like object over the bank of old-fashioned pinball machines. Sounded like something he would do, but Mario was wearing the belt now.

"I got it back in all the confusion," Mario said in response to Kordell's narrow gaze. "Before I ran. Dammit!" Mario made a fist and was about to pound it into the fallen tree trunk until he realized he'd end up with a bloody fist. "I know I'd never abuse a kid. You believe me?"

"I can believe you till my dying day, but what about how Fredito and his family are gonna see it? Especially after you ran. After I ran. His mother Sal has been my best friend for years. She wanted me to father Fredito."

"Then let's go back," said Mario. "To explain things before it gets more outta hand. I'll speak to the grandmother in Spanish and tell her that, even though I'm a little f'ed up in the head right now, I would never hurt her Fredito. I guess I'll leave out the f'ed up part, but I'll convince her I didn't harm him. Fredito can vouch for me. Dammit, they gotta believe me. And believe you. You said you'll stick by me, right?"

That wasn't *exactly* what I said, Kordell thought, but he knew there was no other choice.

Kordell was filled with both trepidation and a strange sense of relief as they headed back to Batter Up. He had no idea what awaited them, but the prospect seemed better than Mario's dismembered body scattered along several miles of train tracks. To avoid

another run-in with a locomotive, they took a different route back, walking along a side street filled with bed-and-breakfast joints. On the way, not one word was spoken between them. What do you say before hoping to exonerate yourself from child molestation?

As Batter Up came into view, the first thing they saw was a parked police car, its muted siren lights swirling. The car was empty and another empty police car sat behind it. And all around Batter Up, there were another half dozen black-and-whites. Ten or twelve policemen milled about, taking notes, dusting doors for fingerprints, speaking on radio units—all in the name of looking for two alleged sex offenders, one of whom owned the place, a kids' establishment at that.

Wordlessly, Kordell and Mario came to a stop on the corner of the side street. Instinctively, they slowly retreated, just enough to avoid being seen while still being able to scope out the scene. The law was everywhere. And the law didn't listen to explanations like, *I'm a little messed up in the head right now, but I'm sure I didn't try to sex up the eight-year-old boy I had my arms around.*

"Let's get out of here."

Kordell wasn't sure who'd said it first, Mario or him. It didn't matter. They both had thought it, said it and now, decided to do it.

Sal's house was dark and quiet. It was a modest, one-story, two-bedroom number on the eastside of Santa Barbara, not far from Batter Up. Even though it was mid-morning and the sun was out, the curtains were drawn and shadows lurked everywhere: on the blue tile kitchen countertop, in the narrow stucco hallway between the bedrooms, over the collage of family photos on the living room wall. Fredito in his baseball uniform. Fredito in his second grade class picture. Fredito in a pointy birthday hat.

The silence was broken by the creaky sound of the front door opening. It was Sal. Alone. She had a worn look on her face and a brown paper bag of groceries in her arms. Her hair was uncombed, her forehead sticky with sweat, her posture battle-fatigued. A mother in the midst of a major life crisis, the kind they didn't prepare mothers for.

She labored toward the kitchen to get rid of the morning's after-thought, groceries she had been in the middle of paying for when she got the call on her cell phone. She dropped the bags on the counter-top near the kitchen sink and shook her head. Should she even concern herself with putting away the perishables?

She heard a noise. Paranoia? No, there it was again, a creak. In another room, the hardwood floor had creaked, similar to what she might hear when Fredito made a late night trip to the bathroom. What now, she thought, I'm being robbed?

She grabbed a large butcher knife from the dish rack and exit-ed the kitchen. The noise had come from one of the bedrooms, she decided. Heart racing, stomach churning, she made her way down the hallway, creeping and cautious. It was dark, but she didn't dare turn on the light or make a sound. Catch him by surprise. Slice off his nuts. See if he fucks with a pissed-off Latina ever again.

Halfway down the hall, she neither saw nor heard anything out of the ordinary, just the eerie, lingering stillness of what might or might not be there. She gripped the knife tighter and decided to check her son's bedroom first. The door was ajar, nothing unusual about that. Still moving at a snail's pace, she peeked around it.

A hand grabbed her from behind, capturing her right arm, the one holding her weapon. She tried to scream, but another hand cov-ered her mouth. It was the same man. He had her from behind and pulled her backward until they both hit the wall. Sal fought back, struggling against his forceful limbs, trying to sink her teeth into the man's black hand.

"Drop the knife, don't be foolish, drop the knife!"

Sal was determined to teach the intruder a lesson. She elbowed him in the gut. He flinched long enough for her to regain control of the knife. She swung around, ready to slice him up, and came nose to nose with—

"*Kordell?*" Her eyes were full of adrenaline. "Where is the bas-tard?" She looked around the hallway, brandishing the knife as if it were a flashlight. "I'm gonna show you both what it's like to have your heart and soul ripped out of you, you irresponsible, inconsid-erate, heartless, sorry-ass excuses for human beings."

Kordell grabbed her wrists and led her backward through the hallway, pleading the whole time:

"Sal, I know things are way beyond insane right now, but you've got to listen to me and not do anything that will just make things worse."

"Fuck you!"

"Think of your boy. You don't want to go to jail and be without him. Or him without you."

"I am thinking of my boy. Now, let the fuck go of me or I'll cut your arms off and you won't be able to hold your prick ever again."

She stared Kordell dead in the face, her admonishment as serious as he'd ever seen her. They had reached the kitchen. He unhanded her. She moved the knife to her left hand and took hold of the tip of the blade. She hurled it past Kordell's ear. The knife landed like a dart in the wall behind Kordell.

"You've been like a brother to me for almost half my life." She was trembling with rage. "You are going to tell me what happened this morning and tell me *now.*"

"Sal, I don't know what happened. Yet. But I want to find out as much as you do. How did the cops get wind of this?"

"Mommy used my uncle's cell to call them and me while he was trying to drive her to the hospital. She was so hysterical, the police could barely understand her. Who is this guy? You tricked with some psycho from Liquid and left him alone with my son? *My son!* My whole life!"

"It was nothing like that—is Mama Carlo all right?"

"She'll be here any minute." Sal saw Kordell's eyes panic at what was suddenly behind her. She turned around and saw what he saw. "*Him.*" It was both a question and a statement, as if it explained so much and so little. "You touched my boy?" Sal asked Mario.

Mario stammered. Kordell hastily interceded:

"Sal. It's not that simple."

"He touched my son, it's simple enough." Sal inched toward the knife in the wall, never taking her eyes off Mario.

"It's not like you think, ma'am," said Mario, but before anyone could react, they heard the sound of a car pulling into the driveway.

Judging by the fear in Sal's face, Kordell understood that Fredito and company were seconds away from entering the house.

"I don't want my son seeing either of you," said Sal.

"I think we should go." Mario moved toward the small enclosed porch just off the kitchen. Through it was the back door they'd used to get into the house.

"Go, my ass!" Sal reclaimed the knife. "You're not getting away."

"Hold on!" Kordell took Mario by the shoulders and literally placed him inside the enclosed porch. "Don't move," he commanded Mario, then returned to Sal, keeping his distance from the knife. "If Mario did this, he should pay. And I should pay for my part in it. And I swear to you that I will not let this go unpunished. But Sal, something isn't right."

They heard the sound of bodies in motion on the front porch steps.

"I don't give a shit," said Sal.

"What has Fredito said?" asked Kordell.

"That's the one thing I can thank God for," said Sal. "He had no idea he was about to be the victim of Bad Touch."

"Mario didn't touch him?"

"You don't even know for sure," said Sal. "Where were you?"

"Asleep in my office. I walked in a second before your mother. Are you saying he's okay?"

They heard the front door opening.

"Fredito's not traumatized?" Kordell asked in a hush. " He doesn't think he's been violated?"

"Mommy saw what she saw," Sal whispered harshly.

They heard footsteps on the hardwood floor of the living room.

"What if this is a misunderstanding I can clear up with time?" asked Kordell.

"*Time?*"

"Salina?" It was Mama Carlo's voice.

"What is *he* claiming?" Sal nodded to Mario.

"He's messed up in the head. He has no idea what happened," said Kordell. "But he swears—"

"Mommy?" This time it was Fredito, his voice sounding closer.

"Here I come, *mijo*." Sal shot Kordell a pensive look, then shooed him toward the porch and shook the knife to encourage him to remain put. Then she went into the living room. Kordell and Mario heard the muffled voices of Sal dealing with her family. There was a man's voice—probably the uncle—as well as Mama Carlo and Fredito, who were probably the intended targets of what sounded like, "You need some rest now."

When Sal came back to the kitchen, Kordell was alone on the back porch. She panicked at the thought of Mario escaping again but saw him through the window of the back door. He could have tried to flee—say "fuck you" to her and Kordell—but he was in her backyard, standing by the swing set, hands inside his baggy shorts, looking like a lost little boy.

"I did see him at the coffeehouse," she said, still angry but more collected than before. "One time, weeks ago. Who is this guy? How do you know him and are you still insisting he's straight? And what the hell do you mean messed up in the head?"

"We grew up together," said Kordell. "He was a good person, but something's gone wrong. He can't be a child mol—that way. I need some time alone with him to get to the bottom of this."

"You trying to tell me you wanna whisk him away for a little therapy session?"

"He was straight when I knew him and straight now or … not. Or mostly. I've got to find out why we're in this … misunderstanding. Before the law gets anymore involved and blows this way beyond our control."

"What's this guy to you?" asked Sal. "What does it matter if he's straight or a child molester or both?"

"This alleged act took place at my business. My *family* business. If this goes public, even if your mom's perception turns out to be wrong, we might as well douse Batter Up with gasoline and light it with a match."

"Bullshit," said Sal.

"You know it's true."

"I mean, why are you trying to cover this guy's back? What aren't you telling me?"

The question killed any momentum he thought he'd gained with her. They heard Spanish from the living room, possibly getting closer to the kitchen.

"If it is a misunderstanding," Kordell said, "wouldn't it be better if Freddy didn't have to go through any legal hassles, especially since he's clueless about what's happening?"

"He's not that clueless," said Sal. "He knows we're all furious with Uncle Kord and that it's got to do with him and the freak he was playing Monkey Warriors with."

"Salina?" It was Mama Carlo's voice. "*Su chico se acuesta.*"

"Give us some time," begged Kordell. "Give *me* time. To take a breath and sort this out."

"Just let you walk out of here?" Sal said. "You haven't even told me his name."

"Mario Cervantes. His family is from the Oxnard area. And me, you've got everything on me except a hard copy of my DNA."

All the years they'd had together—all the peaks and valleys, triumphs and defeats, support and love—resonated in the space between them.

"You think I'd let someone get away with hurting your Freddy, *our* Freddy?" Kordell knew he had run out of testimony. His life was in the hands of the jury now. At least this jury at this moment.

Sal looked away from him as she began to speak. "My baby's supposed to go to his first baseball camp in three days, if all hell hasn't broken loose by then. And if it has and he's caught up in a sexual abuse investigation and can't go, he'll be devastated. I'm only doing this to preserve some kind of normalcy in his life until he goes to camp."

"Doing what?" Kordell asked hopefully.

Sal eyed him. "I'm putting my son on that camp bus on Wednesday so he can live his dream. But if you haven't come to me by then with every single answer me and my mother need, my next stop is the police station, a private detective's office, the newspapers, TV, radio, whatever it takes. And your friend better get himself a lawyer, a shrink and a fulltime bodyguard because I will prosecute his sorry butt myself."

"Thank you, Sal. I will not let you down." He wanted to hug her but stopped short. She still had the knife in her hands. "We will get through and beyond this, I swear."

"You've got seventy-two hours," she said.

"I love you." He opened the back door and started to leave.

"The police are looking for you two," she warned him.

Kordell turned back. "I figured."

"Remember this: my child comes before my best friend."

"As he should," Kordell said, then left before Sal changed her mind or her relatives discovered him in her house.

Sal watched through the window as Kordell hurried to Mario, who was still by the swing set. The two men spoke hastily, then left the backyard through the gate leading to the alley. Sal watched until they were gone, her forehead resting against the glass pane as she whispered:

"Don't make me regret knowing you, Kordell Christie."

THREE

The mouth of the cave framed the Pacific like a jagged picture frame. So blue and light out there, Kordell thought; so dark and damp in here. This same cave had been a sanctuary after the breakup with Toxic Tommy. For weeks, Kordell would awaken involuntarily before the crack of dawn, slip on some jeans and take a long, lonely walk along the beach, always ending up in tears inside this natural tent in a gigantic rock formation on the coast. The jagged opening resembled an upside-down V and blocked out the world except for the view of the ocean. A good place to grieve. A good place to hide.

"You realize the severity of the situation," said Kordell.

"I'm not that fucked up in the head," said Mario. Like an impatient authority figure, Kordell folded his arms and stood over Mario, who had squatted down and was staring at the sand beneath his feet. "Yes, I realize how much deep shit we're both in," Mario added. "Thanks to me."

"Blame is pointless right now," said Kordell. "We need to figure this out."

"Fair enough."

"You skirted around this subject last night, but I've got to ask you this and I need a straight-up answer: are you gay? Straight? Bi? Other?"

Mario paused. "Somewhere between bi-curious and plain ol' bi."

"Bi-curious. What does that mean in your mind's dictionary?"

"It means … hell, I could be bi, I don't know—not because it's a memory thing, I mean, I've always felt I could end up bi someday."

Kordell swallowed hard. "Have you ever been with a guy?"

"I don't know. I can't say."

"Can't or won't?"

"Can't say because I don't remember. I mean, I know that I haven't been with a guy as of … the thing is, I can't remember much about my life in the last few weeks … or months. But I know I was never with a guy before that."

Does that include playing around as kids?

Kordell, can I see your dick?

"Why can't you remember?" asked Kordell.

"Your guess is as good as mine," said Mario.

"Who's the last person you remember having sex or a relationship with?"

"That's easy: my girlfriend—although she's not anymore. Her name was Yolanda. We were together off and on for about eight months. We split up for good last winter. I know that for sure. She went back to her ex-husband. I remember being kinda relieved."

"Relieved?"

Mario drew a circle in the sand with his index finger. "We weren't getting along too well and I've been thinking about guys more lately. I figured if I was single, I could sort some things out, or at least have more freedom to."

"When did you realize you were bi-curious?"

"I don't remember that, not because I have no idea, because … *that's* a memory thing."

"Think, Mario. Can't you remember the first time you thought about guys or wondered if you might be gay? Or bi? Or anything other than a typical hetero dog?"

"Why is that important?"

"Because it just is, Mario. Think."

Mario stood up. "Man, I don't know shit about that right now. I just don't know. I don't know anything. I wanna ... everybody ..."

His fist were clenched, the veins in his neck visible. Kordell stepped back out of fear.

"I'm not gonna hit you, dammit!" Mario shouted, his surging fists betraying his words. "Why are you looking at me that way?"

"What way?" stammered Kordell.

"Like I'm a fucking crazy person. I'm not crazy." Mario realized that his quaking voice and aggressive posture weren't helping his cause. He stuffed his hands into his pockets. "I feel like a fucking retard."

Kordell breathed a sigh of relief but offered nothing in the way of comfort.

"I'm sorry," Mario lowered his head in shame. "I'm not a violent person. I haven't been violent since ... since ..."

"Since what?"

"Since I ..." Mario began, encouraged that he was about to dig up a memory. But whatever it was, it vanished. "Can't remember." He slumped back against the hard rock of the cave walls. "I'm gonna fucking fry for something I would never do!"

"You don't have to, if you're innocent."

"Why can't it be like last night?" said Mario. "We were having so much fun, connecting and playing."

"That was before hell paid us a visit." Kordell leaned against the opening of the cave and stared at the Pacific for inspiration. Last night at the arcade, Mario seemed like the perfect catch: the manly, sensitive, youthful stud-buddy Kordell couldn't have ordered up any better had he found a magic lamp and been granted one wish. But that was last night when they were caught up in the moment, not before *and* after, when it seemed as if Mario was just the opposite of a perfect catch.

The thought gave Kordell an idea.

"Last night," he began, "our only worry was how many times I kicked your ass in air hockey and Ms. Pacman and Boxorama and everything else."

"You kicked my ass?" Mario asked incredulously. "Whose mind is tripping now? I beat you seventy-five percent of the time, homie."

"You mean when you weren't cheating?"

"Cheating? Man, you're buggin'!"

It was working. Mario was grinning, lightening up.

"You the one," said Kordell. "What do you call shooting the puck when I wasn't looking or bumping up against me when I'm trying to shoot hoops?"

Mario nudged him. "I did no such thing."

"Just like that." Kordell nudged him back.

"Man, you crazy. It was more like this, fool." Mario nudged him harder.

"Exactly, damned cheater." Kordell pushed Mario so hard, they both lost their balance. To keep from falling, Mario grabbed Kordell. It didn't work. They both fell to the sand and began wrestling. When Mario won and had Kordell pinned down, he declared:

"I remember last night, homie, and I kicked your ass fair and square."

"Then why can't you remember this morning?"

The frivolity vanished. Mario's face turned somber as he stood and planted himself at the cave's entrance.

"I'm not a child molester," Mario said, his icy stare fixed on the ocean. "And neither is my brother."

"He's not in jail for actually molesting a kid, is he?"

"Just trying to meet one online. Supposedly."

For the first time since this madness began, Kordell realized that both Cervantes brothers were facing the same brand in life: child predator.

"Last night at the bar," Kordell began, "you said you knew for sure that Javier didn't do it. With the way your memory is fading in and out, how can you be so sure?"

"I told you: twin instinct. That's strong. It never fades." Mario stepped back inside the cave. "Plus, I do remember my past. Most of it anyway. It's just right now that's foggy. By 'right now' I mean the last days. Or weeks."

"Your short-term memory," said Kordell. "But how can you be so sure about Javy?"

"My dad … you remember my dad."

"Sorta. I remember he moved out abruptly a little before

your whole family disappeared from the neighborhood."

"Javy was never the most manly of guys," said Mario. "Everyone used to joke that he was supposed to be a girl twin and that I got all the masculinity between the two of us. My father used to treat him like a girl." He turned to Kordell and emphasized: "In every way."

"I don't understand."

"*Papi* used to molest Javier. In grade school. I didn't know about it for a long time, but I knew Javy was hurting inside."

"Did your father ever try to—"

"Hell, no," said Mario. "He never touched me. When I found out what he did to Javy, I took a fireplace poker to his skull. Only my mother, my aunt and my sister all holding me down stopped me from killing him. I was only thirteen and my whole life would have been screwed, but I didn't care."

"*That's* why you guys left the 'hood in such a hurry," Kordell realized. "I remember the owner of the house you were renting going up and down the street, asking everyone where you guys had taken off to."

"My dad moved out the night I smashed his head. My mother was gonna move us across country, but first, we went to her sister's in Thousand Oaks to hide in case my dad went to the police to press charges. He never did and my aunt talked my mom out of leaving California. We moved around a lot of places after that. My father messed up Javy emotionally for years. But Javy got over it, moved on. He spent his whole twenties in therapy. That's why I bet my life that he would never try to corrupt a kid."

"Not to imply that he's guilty," Kordell said gingerly, "but kids who were molested tend to be the ones who grow up to be—"

"Trust me. I know my brother," said Mario. "Besides, he was straight."

"Javy? *Straight?*"

"Ironic, huh? *He* was always the one sure of his sexuality." Mario seemed more clear on that point than any other in the last twenty-four hours.

"When was the last time you saw Javy?" asked Kordell.

"That's kinda hazy. We both live in Ventura, but we don't hang out a lot. He's busy with his detailing business and I got my own

thing going deejaying Latino parties. That's why I'm looking forward
to Friday the eleventh, to see him. That's when he gets out on bail."

"Mario, today is Sunday. The eleventh was last Friday. At the bar
last night, you said you thought he got out soon, but your mind …
well, I guess your memory …"

"Javy can help me," Mario said, thinking out loud.

"Maybe he can fill in the gaps," said Kordell. If Mario had this
twin instinct, maybe Javier had it, too, and could shed some insight
into Mario's behavior and alleged crimes. "Finally, a light at the end
of this dark tunnel."

Mario turned to Kordell, his eyes watery, his fear unmasked,
and said:

"If for some reason I did try to touch that kid in the wrong way,
God help me. I know I'm not a pervert, but I don't know what else
to do. I can't go to anyone else in my family. I can't trust anyone else
but you and Javy."

He trusts me.

"He's been out of jail three days," Kordell said aloud. "Where
would he be?"

"His pad in Ventura."

"We've got to find a way to call him."

"No," said Mario. "I can't bring this up on the phone. It's got to
be in person."

"I don't dare go back and try to get my car. The cops have a couple hundred questions and neither one of us is ready to answer them."

"You got that right," said Mario.

"You're not talking about walking twenty-five miles, are you?"

"No." Mario walked around in a circle. When he was back where
he started, he said: "I don't even know how the hell I got up here."

"Think," Kordell commanded the both of them. "There has to
be a way."

"Can you duck down more and still keep a lookout?" Kordell was
on his back, his body halfway underneath the front half of a
green Ford Taurus, his arm feeling around the greasy underside.

"I'm cool, homie, just hurry." Mario hunched farther down

between the Taurus and an adjacent SUV. The small parking lot off the alley was otherwise empty, but for how long? "You getting it? You sure it's there?"

"Sal and I told Arthur to get rid of this invitation to theft years ago, but he never listens."

Mario eyed the backdoor of the coffeehouse, then the whole row of small businesses that used the lot and the alley. So far, they were alone, but they'd been there five agonizing minutes. "Maybe this was a bad idea. Let's walk there. We can walk twenty-five miles."

Kordell popped up, his shirt and face speckled with dirt and grease. "*You* can walk." He held up a little metal box. "I'll drive and meet you there."

Relief washed over Mario's face. "Shotgun."

Kordell took a quick look at the back entrance to the Mission, the gay/alternative hangout where Arthur—his extremely heavyset best male friend and manager—had served him hundreds of free lattes. Kordell himself hadn't been inside of his former hangout in over a year. His ex, Toxic Tommy, won custody of their table in the settlement.

"Unless Arthur takes off his nicotine patch and steals a cig break, he won't notice his car has gone AWOL until he gets off around four," said Kordell. "Just enough time to get to Ventura, talk to Javy and get back up here."

"And then what?" Mario asked. It was the first time either one of them had brought up life beyond the quick trip to Ventura.

"Let's just do like they do in AA," Kordell said. "Take it one step at a time."

They nodded in agreement and turned toward the car. But the precious seconds they'd taken to converse had cost them. A man was standing on the other side of the Taurus. He was ghostly white, tall, thin, mid-forties. His face was gaunt, his leather jacket unnecessary in such warm weather.

"Mario!" was the first thing the man uttered, followed by a long, drawn-out beat. "Where have you been, buddy?"

Mario looked to Kordell. Kordell looked to Mario.

"Where have I been?" Mario stammered.

"You pulled a disappearing act yesterday at the festival." The man began a confident stroll around the car and came to a stop in front of them. "You said you were going to use the facilities before the musical concert and I never saw you again. And who might you be?"

Kordell was at a loss.

"A friend," Mario answered for him. "From my old neighborhood. Kordell, this is ..." Mario struggled to locate the name in his scattered brain.

"Pizarro," said the man. "Victor Pizarro. I see, Mario, you're still suffering from the aftereffects of your little tumble off the wagon." He turned to Kordell. "You have to forgive my friend. Mario is still in the midst of cleansing himself from certain impurities and illegal substances. I'm what you might call his sponsor and mentor rolled into one."

"This is who you came up here with?" Kordell asked Mario, but Mario's confused expression said he didn't know himself.

"If his mind were clear, he'd say yes," said Pizarro. "But I'm afraid it isn't, as you can see—which is why, Mario, I need to get you back to get some rest now." Pizarro grabbed Mario by the elbow just as the backdoor to the Mission opened, prompting all three of them to freeze. A thin black woman headed straight for her car without paying much attention to them, but the scare served as a warning to Kordell and Mario: they needed to get the hell out of there.

"Uh, Mario," Kordell began.

"Yes, Kordell." Mario reclaimed his elbow from Pizarro. "We need to, uh, if we're going to make that, uh—"

"Make what? I promised I'd give you a ride," Pizarro said a little too eagerly. He grabbed Mario's elbow again and took a step, only stopping when Mario stayed put. "I brought you here," Pizarro insisted. "I'm obligated to escort you back. Let's not make a scene."

The backdoor to the Mission opened again. A college-aged kid with a backpack made a beeline for the bike rack. He was too distracted by the music in his Walkman to care about their stalemate.

"Mario's a grown man—" Kordell began.

"I'm afraid I have to insist." Pizarro glared deep into Mario's eyes. "Now."

"I choose to go" —Mario yanked his elbow free— "with my friend … Kordell."

He trusts me.

"But …" Pizarro began.

"Goodbye," Mario headed for the passenger door.

"Free country and all," said Kordell.

"Mario," Pizarro called out, but Mario ignored him. "Mario … Mario … Mr. Cervantes!"

Kordell waited until Mario was safely tucked away inside the Taurus before getting in. As they drove away, Pizarro stood with his hands on his hips, the furious look on his face never changing.

They didn't talk much on the way to Ventura, perhaps because they were too busy checking out each vehicle that approached and passed, paranoid that it might be The Law catching up with them or this Pizarro man following them. If they were lucky, Arthur hadn't discovered or reported his missing Taurus, but luck, at least good luck, was a commodity in short supply. So it felt as if they were holding their breath for the entire stretch of Highway 101 that ran between Santa Barbara and Ventura County. Not even the dusty mountains on one side and the sprawling blue ocean on the other did much to calm their nerves.

Mario did confirm a few things about Pizarro, but like everything else in Mario's mind, the facts were hazy: Pizarro had indeed been Mario's ride to Santa Barbara and they had spent some time together at Pride, but Mario knew little else about the man. Nor did he have a clue what all the drug and mentor gibberish was about. In fact, Mario was adamant about the following: he did not have a substance abuse problem, not now, not ever. "Like I said before, homie," he reiterated as they passed the huge replica of Santa Claus hovering over the freeway just outside the Santa Barbara city limits, "I experimented in my early twenties, but never again after that. I stake my life on it."

One of them had to be lying. Kordell desperately hoped it wasn't the man in the passenger seat.

"I do remember him saying something about living near

Goleta," Mario added as the freeway ran through Carpinteria, the surfer town that was one of the last signs of life before the 101 turned into an isolated stretch of concrete mimicking the curves of the coast. "Oh, yeah, I have this feeling he works at the Mission."

"The coffeehouse?" Kordell blanched. "Impossible. Not exactly the type Arthur would hire. He tries not to scare away the customers."

Mario didn't argue. With his churned-up memory, he didn't have a leg to stand on.

"By the way," said Kordell. "Sal says she saw you at the Mission. Does that ring a bell?"

There was a long pause before Mario said, "I wish it did."

Later, after riding in silence for a while, Kordell asked, "Why did you choose me? Why not just go with Pizarro, the man who brought you to Pride?"

"You're cuter," said Mario. That brought the only laughter of the trip.

"But really, why?" insisted Kordell.

"You're putting your whole life on the line for me," said Mario. "And I know who you are."

They rode for a moment in silence before Mario added: "And you are cuter."

Not knowing what to say, Kordell let the comment hang until he turned on the radio to drown out the silence.

They reached Javy's apartment complex without incident. It was a small, two-story adobe building on the other side of the freeway from the beach—what the locals called inland. When they got out of the car, Mario had to think hard about which unit belonged to his brother. Eventually, he indicated the second floor at the back of the property.

"Will he be happy to see you?" Kordell asked as they climbed the stairs.

"Always," said Mario.

Upstairs there were four apartments. Without hesitation, Mario went to the one on the far right. He knocked, then rang the bell.

No answer.

"Javy," he said in a partial whisper.

Kordell was about to suggest they wait in the car, but Mario grabbed the doorknob and turned it. It gave way. Mario opened the door and they walked inside.

Sunlight filtered in through the blinds, exposing dark living furniture that was cluttered with newspapers, magazines, soda cans and remotes. Two VCRs sat on an orange milk crate. A small television hovered halfway off its stand.

Mario entered a short hallway, then the bedroom. Kordell followed. Near the bedroom door, something in his periphery caught Kordell's eye. It was on the opposite side of the hall, next to the bathroom door, which was ajar. Actually, it was on the bathroom floor. Red. Blood. A bare foot.

Kordell stopped in his tracks.

"Mario," he barely uttered.

"What is it?"

Kordell froze, his gaze locked on the bathroom floor. He felt Mario coming up from behind, then saw Mario approach the door to open it. The door didn't budge much. The rest of the body was blocking it. Mario pushed harder. The door gave, revealing a blood-soaked floor and another foot, then thighs, a naked male torso, limp arms and, finally, a lifeless, ghost-white face.

Javier.

Kordell thought *suicide* as Mario knelt to feel his brother's throat.

"Is he all right?" Kordell asked, already knowing the answer.

"The killer might still be here." Mario made a series of quick gestures that said: I'll take the bedroom, you check out the living room and kitchen. They bolted in opposite directions, Mario straight to the closets in the bedroom, Kordell to the living room, head swirling, heart pounding. The living room was clear. He checked the closet next to the front door. Clear. The kitchen was next.

What if Mario is in the bedroom being bludgeoned?

He'll yell.

Focus.

The kitchen was empty.

Check the broom closet. Check everything. You could be killed.

Empty. He was about to turn and go find Mario, but he glanced out the kitchen window, half-expecting to find cop cars and cops, who would then add murder to their rap sheet.

There were no cops, but a man with a bald spot on the top of his head was coming up the back staircase. His back was to Kordell. He had a briefcase. Leather jacket. The man turned to ascend the next flight, the last flight. Kordell saw his face. It was Pizarro, Mario's sponsor or mentor or whoever. Kordell swung around to fetch Mario. Mario was already there. They almost collided.

"That man Pizarro is coming up the steps," Kordell told him. Hastily, Mario moved to the window to see for himself, then turned back to Kordell. They didn't even have to say: let's get out of here as quickly and quietly as possible. They took off for the front door, then the front stairwell, picturing Pizarro coming up the back stairwell. They tried to be silent, but speed was the more important factor at this point.

When they reached the bottom step of the front stairwell, they looked up and saw Pizarro reaching the top step of the back. They ducked underneath the stairwell and listened as Pizarro's footsteps stopped at Javier's apartment door. Kordell and Mario had left it ajar. They heard Pizarro walk inside, then close the door. Then they heard sirens closing in.

"The car," said Mario, and he and Kordell sprinted to the Taurus. They reached it and ducked down beside it. Then, seeing no one, they quickly got inside. Kordell was shaking so much, it took a couple of tries to start the engine. The only way he knew he had actually succeeded was when he cranked the key and the engine made that awful, angry sound that said: *I'm in idle already!*

The noise forced them both to take a quick breath, but they didn't have much time. The sirens were getting closer. They drove away from Javier's complex just as an ambulance was coming down the street, unaware that it was too late to save Mario's twin brother.

FOUR

"Stay here," Kordell told Mario as the blue Volkswagen pulled into the other end of the dirt parking lot.

"Count on it," Mario said sarcastically, making clear his preference not to come face-to-face with one of Kordell's suspicious friends.

Kordell approached the Volkswagen and his best male friend, wondering if Arthur would still be his best male friend when this was all over. *If* this was ever going to be all over.

Using the "least public" pay phone he could find, Kordell had called Arthur before making the trek back to Santa Barbara. They had both agreed the small dirt lot on the outskirts of town—the one horny men sometimes cruised—was the most discreet place to meet.

"This is the second time my roommate has ever lent me anything," Arthur said as he struggled to get his big body out of the pint-sized car. "I didn't even tell him about the clothes I swiped."

"Arthur," Kordell began, "to say thanks would be a monumental understatement right about now. I guess saying I'm sorry for stealing your car fits into that same category."

"If you're handing out humility and apologies, I'll get in line."

Arthur pulled his cell phone from his pants pocket and scrolled the mini-display. "Besides, I didn't miss my car until you called and told me you'd carjacked it." He found the number he wanted, pressed TALK and put the phone to his ear. "How's *he* doing?" He nodded toward Mario, who was leaning on the driver's-side door of the Taurus.

"About as well as can be expected for just finding out his twin brother can't help him straighten his life out because he's dead."

"Hmmm," Arthur murmured, paying more attention to his phone.

Kordell turned to Mario in the distance and tried to give him a reassuring smile, as if to say, "Arthur is okay. Everything's going to be okay." Did Mario see it? He was looking at Kordell and Arthur, but perhaps he was too far away to notice.

On the drive back from Ventura, Javy's death caught up with Mario. He climbed into the back seat of the Taurus and cried the entire time, wailing about the loss of the only family member he really cared about and who really cared about him. "Why'd you kill yourself, Javy?" he repeated several times, prompting Kordell to also think of Javier's death as suicide. "Every little homo," Mario must have also said a few dozen times. Kordell let him grieve, putting questions about Pizarro on the back burner for the time being. He was confident the so-called mentor hadn't followed them back up the coast. Whatever Pizarro's schedule and agenda, he was most likely detoured by what he saw in Javy's apartment. Perhaps he had been the one to call the authorities.

"Hey, girl, it's me," Arthur said into the cell phone. "Here he is." He handed the Nokia to Kordell.

"Girlfriend," Kordell said weakly. He tried for lightness and familiarity but failed miserably. "Did Arthur tell you what happened?"

"I don't know squat," said Sal. "Just that he's meeting you somewhere."

"I thought it best if you debrief her," Arthur informed him.

"Sal, something is definitely not right. Mario's twin brother Javier is dead and there's this man" —he turned to Arthur, anxious

to ask him about Pizarro working at the Mission, but that wouldn't mean anything to the worried mother on the other end of the line— "Javy just got out of jail for" —no, that won't sound right— "we just found him dead in his apartment and it might be connected. There's a good chance that whatever happened at Batter Up was not Mario's fault, one way or another."

There was a long pause until Kordell broke the silence:

"Anything new with the police?"

"Just the APB so they can bring you and your friend in for questioning," said Sal. "And they're waiting for me to talk to my grandmother when she's calmed down and not having heart palpitations so we can get her story and decide if she really saw something or was just confused. Come talk to the cops, Kordell, tell them what you know."

"That's just it, Sal. All we know is that Mario's mind is fucked up right now and that's it. And this man. I think he may be the lead that we need."

"Then let the police talk to him," said Arthur.

"Exactly," said Sal.

"And do what?" said Kordell. "This man claims Mario was in rehab and Mario swears up and down it isn't true. Then we see him—the man—in Ventura at the dead brother's apartment. He's a white man—no offense, Arthur—but who are the cops gonna listen to?"

"None taken, Counselor Johnny Cochran," said Arthur.

"Please, Sal," Kordell said, knowing she'd understand his lack of trust in the legal system.

"Mommy is not claiming you had a part in this," said Sal. "Fredito says he didn't even see you until she came in. You don't have to pay for a crime this person from your old 'hood committed just because it was in your establishment."

"But what if he didn't do it?" asked Kordell. "Should he have to go through all the social and legal crap before proving himself innocent? Or what if he needs emotional help?"

"What—you're gonna try to be his fucking therapist?" asked Sal.

"No." Kordell turned to Mario in the distance. "I swear."

"Then why are you doing this?" Sal asked at the same time that Arthur said:

"So why are you doing this?"

"Because I have to," said Kordell. "I know that sounds lame, but can't both my best friends in this whole world trust me? At least give me a chance?"

"The friend in me says yeah, sure," said Sal. "But the mother in me says you've got until Wednesday to come clean, with or without your friend. After that, I'm putting it all in the hands of the SBPD."

Kordell started to say: if I haven't found anything by then, *I'll* put it in the hands of the SBPD. But he didn't get the chance to say anything else to Sal. She hung up.

"T minus three days until my ass is fried." Kordell handed the phone back to Arthur. "And in a few hours, it'll be T minus two days."

"You do see her point," said Arthur.

Kordell sighed. "Were you able to get everything I asked for?"

Arthur reached in the Volkswagen and fetched a black rolling carrier from the passenger seat. "One on-the-lam kit to go," he said, setting the baggage between them.

"Very amusing."

"Sorry."

"Oh, shit," said Kordell. "So many things going on—Pizarro—is there someone who works at the Mission by that name?"

"Pizarro?" Arthur asked incredulously. "No way."

"Figures," Kordell said dejectedly.

"He works upstairs."

"At the Internet grocery store office?"

"See what you miss by letting your ex rule the town? That's another dot com that is now a *not* com. This Project H.O.P.E. séance group or whatever set up shop there a few months ago. Gay—mind you—like a counseling thing, I guess, or a wellness center or spiritual guru summit or something."

"Why haven't I heard about it through the Business Alliance?" asked Kordell. "I'm the president for Christ's sake, how could I not know about this?"

Arthur shrugged.

"And this Pizarro works there?"

"Victor Pizarro. He's like the supervisor or something." Arthur shuddered. "And very creepy."

"Tall guy?"

"White as a ghost. I know who you mean."

"What do you know about him?"

"You know me, I don't go for that spooky spiritual stuff," said Arthur. "The coffeehouse stays outta their way and vice versa. Of course, business is always booming right after they have their little meetings, which suits me fine. And, of course, they like being on top of us, so to speak, you know, get us where we hang out, recruit the natives in their natural habitat."

Kordell fell silent. This wasn't good, made no sense. Why would a man who worked at a place promoting good mental health for gays and lesbians be doing ... what? Befriending Mario and his brother? Lying about Mario being in rehab?

Maybe Mario's the one who's lying.

"One ration of gas was all I could get on short notice." Arthur retrieved a gas can from the trunk. "And I want you to swear on your next boyfriend's life that you will take perfect care of my almost new Taurus."

"Cross his heart and hope to die," said Kordell.

"I put some day-old Mission sandwiches in the suitcase and some bottled water."

Kordell smiled a grateful smile. "I know 'I'm sorry and thanks for everything' doesn't begin to cover it."

"I'll figure someway for you to return this very huge favor." Then Arthur had an idea. "Hey, consider this payback for the two thousand dollars I owe you."

"Deal."

"I was just kidding."

"I'm not. I mean it: consider all your loans paid in full. Right now."

Arthur regarded his friend curiously. "You're in this deep, aren't you?" he asked with a rare seriousness.

Kordell licked his lips and turned away.

"I'm afraid you have no idea," he said.

Mario folded and unfolded his arms yet again, thinking: what could they be talking about all this time? How long before someone comes by and spots us?

He vowed to honk the horn if Kordell wasn't back in sixty seconds, but he didn't have to. Kordell started walking toward the car while Arthur got back in the Volkswagen and drove away.

"One on-the-lam kit to go, complete with petrol." Kordell raised the gas can in the air. When Mario didn't laugh, Kordell added: "Sorry, that was Arthur's lame joke."

"What? Oh, it's okay," said Mario. "I was just getting nervous. And more frustrated."

"Well, in here we've got a couple of hats, sunglasses, toiletries, what money a broke guy like Arthur could scrounge up, and some of his roommates clothes 'cause Michael is a little closer to our size than Arthur." Kordell held up the cell phone he used to talk to Sal. "I even got him to give us this."

"That's great," Mario said absently. "We're really plugged in now."

It was clear that his brother's death was still on his mind, if not both his brother's death and his own dilemma, which had to be connected, somehow, some way.

"Think you're ready to talk now?" asked Kordell.

"What other choice do I have?" said Mario. "Javy wouldn't want me in jail like him for something I didn't do."

They did a quick inspection of the gear in Arthur's rolling carrier and placed it in the backseat of Arthur's car, now their car for however long they needed it. They also topped off the tank, leaving them with about half a can of gas. Once finished, it was time to decide their next move. For this discussion, they sat at the dirt lot's edge, facing the pond that sat in the middle of a field of tall grass. In the distance, the Santa Ynez Mountains reigned over all, and despite the scenic nature around them, deep relaxing breaths were in short supply.

"I was so counting on my brother to clear me up," said Mario.

"Now we're back to square one. Correction, we're not even *up* to square one."

"Not necessarily," said Kordell. "When I saw Javier's body, I thought suicide. You know, maybe he was distressed over the prospect of being known as a sex offender. But when you saw the body, you thought it was murder. Was that your gut feeling?"

"What do you mean?"

"You only called it suicide in the car. Your first reaction was that he'd been killed. Was that your intuition? Oprah's always telling us to go by our intuition. You say you know your twin. Think, Mario: was it suicide or murder?"

Mario stood up, racking his brain, his heart, his twin instinct.

"It wasn't suicide," he said.

Kordell perked up.

"It wasn't murder either."

Kordell sank.

"It …" Mario trailed off, walked around some more. "It was not suicide. My brother did not commit suicide."

"You're sure?"

"As sure as I can be."

"So who wanted him dead?" asked Kordell. "Who even knew he'd been out on bail?"

"Pizarro knew. Why else would he have been at the apartment? Who the hell is this guy that I rode down to Santa Barbara with?"

"*Down* to Santa Barbara?" asked Kordell.

"Yeah, I told you that, didn't I?"

"You never used the word *down*. If you came to Santa Barbara from Ventura, wouldn't you have said—"

"*Up*," said Mario, the wheels in his mind accelerating. "I like going *up* to Santa Barbara," he added as an example of his normal speech.

"Down from where, Mario?" Kordell extended his hands, as if to reach *down* Mario's throat and retrieve the information. "You and Pizarro drove down from …"

"From—" Mario tried to finish the sentence with the utmost confidence, but couldn't. As usual, the facts slipped through his fin-

gers and were now floating in the wind. "*Damn!*" He slammed his fist down on the trunk of the Taurus.

"It's okay, it's okay." Kordell jumped up. "Maybe it will come to you. Don't force it."

Mario leaned against the car, his face buried in his chest.

"Your mind isn't that screwed up," Kordell said. "Pizarro does work—not at the Mission—but above it, for this wellness outfit for gays."

"I knew it," Mario said enthusiastically, as if he'd just followed a hunch on a quiz show and answered the question correctly. Then, just as quickly, his face turned shy and unsure. "So what does this mean?"

"Well ..." Kordell had to pause a moment to absorb the cute, innocent look on Mario's face. *How could someone who was capable of making that face be evil?* "For one thing, it means maybe he lives in Goleta like you thought, and Goleta is *down*. Maybe you drove *down* to Santa Barbara from Goleta."

"Yeah, but it's *next* to Santa Barbara. I don't know if I would say *down*. I don't know."

Kordell indicated the cell phone. "We need to find out where this man lives and pay him a visit."

"But he won't be home," said Mario. "He's probably still in Ventura, doing God-knows-what in my brother's apartment."

Kordell flashed him a sly smile. "Is it my imagination or is your mind starting to clear up more and more?"

It took a beat or two for Mario to catch on, but when he did, he too wore a very sly smile.

The Taurus pulled onto Albatross Lane, a paved but dusty road in the hills east of Goleta, the city adjacent to Santa Barbara. There was no Victor Pizarro in any phone book in the county, but thanks to Arthur's cell phone and a call to Arthur, who was back at work underneath Project H.O.P.E., Kordell and Mario had hit pay dirt. It pays to have friends who have friends who work at the telephone company.

They drove by Pizarro's house once with Kordell slumped down

in the passenger seat and Mario driving (a Latino was slightly less conspicuous than a black man in this neck of the woods). There were no cars in the driveway or signs of life inside the ranch-style home. They used the cell phone to dial the number Arthur had provided, but got a machine and quickly hung up.

Next, they parked farther up the mountain on a clearing that served as a lookout point for anyone wanting to take in the scenic view of the hills and valleys. Then they circumnavigated the surrounding woods on foot, traveling over hilly terrain and rocky slopes—the long way to Pizarro's little hideout.

Hideout was a good name for it, too. Like many of the homes in this area, Pizarro's was secluded from the neighbors, thanks to tall trees and high wooden fences. The better to break in and get information.

When they reached the front door, Kordell stayed out of sight while Mario rang the bell. That way, if someone was home, Mario could make up an excuse for being here to see his "mentor" and they'd resort to Plan B. The first part of Plan B was to actually come up with a Plan B; but they didn't have to. No one answered. Mario gave Kordell a "okay" signal and they met up around back.

"Any alarm?" asked Kordell.

"Nope."

"White people."

"No doubt." Mario made quick work of the bathroom window, prying it open with little effort.

"Thank God you're Latino," Kordell joked.

"It was unlocked." Mario was not amused.

"Forgive me," said Kordell. "I'm about to shit in my pants. I've never broken and entered before."

"Neither have I, my African-American homie."

"Let's just do this."

They climbed through the window, Mario first, which was good because he cushioned the fall that Kordell took once he squeezed his big black ass past the tiny window frame. Kordell fell on top of Mario in the tub. They were too scared of being heard to worry about the awkwardness of their bodies entangled. They listened for a moment,

heard nothing, then freed themselves from one another and the bathtub.

"Dude," said Mario. "Next time you're going to do an imitation of Laurel and Hardy, let me know first, okay?"

"I said I was sorry," Kordell barked in a whisper.

"It's cool. You're not the only one who's scared shitless."

They left the bathroom, but unlike the search at Javier's place, they decided to stick together. They searched the living room, the den, three bedrooms and the kitchen. All they found were the remnants of a normal life: computer, computer books, a small aquarium full of goldfish, childhood photos of Pizarro with his mother, photos of the mother alone, copies of *TV Guide, Newsweek,* Hawaiian vacation brochures. The only odd artifact they found was on top of the toilet tank in the master bathroom. There they spotted several straight men's magazines, the kind that featured busty young Hollywood starlets in as little clothing as possible, surrounded by miniature headlines that promised sex tips, sports scoops and previews of the latest high-tech gadgets.

"Isn't this a little strange for a man who works at a gay wellness center?" Mario wondered.

"Unless he's straight and heals people regardless of orientation." Kordell wandered into the master bedroom for one more scan. "Does any of this look familiar?"

"Hell, no." Mario joined him. "I've never been here."

"You know that for a fact, or you just don't think so?"

"I definitely don't feel it."

Just then they heard the sound of car tires crunching up the gravel driveway and looked at each other with *heart attack* in their eyes. Mario was the first to move. He swung open the closet's double French doors and disappeared behind the rack of suits. For lack of a better suggestion, Kordell followed and closed the doors behind him, settling down seconds before they heard the front door open.

At first they didn't hear much. Whoever was there was in no hurry to get to the master bedroom. But a few minutes later, the sounds of a single body stirring grew closer and closer. First there was a toilet flushing in a hallway bathroom, then steps on the car-

peted floor in the hallway, then steps on the hardwood floor in the bedroom. Kordell and Mario eyed one another, which wasn't easy since their faces were inches apart, their hot, nervous breaths merging as one.

The footsteps had to be those of a man's—heavy and labored. He crossed the room, back and forth once, twice. Through the French doors, Kordell and Mario could make out legs in black pants. Going over to a bookcase. Stopping at a chest of drawers. Bending down. Looking underneath the bed. Then all movement stopped. The legs were standing in the middle of the room, but which way were they facing? Kordell and Mario held onto each other, bracing themselves.

The next sound they heard was an old-fashioned telephone, blaring out atop the dresser. It was like a bomb exploding. Each one felt the other's claw-like grip sink into his own skin. The phone rang again. And again. It rang until the machine picked it up. They listened, as did the pair of legs, which hadn't moved from its position in the middle of the room.

First came the greeting: "Victor Pizarro. What can I do you for?"

An abrupt beep sounded, then came a young man's soft voice: "Victor, hi. It's Brother John. I'm done *cleaning*—hint, hint—and I'm on my way to your house to feed the fish. I'm not sure what time you're going to be there, but I'll hang for about an hour and try calling you on your cell. Turn it on, will ya? I'm dying to find out what's the 4-1-1 with the brother that's left."

A long beep ended the call and the legs in the bedroom began pacing the room. Seven more short beeps emanated from another source. It wasn't long before Kordell and Mario realized that was Legs using his cell phone:

"McPherson. Yamo. No time." Legs was a man all right. A white man, judging by the voice. "Company coming. Office."

The man scurried out of the bedroom. Seconds later, the front door opened and closed. Shortly after that, a car engine started and hightailed it away from the house. Only then did Kordell and Mario open the French doors that had kept them hidden. As they did, Kordell searched for some kind of joke about coming out of the closet; but Mario upstaged him.

"Look what Pizarro's hiding in his closet." He was holding up a gay skin magazine. *Torso.* "And that's not all."

"You don't say," Kordell deadpanned. They rummaged through a cardboard box on Mario's side of the closet and found all kinds of goodies: more gay magazines and porno, DVDs of every gay movie Hollywood had made in the last forty years, DVDs of documentaries on homosexuality.

"Why would he hide this stuff?" asked Mario. "He works at a gay place. We went to Pride together. What kind of man would hide this stuff in his own house?"

"A man leading a double life?" Kordell dug deeper into the box. Fetish catalogues. Bondage books. Kink videos. Circuit Party music mixes.

"Or a man doing research?" Mario held up a book. WHY HOMOSEXUALITY? THEORIES AND HISTORY, A PRACTICAL APPROACH WITH PRACTICAL ANSWERS.

"Practical answers?" said Kordell. "There's a stretch."

"This is the kind of book I was looking for! Wait a minute" — Mario held his hand up to stop Kordell from interrupting his train of thought— "A memory ... I've been curious about gays ... I did research on what makes a person gay."

"And?" Kordell said softly, trying to pull the memory out of Mario, especially since they didn't have much time.

"The Internet ..." Mario said, then paused a lifetime before adding, "Fuck. Lost it!"

"We've got to get out of here," said Kordell. "You heard this John guy."

"Talking about *me*, the brother's that's left." Mario stashed the book back into the box, then snatched up a colorful postcard. "Wait ... I've seen this before!"

"Something about Project H.O.P.E.?"

"No, *this* place. I've been here." Mario's hands started shaking, his eyes blinking excessively. Kordell took hold of the postcard and saw a sleek glass building in the middle of a picturesque meadow. He turned the card over.

"The Facility. Doesn't say anything else. What is it?"

"I—I don't … it has to do with wellness," Mario said, still stumbling through his memories. "Wellness and … and … fuck, I don't know!"

They heard a creaking sound. It was only the house shifting, but it was as good an excuse as any to get the hell out of there.

"I'm taking this," Kordell said of the postcard.

Hastily, they put the rest of Pizarro's goodies back the way they found them, then raced to the bathroom window to make their escape. This time there was no Laurel and Hardy routine, just stealth and grace as they slipped through the window and into the woods. Good thing, too. Just as they hurried away, they heard another set of tires crunching up the gravel driveway.

FIVE

"What time is it?" Mario lay on the ground on his back, head resting in his hands, gazing at the sky. Kordell looked at the display on the cell phone. "Nearly eight, why?"

"Wasn't this about the time this whole mess started this morning?"

"If you wanna get technical, all this started before this morning." Kordell rolled over on his stomach and peered through the digital binoculars they had purchased at a small camping store off the highway (only Mario went inside and even then he was buried underneath a baseball cap and sunglasses, thanks to Arthur's on-the-lam kit). "The question now is *how* it got started. And why."

A large valley separated them from the Facility, a one-story structure whose exterior consisted of long horizontal stripes of green and silver glass. They were camped out on a grassy ridge several miles east of Santa Barbara proper, nestled in a secluded canyon in the mountains. There were no other signs of civilization in sight. Everything else around them—the barren hills, the rocky slopes, the towering cliffs—was courtesy of Mother Nature.

"You sure you've never heard of this place?" asked Mario.

Kordell shook his head. "You sure you don't remember anything about it?"

"Just the feeling that I never wanna go back there." Mario shuddered. "Still nothing happening?"

Kordell surveyed the dimly lit parking lot through the binoculars. "Not a damned thing."

"You think we're in over our heads?" asked Mario.

"You're not enjoying hiding from the law and playing Columbo?"

Mario let out a half-hearted laugh.

"I'm sorry." Kordell brought the binoculars down. "I'm trying to make light and you lost your brother today."

"It's actually good to joke a little," said Mario. "When my nana died when I was nine, I cried my eyes out for three straight days. Then, on the fourth day, I started watching cartoons for something like a week straight, all my favorites: Spiderman, Road Runner, Masters of the Universe—remember them?"

Kordell let out a small laugh.

"My aunt said I was burying my pain," Mario went on, "but I got through it better. I loved my Nana." He rolled over so that he was lying on his stomach, facing the Facility. "Man, if Fredito's nana loves him as much as mine loved me, it must be killing her to think her grandbaby was abused. Her eyes this morning …"

"Her eyes are full of relief. She knows that Fredito doesn't think anything happened. And hopefully soon, we'll all come to realize that."

Mario propped himself up by the elbow. "You've been like an angel to me, who came down from the sky and is helping me out for no reason. I don't know if I deserve it. Maybe I should turn myself in and get this over with."

"We owe it to ourselves to find one morsel of truth before we give up."

Mario eyed him curiously, unsure why this angel wasn't saving his own butt. "It's still Gay Pride weekend. You should be out with your boyfriend or something."

Kordell scoffed. "I don't have a boyfriend."

"A good-looking guy like you? Then you should be out getting one."

"Sure." Kordell rearranged himself so that he was resting on his back. "I'll just click my heels three times and before me will materialize a wonderful guy who isn't a lying, cheating, immature drama queen and we'll live happily ever after."

"You don't think Mr. Right is out there?"

Kordell thought about it for a good long while, then said: "No, he's not out there. Mr. Right has left the universe."

"Man, you can't think like that."

"Call it the voice of experience," said Kordell. "And don't tell me you know about these things."

"Cold shot. And not fair."

"Neither is the dating scene. If you don't look like you belong in a circuit party ad, you can *fuggedaboutit.*"

"You're in good shape," said Mario. "What's wrong with a little meat on dem bones?"

"In the gay world, I might as well look like Arthur." Kordell sighed. "That's not fair, to me or Arthur. Sorry, Arthur." He paused to take in the fading sunset. "I don't know. Sometimes it's hard not to think we gays are just like the homophobes say we are: sex-crazed, body-obsessed, drag-wearing, effeminate, child-molesting freaks." He stopped himself when he realized what he'd said. "But I know we're not all child-molesting freaks. Or any of the other stuff."

It was a while before Mario broke the silence.

"What if ..." He stopped himself.

"You did try to molest Fredito?" Kordell finished the thought. "Just for the sake of argument, why? Why would you do it?"

Mario sat up but remained silent, gently rocking back and forth.

"Do you have an attraction for younger boys?" asked Kordell. Silence.

"Would you tell me if you did?" asked Kordell.

"Would you tell me if *you* did?" asked Mario.

"I haven't been accused—"

"What difference does that make?"

"You're right. Okay, I'll go first." Kordell sat up and took a deep breath, then another. "Let me see if I can make this make sense. Humans are sexual beings, both adults and children. They may not be sexual in the same way as adults, but children have a sexuality and sexual feelings."

"*I* sure did."

Kordell blanched at Mario's admission, then collected himself and went on:

"Children at some point—of course, everybody develops differently—but at some point, children are sexual, meaning they have sexual feelings. Toward themselves, toward each other, toward adults."

"Toward the family dog," said Mario.

"Let's stick to *homo sapiens* for the sake of this discussion."

"Carry on."

"So if children are sexual and adults are sexual, aren't some members of both groups bound to zap some of that sexual energy toward the other group, for whatever reason? But—and I can't emphasize this *enough*—I am in *no way* saying adults and children should be appearing together on the same episode of some TV dating show. Or that children should be set up on blind dates with each other. Or that any adult should have *any kind* of sex with *any* kid— that's not at all what I'm saying."

"Then what are you saying?" asked Mario. "Because I'm kinda getting weirded out here."

Kordell took another deep breath. "There's no way in our society—our Judeo-Christian slash Western slash modern world—that a child can have a healthy sexual relationship with anyone, be it another child or an adult. Why? Because we disallow even the possibility of children having legitimate sexual feelings that need to be explored and dealt with and we brand anyone who goes there, even in an intellectual discussion like this, a pervert or a lunatic."

"Or a predator," added Mario.

"Well, look around, my friend, the world must be full of mostly perverts, lunatics and predators because—what are the statistics

about child molestation?—they're astronomical. It seems like more people in this world were molested as children than not. And the molesters are not all evil Cyclopes or twisted psychos that can be eliminated with bigger, better law enforcement. They're fathers, relatives, teachers, priests, the people you see at the grocery store, the mall, the school recital. Many of them have been molested themselves—the legacy of shame passing itself on."

"Because we got the devil in us," said Mario.

"Noooo," said Kordell. "Because we don't approach the sex and sexuality of adults in a healthy way, let alone the sex and sexuality of children. All this denying, manipulating and demonizing of sexuality makes our desires come out in twisted, unhealthy ways that fuck us all up, man, woman *and* child."

"We got the devil in us," said Mario.

"You don't really believe that."

"Hell, yeah, I do." Mario stared into the forest beyond the ridge. "Everyone who molests is evil. A devil. And if I did it, I'm one, too. Every little one of us is the devil."

Kordell searched Mario's face as if looking at him in a new light. "This isn't the first time you said something like that."

"Like what?" asked Mario.

"*Every little homo or every one of us.* You never said 'devil' before—at least I don't think—but is that what you meant? In the car on the way back from Ventura?"

"That's what I believe." Mario's voice trailed off, not sounding as convincing as he could have.

"Do you really, Mario?"

"You didn't answer my question," said Mario. "Really, it was your question: do you have a thing for younger boys? I'm talking, like, pre-adolescents."

"Honestly? No. I don't have a thing for them; I don't want to have sex with them; and I don't believe anyone should because we're just not emotionally equipped for that in this go-round. And I'm a sane, rational adult and I know the difference between right and wrong, and it would be *way* wrong to intrude on some kid's life and send him down a dark path from which he may never recover."

"Hmmm," Mario seemed lost in his own thoughts.

"I know that as an adult," Kordell added, thinking to himself: *I
didn't know that as a kid.*

"I hear ya." Mario still seemed miles away.

"What about Mario?" asked Kordell. "Does he have an attraction for younger boys?"

"I'd kill myself before I touched a kid that way, male or female."

"Is that answering the question?"

"I do not have a thing for them," Mario said decisively. "I do not
want to have sex with them, okay?"

"Have you … ever …"

"Been molested?"

Kordell swallowed hard, then nodded.

Mario shook his head. "My brother was the only one who suf-
fered that way."

*What's your definition of molestation? What we did as kids? Do
you remember? You don't seem to remember. Or was that just two kids
in your mind, even though I was a few years older?*

"I do have this memory though," Mario added.

"Yeah?" Kordell's gut went tight.

"There's this group of kids—some guys, some girls, all kids
though—and I think some of the older kids were making certain
people, including myself, kiss and play with each other's, like, geni-
tals and stuff."

"People from our old 'hood?"

"Dunno." Mario wiped his brow. "Maybe. But see, I don't know
if it really happened or I just dreamt it. It's like an image from my
childhood, kind of like a moving painting."

"Moving painting?"

"You know, it's frozen in time, but still breathing, like it still has
life. But is it based in reality? Did it really happen? Maybe I don't
want to know."

"Because?" Kordell couldn't look at him, couldn't take his eyes
off him.

"I don't know if we should have been doing that," said Mario. "I
have a lot of shit like that, faint memories from when I was real

young. This is stuff that's been fuzzy forever, not just recently. Like there's this other time I might have been messing around with this guy—an older kid—but see, I don't know if that was real or a dream. You know what I mean? It's weird like that."

"I think I do." Kordell lay flat on the ground. The sky was pitch black. So was the void in his mind.

"You have crazy images from your past in your head?" asked Mario.

Kordell puckered his lips, his breath barely seeping through the wrinkled opening.

Kordell, you wanna see my dick? It's huge, man.

The invitation had come from Jamaal, his dad's partner in the roofing business, which was strange in and of itself because Jamaal was in his late teens/early twenties. When Kordell was still prepubescent, he walked in on one of those adult conversations that promptly cease when a child walks into the room. His mother and aunt had been discussing the fact that Jamaal was his dad's bastard child. Or was that his dad's brother's bastard child? Or did anyone really know the truth? It was never discussed in the open, before or after Jamaal's death in a freak roofing accident.

Kordell thought of Jamaal now because he starred in one of Kordell's moving paintings from childhood, namely the one where Kordell first saw and touched another male's dick. If Kordell let the "painting" breathe on its own, he could remember being shocked at how steely the teenager's rod felt; he could visualize a playful Jamaal zipping his pants back up as if to leave, then changing his mind and wrestling Kordell to the ground; he could almost feel a fully-clothed Jamaal humping him and, soon after, a breathless Jamaal abruptly stopping and remaining very still, as if afraid to move. Of course, the adult Kordell was all too familiar with the actions of a man trying to blunt the intensity of an orgasm. But had it really happened it all?

"How's your sister?" Mario suddenly asked.

"She's married and living in LA. No kids yet. So you do remember her?"

"Man, I'm not a retard."

"And you remember her babysitting?"

"Everyday that one school year." Mario threw a small stick at him. "You're starting to piss me off, thinking that my whole mind is whack."

"I'm just playing with you." Kordell lied.

"Yeah, right," Mario said, half-bothered, half-joking. He turned toward the Facility, his way of letting it go.

They lapsed into silence while keeping an eye on the parking lot. No one came in or out of the place and darkness descended on the ridge before long.

"Where are we gonna sleep tonight?" asked Mario. "We can't exactly get a hotel room."

"I guess we find a secure place to park the Taurus."

"Look!" Mario pointed to the parking lot. "Somebody's shift is over."

Kordell grabbed the digital binoculars, hastily switched them to night vision and power zoom, and had a look. Several people were coming out of the Facility. "It's mostly men," he told Mario. "Check it, all men, seven, eight."

"What are they doing?" Mario sat on his knees. "What are they wearing?"

"They look like they're getting off work," said Kordell. "White lab coats."

"Lab coats?" Mario asked incredulously. "You sure it's not some kind of green outfit?" Mario took the binoculars from Kordell. "Lemme see ..."

Kordell strained to get a good look with the naked eye. "What is it, Mario? You remember something?"

Kordell heard the binoculars drop to the ground, then turned in time to catch Mario, who was falling backward. The unexpected weight caused Kordell to stumble to the ground while holding Mario, who had fainted. Kordell laid him down gently, then grabbed the digital binoculars to see what Mario had seen.

Most of the men were getting in their cars and driving toward the security gate, where they slipped a card in a box, which freed the gate long enough to let out one car at a time. But two men lingered in the parking lot, one patting the other on the back. One of them got

into his car and the other man turned toward the security gate to wave to another car going through. It was then that Kordell got a good look at the lone man standing in the parking lot.

It had been years since Kordell had seen that face. It was much older now, but the skin was still smooth as silk, even if the face was slightly fatter now. There was no mistaking his identity. Kordell had had a crush on him all those years ago. It was him all right, and without a doubt, that was the reason Mario lay passed out on the ground. He had been shocked to see his own father, Giovanni Cervantes, after all these years.

Kordell couldn't remember the last time he'd paid attention to the sound of birds chirping. Or the wind swaying through the trees. Or the last time he'd slept outside in the open air—if ever. He stared at the clear sky and imagined for a moment that he and Mario were waking up from a romantic camping trip: the night had been so warm, they had decided to sleep under the stars instead of inside their tent. Now, with morning, Kordell would light a fire and make a big, hearty breakfast, giving them enough fuel to make it through a day of hiking through the woods, skinny-dipping in some secluded pond, then returning to the campsite by nightfall to make love under the stars.

Mario, his big, strong, ruddy-skinned warrior-stud, a throwback to some time long ago, when only his tribe roamed these lands. Mario, all grown up, the same confident Super Mario from the old neighborhood evolved into a youthful, mature man who enjoyed air hockey and video games just like Kordell. Mario, who didn't let on if he remembered the two of them experimenting as kids. Who, twenty-four hours ago, may have been trying to molest Fredito. Who denied he was ever in anything remotely resembling rehab, even though the Facility could easily pass for some kind of rehabilitation joint.

Kordell rolled over on his side and regarded Mario, who was still sleeping on the ridge, who, after passing out upon seeing his father exit the Facility, awakened only long enough to mumble those contorted words again: every little homo ... kill every one ... devil. Then he fell asleep in the dirt, no doubt exhausted from a day where

his mind must have felt as if it were suffering from a really bad case of the 1960s.

How could he not remember? Only his short-term memory is supposed to be messed up. Is he merely waiting for me to bring it up? Is this like those straight guys you hear about who get drunk and blow each other, then, the very next day, act as if it never happened?

"Mario," he whispered, testing to see if the confused man was truly asleep. Maybe he was faking that, too. Mario didn't respond. Kordell rolled back over on his back and closed his eyes.

The three of them—Kordell, Mario and Javier—would come bounding into Kordell's house everyday just in time for *Batman* reruns—the campy series, not the dark, animated version and not the big-budget movies, of course. Adam West and Burt Ward. Eartha Kitt and that queeny Joker, who in retrospect looked like a combination of Prince and Little Richard.

Kordell's sister Mimi was supposed to be watching them. Kordell was only eleven or twelve. The twins were seven or eight. Somebody should have been watching all of them.

By the time *Batman* was over, Mimi's boyfriend, Tall Greg Warren, was there and the horny teens had made a beeline for her bedroom. Javier would fall asleep and be dead to the world. Kordell and Mario were left alone to watch more late-afternoon TV, play Chinese checkers or …

"Kordell, can I see your dick?"

How did I know he would go for it? How did I know that if we went back to my bedroom and I stripped to my underwear—in the name of changing my clothes—and lingered forever, he would ask?

"Kordell, can I see your dick?"

Of course, Kordell showed Mario. And from there, it was a short walk to Mario sucking Kordell's adolescent dick. And Kordell putting his mouth on Mario's very small *pre*-prepubescent dick. It was an even shorter route to the two of them doing this for—how many times? A couple? A handful? Half a year? Kordell had no idea. Kids didn't know from time. What he did remember quite accurately though was the fact that sometimes they did it right in front of Javier, who'd be asleep on the couch, oblivious.

Then, at some point, for some unknown reason, Mario wanted to stop. They'd start and Mario would hold his arms over his face, blocking Kordell from penetrating his mouth. That was when Kordell learned that he could get off by rubbing his dick on Mario's head. "Get off" might be the wrong phrase, however. Kordell couldn't remember if he was even capable of ejaculation at that point. He also didn't remember how it all came to a halt, just that it did, most likely due to a combination of Mario's resistance and the fact that Mimi went off to San Diego State and the Cervantes family found other sitters for subsequent school years.

But it was no moving painting, as Mario had suggested. It was reality. Kordell had done it with Mario. The only boy with whom Kordell had ever initiated those "boys-will-be-boys" moments. Only was it really "boys-will-be-boys"? Or was it more like, "older boys will corrupt younger boys, younger boys who start out liking it, but who eventually cover themselves as a way of hiding from your lecherous advances"?

He turned toward Mario, head only, while his body still faced the morning sky.

"Did I do this to you?"

Years ago, I heard a rumor about you and your brother both being a little sweet, as Lil' Casper—the older white boy from the 'hood—put it when I saw him at the mall during my junior year in high school. Everyone had labeled Javy a little queen long before that, and during that summer, when you two were still preteens and inseparable, Lil' Casper said that they—the people who talk and become they—they also "wondered about you." I hadn't seen you in years by then and I tried to attribute the comment to Lil' Casper's penchant for nasty gossip and his own inferiority complex, due in part to the fact that he was a 5'3" wigga that nobody liked. Not to mention the fact that he was always questioning everybody's sexual orientation, which, in retrospect, of course, was a good sign that he probably questioned his own most of all.

But none of Lil' Casper's motivations mattered to me that day in the mall. Just the mere possibility that you might be the subject of sissy rumors was all it took for guilt to course through my veins and take up

permanent residence in my head. I felt guilt and guilty right away, remembering what you and I had done—what I had done to you. For months after that run-in with Lil' Casper, I agonized over whether or not you were confused and trying to live up to the label I pinned on you when I seduced you into asking to see my dick. But then later—while I was in college—I heard that you were a stud athlete breaking all kinds of school records. I breathed a great sigh of relief then, a sigh that lasted until I saw you again, at Santa Barbara Gay Pride.

And I see it now for the first time with my own eyes. Yes, you do have a little "sweetness" in you, especially when you get all goofy and start laughing and joking around, especially when you do that crazy victory dance. Don't get me wrong: it's cute, and I could love you for it. I could love you, period.

But did I do this to you? Did I make you sweet? Did I make you bi-curious? Or gay, deep down inside? Did I make you want to do to kids what I did to you?

You called me an angel, but why do I feel like a devil to you? Why do you insist we all have the devil in us?

He stared at Mario until he didn't see Mario anymore, just a shapeless object. He wasn't even sure how much time had elapsed before he began to focus again, but when he did, he saw that Mario's eyes were open, looking back at him.

"How long have you been awake?" asked Mario.

"Not very. You looked like you needed the sleep."

"I do remember seeing my father last night. I know that's what you're wondering."

"Not necessarily, but my mind would have gotten there eventually."

"That's the first time I've laid eyes on him since the day I try to put him out of his misery with a fireplace poker when I was a kid. I think. I don't know. I'm not that awake."

"He never contacted you guys again after that?"

"He came around every once in a while to give my mom money, but he only did it when me and my brother weren't around. My mom didn't want the money, but I made her take it."

"Did you have any idea what he was up to all this time?"

"Never cared or wanted to know." Mario stood up and looked at the Facility. "I can't remember seeing him there. Or Pizarro. I was led there. My hands were tied … no, they weren't tied … damn, maybe they felt that way."

"So this place," Kordell also stood up, "is some kind of … facility. They facilitate something. You've been there before, you think. Your dad and Pizarro are tied to it, and Pizarro is tied to Project H.O.P.E. above the Mission."

"And to me and my brother somehow."

"Just like your dad is."

The thought hung in the air for a moment, then the cell phone rang.

"It's from the Mission." Kordell recognized the number on the Caller ID display. He pressed talk, put the Nokia up to his ear and said nothing.

"Hello? This is the owner of a Ford Taurus looking for his vehicle."

"Arthur." Kordell breathed a sigh of relief, as did Mario.

"I can't believe I remembered my own cell phone number," Arthur said. "Just calling to see how you and your little buddy are. And more importantly, how is my steel green friend?"

"All three are safe and sound." Kordell gave Arthur a brief update and half a dozen assurances that his car wouldn't be starring in any upcoming episode of *World's Most Dangerous Police Pursuits*. As he did, Mario walked over to the ridge and studied the Facility, trying but failing to dig up some artifact of memory.

"Good news," Kordell said after hanging up. "Fredito is doing just fine, can't wait to go to baseball camp on Wednesday. He didn't feel he was getting the Bad Touch from you and Sal has told him that Mama Carlo might have been mistaken and Uncle Kord is checking into it. "

"That's good to know," Mario said, his eyes still trying to pierce the walls of the Facility. "At least one of us is at peace."

El Destino Beach was farther up the Central Coast but not far from the Facility. It was just after dawn and the beach was all but empty. A few joggers were getting in their morning exercise and a

mother and her two small children were setting up a beach canopy, but that was it. A good place to shit, shower and shave, Kordell and Mario had decided, only there'd be no "shave" because Arthur hadn't included a razor in their on-the-lam kit (and neither one of them really needed it anyway). There'd be no "shower" either, because they didn't have towels or bathing suits, which would have been a must since the showers were located outside in plain sight. So, making do, they grabbed Arthur's toiletry bag and headed for the restroom, where they could at least wash their faces and underarms and brush their teeth. And use the facilities.

Mario went for the tin sink right away, taking off his shirt and throwing water on his dirty mug. Kordell had a different Priority Number One: brushing his teeth. He fished around the toiletry kit and took out the lone toothbrush.

"I guess Arthur figured one of us doesn't care about dental hygiene," he said.

"We can share." Mario paused as if to reconsider. "Are you ... you're not ... do you know your ..."

"Yes, I do," said Kordell. "I've been positive forever, but very healthy. Not one real serious problem, just that I am positive."

"That's cool with me," Mario said hastily.

"You use this." Kordell handed him the toothbrush. "I'll brush the way *Starsky and Hutch* brushed in the episode where Kristy McNichol was an orphan on the run. 'You just put the toothpaste on your finger,' Hutch told her." Kordell demonstrated. " 'And use your digit like a brush.' "

He didn't wait for a response. He cleaned his mouth with his index finger, refusing to wait for the awkward moment to resonate.

"*Starsky and Hutch,*" Mario mumbled while brushing his teeth with the toothbrush. "I figured you for a closet detective."

"I ain't a closet anything," Kordell shot back, grateful for the levity.

When they finished washing, they split the one sheet of paper towel that was in the dispenser and used it to dry themselves.

"You know, it wouldn't stop me," Mario said when they finished.

"From?"

"Getting to know a person, that way. Your being positive—well, I mean—I'm not. Positive. But I once dated a girl who had HIV and I'm cool with it."

Kordell nodded in appreciation, then felt like changing the subject. "What I've got to say next is probably not the kind of thing that usually follows this kind of conversation."

"And that is?"

Kordell nodded toward the lone stall. "Providing they have a nice thick roll of toilet paper in there, I'm going to paper the seat a mile high and take a much-needed dump."

They both laughed. They were actually finding laughter amidst all the confusion, grieving and chaos. They were capable of getting along so well, Kordell thought as he went to the toilet.

The stall had an ample supply of toilet paper and after covering every inch of the seat, Kordell dropped his draws and went to work. A little nervous about having a bowel movement within earshot of Mario, he read the walls. Reading material was essential, even in the privacy of his own home. The sound of Mario running water also helped.

All sorts of epithets were carved into the wood. Fuck this. Fuck that. There were drawings of all varieties of sexual anatomy, and even cruising notes. For a blow job call this number, be here at this time on this day, tap on the floor. Men, he thought. Sexual animals that never get enough. What was it Blanche of *Golden Girls* once said? They'd do it in the mud if they had to.

Not that he was any different.

The sound of running water stopped. Good timing. He was done.

As he started to leave, he noticed a drawing of a small arrow on the stall wall, pointing toward the toilet paper dispenser. He touched the metal plate that held the roller to the wall. That side of the plate dropped and began swinging from the hinge that was still attached. The action momentarily startled Kordell. The glory hole he saw surprised him even more.

They'd do it in the mud if they had to.

Sometimes men had to.

He bent over and peered through the hole. Looking through it was like an addiction, a curiosity, an automatic calling of human nature. You see a hole, you look through it. To see what hundreds, if not thousands of men have seen, their POV, their lust, their desperate desire to do it in the mud.

Mario was at the trough, taking a piss. Kordell couldn't see his dick and didn't want to see his dick. He'd seen it as a kid and didn't want to see it ever again, unless they had overcome everything to find true love in each other's arms. And still, Kordell could not stop being a voyeur.

Mario shifted, revealing another body also taking a piss. A lump swelled in Kordell's throat when he realized that the other body was that of a boy close to Fredito's age. Quietly, Kordell sat back down on the toilet seat to get a better look.

Oh God.

Mario had finished peeing and was just standing there, pants still open, dick still out, hand holding dick, eyes like lasers on the boy. The boy was urinating unassumingly. Mario, however, was not unassuming. His hand—the one that had been guiding his hose—reached upwards, as if to move toward his own face. Then it changed direction and inched into the space between him and the boy. Then, abruptly, it changed direction again, landing on the wall.

Kordell felt sick. He froze, saw himself molesting Mario as a kid, saw Mario undeniably focused on the kid. Mario's pants hit the floor, the big belt buckle colliding with the concrete below, a breach in the silence. The kid was now looking at Mario, the energy directed toward the boy finally resonating in his innocent little soul.

"Do you know what devils are, young man?" Mario asked him. Fear flooded the boy's eyes. He pulled his swim trunks up to his belly-button and ran to escape from this depraved pigsty, this rank cesspool that was swarming with the ghosts of desperate, emotionally warped men.

Kordell sat there, never wanting to come out, never wanting to face what men were capable of, what Mario was capable of, what he was capable of. He wanted to flush the toilet and be swallowed up

with the shit, toilet paper and filth. No one would ever be able to convince him that he wasn't partially, if not wholly, responsible for what had just happened, what had almost happened, what just may have happened before this day.

He heard footsteps. Someone else was now inside the restroom.

"Mario Cervantes!" the someone said. A young man's tender voice. "What a relief!"

Kordell leaned back on the toilet seat, raised his feet and quietly covered the glory hole with the toilet paper dispenser.

"Brother John!" cried Mario. "I know you! I know who you are! What are you doing here?"

"Of course, you know me, eh?"

Kordell recognized both the name and the voice from Pizarro's answering machine.

"I told Victor you'd find your way back," said Brother John. "So tell me, did you do it?"

"Did I do it?" asked Mario.

"The boy," said Brother John. "Did you do him? Did you earn a gold star?"

"I ... I ..." Mario began.

Kordell's abs began to hurt. He was in a crunch position on the seat: legs against the door, head against the back wall. He turned ever so slightly and was able to peek through the space between the partition and the wall. He saw Mario's back and the young man's face. Brother John was short, blond and handsome in that pretty boy way. He was in his early twenties, his crew cut covered with mousse.

"I did my ..." Mario stammered. "I couldn't."

"Are we not alone?" Brother John moved toward the stall. "Is that why—"

"No!" said Mario. "The stall is empty. I was alone with the kid."

"Then why did you not do what you were meant to do?" asked Brother John.

Mario didn't answer. There was a prolonged silence, only broken by the sound of more footsteps entering the restroom.

"Look who I found, Victor," said Brother John.

"So you did. What a stroke of good fortune." It was Pizarro. He

was wearing a very smug grin that was visible even through the small slit. "Mario, I knew you'd come back." When Pizarro saw that Mario was confused, he added: "To the Facility. Your mind is out of sorts, I know. That's what happens when you leave before you're ready."

"Leave?" Mario walked around the restroom. "The Facility. That's the rehab. That's why ..."

"Why what, Mario?" asked Brother John.

"Why I hitchhiked this way," said Mario. "I wasn't sure at first, but I knew I needed a ride. A ride to the Facility ... my head ... still shaky."

"Which is why—" Pizarro bent down to look under the stall.

"It's clear," said Brother John. "When I came in Mario had just met a most handsome young boy."

"Indeed." Pizarro became visibly excited. "And?"

Mario remained silent.

"Apparently his recruiting efforts failed," said Brother John. "Don't get upset, Victor. It's not his fault."

"How did you find me here?" asked Mario.

"Fate," said Pizarro. "We were merely scouting locations."

"Locations?" asked Mario.

"For field experiments," said Pizarro. "But that's none of your concern."

"My head," said Mario. "Nothing's clear."

"You should've come with me when I caught up with you behind that coffeehouse," said Pizarro. "What's the black man to you?"

"Nothing," said Mario. "Gay guy from high school I ran into. Gave me a ride. I couldn't remember who you were."

"Where have you been sleeping the last two nights?" Pizarro seemed irritated, perhaps impatient.

"The park, the beach," said Mario.

"Alone?" asked Brother John. "No boys? Not this black man?"

"Alone." Mario rubbed his eyes as if to focus his mind.

"We need to get you back." Pizarro grabbed him by the arm.

"Back?" asked Mario. "I just tried to ... am I a ..."

"Back to the Facility, where you belong," said Pizarro.

"Victor, we don't have much time," said Brother John. "You have that appointment at H.O.P.E."

"It can wait," said Pizarro. "Mario needs some very special attention right now."

"But it's with the anxious man," said Brother John. "The one who keeps calling and hanging up and won't give his name. The one who's full of shame. The perfect candidate."

"Ah, yes," said Pizarro. "Mario, I insist you come with us. I don't have much time, but I should be the one to check you back in and give you something to help you rest."

"Hold on." Mario freed himself from Pizarro's grasp. "My mind is fucked up, you know."

"I couldn't force you to come with me in front of your friend in Santa Barbara," said Pizarro. "That would have caused an unnecessary scene. But there's nothing stopping me now from making sure you complete your training."

There was a long silence while Pizarro gave Mario the chance to come along willingly. Kordell was in pain now, his cramped body slipping on the toilet.

"The idea of going back there makes me sick," said Mario, "but I don't know what other choice I have."

"It's the fastest way out of this mental haze you're in," said Pizarro.

"I know," said Mario. "I have to see things clearly, free myself of this prison my mind is in right now."

"Praise the Lord, let's go," said Pizarro.

"Yes," said Mario. "Praise the Lord. And may his angels watch over me and never let me down. May angels always be by my side, wherever I go, wherever I am, watching my back, helping me."

"Et cetera, et cetera, amen," said Brother John.

"This way to the van." Pizarro extended his hand. Mario stepped between him and Brother John. Both men took hold of Mario's arms and escorted him out of the restroom.

As soon as they were gone, Kordell collapsed on the toilet, his muscles aching and quivering. But there was no time to worry about that. He bolted out of the stall but knew better than to exit the

restroom just yet. Instead he climbed onto the wooden bench in the corner that served as a mini-changing area. There was a grating for ventilation where the wall met the ceiling. Kordell stood on the bench and peered out at the parking lot.

Brother John climbed into the passenger seat of a white mini-van. Pizarro put Mario in the back, then went around to the driver's side and got in. The engine started. The minivan backed up, then drove forward. Pizarro and Brother John were looking ahead, but Mario was looking off to the side, toward the restroom, as if to make eye contact with Kordell.

Didn't work. In the next second, Mario and the minivan were gone.

"In here," said a boy's voice from the door. A mother and child came in the restroom and found Kordell standing on the bench. He recognized the boy from the encounter with Mario. "Not him," the boy said, but that didn't stop the mom from glaring at Kordell with a chilling dose of suspicion and mistrust.

SIX

*T*his is everything The Right wants and needs to put gay culture in the grave. PARENTS' WORST FEARS ARE TRUE: GAY
RECRUITING FACTORY TRAINS PREDATORS IN THE ART OF
CHILD MOLESTING. *The National* Enquirer *couldn't make up
a story more ridiculous if the whole staff smoked crack at the next edi-
torial meeting. We are finished. We will all be finished. Donny Osmond
was wrong: one bad apple will spoil the whole bunch, girl. To para-
phrase REM, it's the end of the gay world as we know it. We might as
well all take a shot of extra-strength HIV and die within 48 hours of this
story breaking. How could we ever recover from something like this?
How could we ever convince ourselves that they were not right about us
all along?*

*And Mario ... how did you get mixed up in all this? Did they find
you or did you seek them out? Were you telling the truth about not seeing your father in years? Is this some kind of "like father, like son" deal?
What is your truth? What the fuck is my truth?*

Tired, worn and overwhelmed, Kordell headed south on
Highway 101, unable to free his mind from the most depressing of
gutters. With all the driving up and down the coast in the last two

days, he felt like a rat on a treadmill, a cog in an experiment in which, at the end of his usefulness, he'd be discarded as easily as one throws away a paper cup. The scientists would then move on, find some other unwitting suckers and toy with their lives until it was time to flush them down the drain.

He exited the 101 and made his way to State Street. His morale went from bad to worse, thinking of all the drama that had played out between him and Toxic Tommy at the coffeehouse.

Their first real date, a film at one of the many movie houses on the street, followed by a couple of nonfat lattes served up by Arthur. An Italian with a body worthy of Colt *magazines walks in. Everyone in the room with a predilection for sucking cock notices him. Tommy excuses himself mid-discussion and approaches the guy. Something about them being old friends. They exchange words. Did Tommy slip him something? A piece of paper? Was Kordell's date trying to pick up on another guy so unabashedly? Of course, he would deny it later that night. Over the next year, Toxic Tommy would do more denying than Bill Clinton did in his eight years in the White House. But the fact that Kordell put up with The Toxin for nearly 365 days—who did that speak worse of, Kordell or Tom?*

Maybe it's not our fault, Kordell thought as he pulled the car into the alley and checked himself in the mirror to make sure he looked somewhat hidden underneath his sunglasses and baseball cap. Maybe we gays never had a chance at being sane, well-adjusted members of the human race. Maybe growing up a pariah in society, where they're always telling you that people like you are lying, sick, immoral, untrustworthy, oversexed pedophiles who deserve to be beaten up and killed one way or another—maybe part of you believes it and fulfills one or more of these anti-social roles the world assigns to you.

Maybe my passing down the act of child molestation to Mario was me doing my bit for society. And now, like a good student, he's gone on to greater heights, or depths in this case, thanks in part to a man named Pizarro and a place called the Facility.

That's bullshit, Kordell. Mario was calling out to you. He needs you. You may have fucked him up then, but he needs you now.

He thought about handing the whole thing over to the cops, leaving it up to them to raid the Facility and sort out all the madness. But where would that leave Mario? What proof did Kordell have about any of this? And couldn't Kordell's accusations be construed as a desperate attempt to extricate himself from what took place at his business?

He parked Arthur's Taurus in the Mission parking lot and surveyed the coffeehouse. *Their* coffeehouse. One of the few places in town where gay men and women could unapologetically feel at home with their friends—relaxed, laughing, drinking, touching, kissing, planning, dreaming. A place where the alterna-kids met up to study, admire each other's piercings and tattoos, and swap instant messages on laptops and PDAs. Even he and Tommy had had a good moment or two there. Okay, more than a good moment or two.

Kordell stopped at the back door. The main door was open. Only a screen door separated him from the place he once treasured. He removed his sunglasses and baseball cap, opened the door and walked down the shadowy hallway. Seconds later, he was in the light.

Arthur was there, back to Kordell at the cash register to the right. Kordell headed straight for him, glancing around the room as he did. Not much had changed. The front section of the room had little square tables and wooden chairs, resembling the many cafés that dotted State Street. Real meals, albeit mostly sandwiches and short-order stuff, was served there. A miniature wall separated the front from the middle section, which was called the living room. It contained old velvet couches and sofa chairs in bright primary colors. Classic post-modern coffeehouse. Then there was the third section, where Arthur stood, which consisted of the cash register and a glass counter full of expensive sweets. Arthur was the only person Kordell recognized. The place wasn't that full, but a few people were having breakfast in the café section, most of them appearing much younger than he remembered.

"Don't panic. It's only me and me alone," Kordell said to Arthur's back.

Arthur gasped, then spun around and said in a low voice: "What are you doing? Have you resolved everything? Is he—you know—did he?"

"Nothing's resolved," said Kordell. "Far from it, *very* far from it."

"Then why are you taking a chance being seen in public? Can you say All Points Bulletin?"

"Desperate times, desperate measures. All roads lead to ..." Kordell nodded upwards to Project H.O.P.E. on the second floor.

"Where is he?" asked Arthur.

"Out of harm's way. Or in harm's way, I'm not sure, but I intend to find out. How dangerous is my being here, has Sal—"

"She's still giving you until Wednesday. But some cops come in here sometimes for the sweets. If the police saw you—"

"Stop whispering." Kordell felt the presence of a body somewhere behind him but didn't want to look right away. "You're making us look suspicious."

"No one but us knows anything about this." Arthur whispered anyway and had guilt written all over his heavyset face.

"How much is this one?" Kordell walked around to the other side of the counter and pretended to inspect the pricey sweets. The body behind him was within earshot. It was a handsome Asian man who was mopping the floor. He was tall with high cheekbones, and despite his smooth, youthful face, he looked to be in his late thirties. Under saner circumstances, Kordell's attraction meter would have been going off.

"Go for the kiwi torte," Arthur said to Kordell. "It's fresher and on sale."

"It is, huh?" said Kordell. The Asian man made eye contact with Kordell. They smiled at each other. Was that a spark in the man's eyes? "Is kiwi in season?" He lowered his voice so that only Arthur could hear. "*What about Batter Up? What's going on with it?*"

"*The cops are done there for now. Lying and claiming I had power of attorney worked. They let me lock it up and post a 'closed for repairs' sign.*" Arthur cleared his throat. "Figured out what you'd like yet?"

"Two kiwi tortes. The large ones." Kordell thought about all the school-aged kids who had just won their freedom for the summer and would be dying to get into the arcade. Business would suffer, but so what? Batter Up might never open its doors again.

"I love kiwi, can't get enough. Is that for here or to go?" Arthur glanced at the Asian man. *"So what you gonna do?"*

"Pay a visit. To go, I can't stay. *Who is that?"*

"New guy. No big. I hired him a few months ago. Five dollars even. They're on special."

"Specials are good. *You sure?"*

"Koji!" Arthur called the Asian man over. "Koji, this is" —he stopped cold, realizing he was about to do a very bad thing to a man who was trying to lay low— "my friend, my good friend. My good friend, this is Koji Yamamoto. He's new here. From LA."

Kordell was too busy trying to stop his heart attack to pay Koji much attention. "Nice to meet you." He snatched the bag of tortes from Arthur. "I'll pay for them later. Better still, you owe me after this." He made a hasty exit, heading for the hallway that led to the upstairs tenants.

Fitting that the door would make a creaking sound as it opened. COME ON IN, GET H.O.P.E. the sign on the glass proudly declared. Underneath, it further explained: MAKING A DIFFERENCE BY HONORING OUR PERSONAL EVOLUTION.

So that's what it stands for.

Kordell inched his way across the threshold and wondered: did they realize that one of their own was coaching gay men on how to be better child predators? How to pick up kids on the Internet? The most effective child lures? The best dark, dank and smelly beach restrooms to find little boys and—

"Hi, come on in and get hope," said a young blonde with long, straight *Brady Bunch* hair. She was all alone, sitting behind a desk amidst half a dozen identical desks.

"I'm—hi—I'm with the Gay Business Alliance." Kordell maintained his ground near the door. "We wanted to—well, I feel like a bad neighbor who's waited much too long to come over and welcome you with a plate of cookies. Except I don't have any cookies, just goodies from downstairs."

"I'm Sunny," she said. "I'm the only one here, but come, come." She motioned for Kordell to sit in the chair in front of her desk. He did as he was told.

"Are things slow today?" He set the bag of kiwi tortes on the desk and glanced around. Project H.O.P.E. looked like any other small business office: file cabinets, computer monitors, piles of paperwork filling in-boxes.

"Pride weekend wiped everyone out, I suspect. Herbal tea?" She held up a mug for him to see. When he declined, she took a sip.

"No one told us—the Business Alliance, that is—that you were here," said Kordell. "You didn't get a brochure from the Chamber of Commerce?"

Sunny thought about it, but waited too long to answer.

"How long have you been here?" Kordell asked. "I mean, did you have an operation somewhere before this? Is your head person here in Santa Barbara? Who is that person by the way?" He saw her eyes widen and knew he was piling on the questions a little too anxiously.

"I've only been here three weeks myself," she said.

"And what do you do, if you don't mind?"

"Whatever they need me to do."

"Oh … cool." *Cool?* Did he actually use that word?

"Want to leave your card?" she asked.

"I ran out. This was more of a I-was-in-the-neighborhood kind of thing, not very prepared, I know. But no one else is here? Or coming?"

A knowing look wiped across Sunny's face. She leaned over her desk and whispered: "I think I know what you want." Then she rose up and went over to a file cabinet. Was that where they kept the weapons? A panic alarm button? "Not to worry," she added smugly. "I know just what to do."

"Maybe I should come back some other … other …" Was there enough time to make it to the door?

"I can take care of you." She opened the top file cabinet and pulled out … *a file.* "Just let me get some basic information and we can get you started."

"Started?"

She sat back down, opened the yellow folder and began filling out the top sheet of paper. "Open up a case file. It's strictly anonymous though. No one will ever know you came to us for help."

"Help? I don't … you don't understand. I don't" —*wait a minute, hold on a sec*— "I don't want anyone to find out I'm doing this. I'm head of the Business Alliance, after all. People expect me to be their leader and I can't always lead when I'm, well, you know."

Sunny looked up with an empathetic look on her face. "Confused?"

"Very," said Kordell. "Which is why I need Mr. Pizarro's help."

"He's not available," she said matter-of-factly.

"He's supposed to be here today." *For the confused man who keeps calling and hanging up.* "For me. We have an appointment, yes?"

"Mr. Pizarro has a very extensive workload that takes him all over the central coast," said Sunny. "We have plenty of other quali- fied—"

"If I can't have him," —Kordell blurted, raising his voice. He settled back in his chair and tried to seem calmer, less anxious— "if I can't have him … I don't want nobody else."

He stopped short of adding: *baby* like the old disco song. Sunny stopped her work and asked: "How did you even hear about Mr. Pizarro?"

Kordell paused, but before he could field this one, he heard a man's voice from behind him.

"As flattered as I am, I'd like to know that, too."

It was Pizarro, standing in the doorway. When Kordell turned around, Pizarro recognized him from the parking lot, when Kordell and Mario commandeered Arthur's car.

"Thank God you're here!" said Kordell.

"Mario's friend," said Pizarro. "Kordell, isn't it?"

"I thought you weren't going to show. Yes, that's right, Kordell Christie." He stood up, deciding to use the nervousness racing through his veins. It fit, added to the character of the Confused Gay Man. He turned back to Sunny. "Told you, I have an appointment with him."

"You know this man?" Sunny asked Pizarro.

"I didn't realize you were the one who's been calling incessant- ly," said Pizarro. "You failed to mention that when we met."

"With good reason." Kordell could feel the sweat cascading from his brow. "My friend. Your friend. I can explain, but" —he turned back to Sunny— "I would feel more comfortable doing this in private."

"That can be arranged," Pizarro said in an ominous voice befitting an evil, queeny villain in an animated family movie.

"I heard good things about H.O.P.E. a while back," Kordell said moments later as he entered Pizarro's office.

"The names of those who spoke so well of us?" Pizarro asked, closing the door behind him and motioning to a chair in front of his desk.

"It was a conversation I overheard at a party." Kordell sat.

"A sex party?" Pizarro sat behind the desk.

Kordell blanched. "No, just a *party* party. Someone mentioned getting good counseling from here and raved that you were the man."

"What about Mario?" asked Pizarro.

"What *about* Mario?" asked Kordell.

"What did he say about me or the wellness center?"

"Said he didn't want to talk about it," said Kordell. "Which was fine with me because no way was I gonna come clean and admit to needing counseling about my sexuality. I'm not supposed to be coming to a place like this. I'm supposed to be out and proud and strong, a pillar of the gay community, the role model, the business leader."

"Is Mario a former boyfriend of yours?"

"First time I'd seen him in over twenty-five years. We both grew up in Oxnard. I take it he's a patient of yours? Is patient the right word?"

"Who our *clients* are is confidential. If he were one, I couldn't tell you."

"So if I become one, you won't tell him? Or anybody else?"

"I don't take on new clients," said Pizarro. "My job is overseer. If someone needs extra help, I may take a case or two as a favor, but I'm quite busy."

"So Mario needed extra help?"

Pizarro's head tilted to one side, his lips forming a tight, snide grin.

"Sorry, that's a no-no," said Kordell. "I know ... know. It's just that Mario did seem, well, a little weird."

"How much time did you spend with him?"

Corroborating stories, eh?

"Just enough to reminisce about the old neighborhood," said Kordell. "And give him a ride. He said he had to get somewhere, but I ended up just taking him up the coast a little and dropping him off near the beach—his request."

"Then why did you insist on helping him ditch me?"

Did Mario hurt poor little Pizarro's feelings?

"I was just following his lead," said Kordell. "He wasn't exactly himself. Or the person I remembered growing up. I was actually glad to drop him off."

"You didn't see him after that?"

"Didn't even exchange numbers." Kordell paused. "Have you seen him?"

"No." *Fucking liar.*

"Will you see me, as a client, that is?"

"What is the nature of your anxiety?" asked Pizarro.

"What isn't? What services do you offer?"

"H.O.P.E. is designed to provide gay men with the resources they need to lead healthy, productive lives that all of society can be proud of. That ranges from counseling to support groups to holistic options to anything we need to do to help you become the person you were meant to become."

"How do I know the kind of person I was meant to become?"

"What's on your mind, Mr. Christie? Or shall I say: what's in your mind? I can't know where to steer you unless I know where you are on your personal journey."

"Where do I start?" Kordell stood up and began walking around the room, figuring he'd better throw out as many distress signals as possible. "I could be called a lot of things. Sexual compulsive. Substance abuser. I feel caught up in a lot of the ... barebacking, hard time making a commitment, being monogamous. I wonder if being gay is a sin after all. I have immoral thoughts. Illegal thoughts."

"Par for the course for today's gay man."

"What can you do about it?" asked Kordell.

"Help you help yourself."

"What if I can't?"

"Do you believe you can?"

"I don't know." Kordell feigned serious contemplation. "I've been living this way for a very long time. I know people change, but it seems like they always slip up, *fall* backward."

Pizarro began playing with one of those big plastic eight balls that tell one's future, rotating it in his pale, bony hands. "What would the last resort be for you?"

"What do you mean?" asked Kordell.

"If all else fails and you couldn't see yourself being happy being gay, would you consider an alternate lifestyle?"

"You mean an alternate lifestyle from *this* alternate lifestyle— that would be ... going ... turning ... straight?"

The look in Pizarro's eyes said: precisely.

"I'd never do that," Kordell said, convinced this was what a sick child molester would want to hear. "I'm a man-smoker for life, a lifer. I couldn't give it up if I tried, and believe me, I don't wanna try."

Pizarro sat up straight and returned the eight ball to its home on his desk.

"Why do you ask?" Kordell sat back down in front of the desk. "Do you believe people can change?"

"It's not for me to believe or disbelieve," said Pizarro. "I was simply asking as a sort of Rorschach test to see where you are psychologically. If you truly wanted to turn straight, we could refer you to places, highly-recommended places."

"That's kind of an odd thing for a gay wellness place, don't you think."

"Do you know how many people we get in here asking if we can make their feelings for the same sex disappear? The number is staggering. That's why I got into this business years ago: young men, not-so-young men—all twisted up inside, wanting nothing more than to procreate with a beautiful girl and have a riding lawn mower and Christmas mornings with lots of children and toys paid for with maxed-out credit cards. It's the American Dream and none of us is

immune from wanting it. If you came in here insisting on achieving that, we do have places we can recommend, but that's not you, or so you claim."

"So the fact that I don't want to change, where does that put me?"

"One way or another, Project H.O.P.E. can cure what ails you." Pizarro stood up. "Make an appointment with Sunny and she'll put you with a good case worker."

"What ails me is eating me up inside." Kordell kicked the *High Anxiety* act into overdrive. Appointments were for people who couldn't be accused of harboring a child molester—*potential* child molester—from the law, for people who had more than 48 hours to prove otherwise to their best friend and that very same law. "I don't know if I can wait. I might explode!"

He was interrupted mid-plea by the intercom on the desk:

"Mr. Pizarro." Sunny's sunny voice. "There's a man here to see you, says it's urgent and that you agreed to see him today."

The *real* Confused Gay Man, Kordell realized.

"Right now!" He stood up. "I have to know that you'll help, that someone will help—oh, God—I'm not going to hyperventilate again, am I?"

"Sit down." Pizarro started toward the door. "Let me get Sunny—"

"*No!*" Kordell cried.

Pizarro stopped his forward progress.

"I have to use the bathroom." Kordell pressed his knees together and squirmed in place. "It's not my breathing. It's my kidney. It's always one or the other when I get nervous and confused. I have to pee, but I don't want to leave."

"You can't pee here!" said Pizarro.

"Where's the restroom?"

"In the hall."

"I can make it I think."

"Are you sure?"

"Promise not to go anywhere?"

Pizarro hesitated.

"I'm nervous!" Kordell squirmed more for emphasis.

"Then go!"

"But don't leave. I need to know you'll be here for me when I get back. That you won't go anywhere—my anxiety." Kordell buckled as if his kidney or bowels or both were about to let go. "I also have abandonment issues. My daddy left me."

"I'll stay," Pizarro cried. "Just go!"

"Promise?"

"*Promise!*"

"Right back." Kordell scampered toward the door, flung it open and slammed it behind him. Then he hurried down the hallway, past the bathroom, and peeked around the corner. *Real* Confused Gay Man was sitting on one of the couches in the waiting area. He was a chubby young cub who truly looked on the verge of pissing in his pants. Sunny was at her desk, head down, reading a newspaper. Kordell drew back and waved to get the guy's attention. It didn't work. *Real* Confused Gay Man just kept rocking back and forth, his hands tightly clasped between his chubby, quivering thighs. Kordell waved again. Still didn't work. Kordell jumped up and down and threw his arms over his head. This worked.

Real Confused Gay Man's eyes became wide with panic when he saw Kordell. Good. Kordell motioned toward the door, trying to warn the man to get out of here. At first the man didn't understand. He was too caught up in his own nervousness. He kept mouthing "what?" and looking over to Sunny, who was oblivious to them. Kordell decided to try another approach: he grabbed his crotch just like another Santa Barbara county resident, Michael Jackson, then made a fist and used it as if he were pumping a cock in and out of his mouth. A new kind of fear morphed in the young cub's eyes, but he still wasn't moving. Kordell started massaging his own body, molesting himself like Jim Carrey might in a stand-up routine. After that, he went back to the "get out of here!" motions. It worked. *Real* Confused Gay Man turned into Scared Shitless Gay Man. Without a word, he bolted from Project H.O.P.E.

A few seconds later, Kordell entered Pizarro's office looking relaxed and refreshed. He felt sorry for the young cub, but he could-

n't worry about that now. He had to take solace in the fact that maybe he'd saved the guy from becoming even more fucked up.

"Can I get you anything?" Pizarro asked, still worried for Kordell.

"I'm much better now, back to normal—"

"Good." Pizarro stood up. "I must leave." He collected his brief-case, cell phone and leather jacket. "I have an emergency some distance away, someone else more dire than you, believe it or not."

"But you said you'd stay."

"Make an appointment with Sunny." Pizarro herded Kordell through the door and locked his office once they were on the other side. "As I explained, you'll be in good hands with our staff."

"But I want you, Mr. Pizarro, please." Kordell followed him down the hallway.

Pizarro turned and looked him squarely in the eye. "You can't have me." Then he was out the door, leaving Kordell standing there in the main office with Sunny.

"Herbal tea?" Sunny asked, holding up her trusty mug.

SEVEN

Kordell stormed down the hallway that led to the coffee-house, wondering: *what the hell am I supposed to do now?* The visit to H.O.P.E. hadn't cleared up a damned thing, except the fact that the time bomb underneath his ass was ticking steadily while the riddles that had invaded his world seemed no closer to being solved.

Arthur was waiting on two customers seated on the blue velvet sofa in the living room. His large frame obliterated their identities until Kordell came closer—too close to back away, as it turned out. He noticed Sal and her lover Jenna before they saw him, but when they did, Sal looked none too pleased.

"*This* is why you got me down here." She shot a dirty look to Arthur and yanked at Jenna's cornrows. "False pretenses."

"Y'all need to talk," said Arthur.

"I had a hunch," Jenna said in response to Sal's suspicious glare. "But I did *not* have a hand in this."

Kordell wondered if Jenna was being sympathetic toward him because they were both black. Whatever the reason, Sal didn't share that sympathy. She looked ready to bolt or call the cops.

"How's Freddy?" he asked her.

"Keeps bugging me about when he can go to Batter Up again."

"What do you—"

"Closed for repairs." Her tone was very formal. "Where is he and what do you know?"

"He's at this place called the Facility," said Kordell. "Any of you heard of it?"

His friends shook their heads.

"Sounds like a mental hospital," said Jenna.

"I'm not sure what it is." Kordell sat on the arm of the sofa. "I don't know what's going on, Sal, Jenna, Arthur. I think I've failed in a big way and now I'm gonna pay for it."

"Hold on, honey." Jenna rose up and put an arm around his shoulder. "Arthur, go get him some water."

Arthur complied.

"Are you saying he did try to" —Sal braced herself— "did he try to molest my child or not?"

Kordell thought long and hard. He was on the witness stand and the judge and jury were waiting. Arthur came back with a glass of water. Kordell took a long sip while his three friends eyed him.

"I don't want to believe he did," he said. "And I don't *think* he did. But even if he's guilty, it might not be his fault."

"*Not his fault?*" cried Judge Sal. "Don't tell me he's got some crazy-assed victim story as his defense. Did he eat too many Twinkies growing up?"

"There are others involved." Kordell was looking down but felt his friends tense up and draw closer. "This isn't just about Mario anymore. Something's going on and it's bigger than him or me. It's sick, really sickening."

"And this has something to do with Project H.O.P.E.?" asked Arthur.

"Project H.O.P.E.?" Jenna backed away from Kordell and retreated to her seat on the couch. "Wait a minute. You're talking about some serious accusations here. Before you say a word to anyone, you better make sure you're standing on some very solid ground."

"I might as well be hopping on one foot on the San Andreas fault," said Kordell. "And for all the good I'm doing, it may as well open up and take me now."

"Okay, time out." Arthur turned to Sal and Jenna. "Now, girls, I mean, ladies—"

"Women," said Sal.

"Whatever," said Arthur. "Kordell, you need help. Let us help. Tell us what you do and don't know. Think of us as your angels, Charlie."

There was that word again. *Angel.* Never had Kordell heard so much about angels and devils than he had in the last two days. He took a seat on the sofa opposite Sal and Jenna.

"Years ago," he began, "a man named Giovanni had two twin boys. One was Javier, who's a little bit—well, to hell with being PC— Javy was a little queen. The other one is Mario, athletic stud but not hyper-masculine, just …"

"Tall, dark and handsome." Arthur sat next to Kordell. "Did you ever find out if he's a chub chaser?"

"Arthur!" said Jenna.

"Innocent until proven guilty, no?" said Arthur.

"He's straight, like I told you at Pride," said Kordell. "Well, not *totally* straight, but bi or … anyway. As kids, Giovanni molested Javy, but not Mario. When Mario found out about it—back then—he took some hardware to his father's head and the father moved out, end of dad's involvement in the family. Supposedly."

His friends all took deep breaths and moved about nervously.

"Flash ahead to now," Kordell went on. "Javy was just bailed out of jail after being arrested for trying to meet a minor online."

"How young?" asked Sal.

"Young," Kordell said, trying to be evasive.

"*How* young?" Sal insisted.

Kordell hesitated. "Preteen. But get this. Mario says that not only is Javier innocent, but he's straight! Little queeny Javier is straight."

"Get out," said Arthur.

"Meanwhile," Kordell said, "Mario shows up at Pride all dazed

and confused—not from drugs, he swears—and the last significant event he remembers about his own life is breaking up with his girlfriend months ago. Cut to yesterday morning—the morning after Pride—when it appears as if Mario's trying to do to Fredito what Mario's dad used to do to Javier."

"And Javier passed on?" asked Jenna.

"We found him in his apartment yesterday and Mario is sure it wasn't suicide. And get this: Pizarro from H.O.P.E. shows up at Javy's place. He knows both Mario *and* Javier, but Mario has no memory of him. But Mario *does* have a vague memory of this Facility place, which Pizarro is connected to somehow. And we saw Mario's dad coming out of the Facility, too. And Pizarro has something to do with—how should I put this?—little boys. What the fuck is going on? How creepy is that?"

"How *Twin Peaks* meets *X-Files* meets NAMBLA is that?" said Arthur.

"What's NAMBLA?" asked Jenna.

"You don't wanna know," said Arthur.

"Men in love with boys," said Sal. "They're always fighting to get into our parades and we're always fighting to keep them out. I'm calling the cops. I know I said I'd give you until Wednesday, but now I don't know."

"Mario is not part of this of his own free will," said Kordell. "I think. And how and why is this all tied to Project H.O.P.E.?"

"Just because Pizarro works there doesn't mean they're all in on it," said Jenna.

"They'll can his ass if a scandal breaks out," said Arthur.

Just then, a man's voice caught them by surprise.

"Project H.O.P.E.? I do stuff for them." It was Koji, the new Asian worker. This time, instead of a mop, he had a broom. "It's a good place, no?"

They all remained mute, like children who'd just been caught plotting something children shouldn't be doing.

"We don't know much about it," Jenna finally said. "Maybe you can tell us."

"They believe in a spiritual approach to mental health." Koji's

tone was very deferential. "Good people doing good work. It changes lives. For the better."

"Does someone work there named John?" asked Kordell. "Or Brother John?"

"I know Brother John," said Arthur. "Talk about *Twin Peaks* meets *X-Files*. Can you say weirdo?"

"Why? Who is he?" asked Kordell.

"Just one of the staff upstairs," said Arthur. "His name is actually Brother John. I made him show me his driver's license and that's what it says. Short fucker, cute, but says he's celibate for life. Yuck. "

"That's two," Kordell nodded upstairs and Koji immediately zeroed in on him.

"I didn't catch your name earlier." Koji extended his hand.

"Kordell." They shook.

"Nice to meet you, Kordell. And your family name?"

Kordell froze. Jenna cleared her throat in a panic. Sal did a spit-take with her cappuccino.

"You know what, gang?" Arthur said hastily. "You three are gonna have lunch on me while Mr. Yamamoto and I get back to work. Y'all have a lot to catch up on and I'll join you when I can. New boy don't wanna get fired on the job, do he?" Arthur led Koji to the kitchen without waiting for an answer, leaving Kordell alone with Sal and Jenna.

A few moments later, they were seated at one of the tables in the café, failing to come up with small talk. It wasn't until Arthur came back to take their order that the tension lessened.

"Didn't know Orientals were so nosy—joking," Arthur quickly added before Jenna was able to scold him for being so un-PC.

"I don't have much of an appetite." Kordell closed the menu.

"You need to keep your strength up," Sal said from across the table. "You've probably been eating like crap, if at all, and you know you're stressed."

"My day-old sandwiches are not *like crap*, thank you very much," said Arthur.

Kordell and Sal stared at each other with a softness in their eyes that had been missing since yesterday morning, a softness that said

this was hard for both of them, that Sal understood that Kordell would never knowingly place her child in harm's way, and that Kordell understood that Sal was doing what she had to do for her family.

"I'll have a club sandwich," Kordell said, not taking his eyes off Sal, who smiled a smile of recognition. It was what Kordell always ordered in the good old days, when they came to the Mission before the breakup with Tommy.

"I'll have—" Sal began, but Arthur finished her sentence:

"Swiss-turkey, no bacon, no mayo, no fun. And chopped salad for Queen Jenna, I presume? Light on the garbanzos?"

"Civility and love in hard times." Jenna clasped her hands together as if in prayer. "That's what makes us human. That's what makes us family."

"I want this to be over," Kordell said, almost breaking into tears as he watched Arthur walk away.

"You think I don't?" Sal scoffed, then segued to a softer tone. "It will be over on Wednesday morning, right? One way or another, you'll find out what you need to know or we'll let the cops do the investigating, agreed?"

"What time is Freddy supposed to leave for camp?" asked Kordell.

"Crack of dawn unfortunately," Sal said, wincing at the idea of an early morning.

"You have my word," said Kordell. "I will give you and/or the cops everything I know by then."

Jenna nodded toward the window and murmured, "Speaking of c-o-p-s."

A small crowd of people passed by on the sidewalk. Among them were four cops. Immediately, Sal and Kordell buried their faces in their menus.

"Breathe," said Jenna. "Deeply. And relax."

"They can't see me," Sal and Kordell said simultaneously.

"… having a meal with him," Sal added, then said, "No offense."

"None taken," Kordell replied facetiously.

"Well, if your body language reads *guilty*." Jenna waved at the cops who were eyeing them through the window. The cops waved

back. "Keep going," she ordered them like a voodoo doctor. "They obeyed," she said after a beat.

Sal's and Kordell's menus came down, followed by sighs of relief and a quick look-see of their own. The cops were drifting farther and farther away, strolling aimlessly through the crowds on the sidewalk. As they passed, they revealed two men heading straight for the Mission and Kordell immediately recognized one of them.

"Oh, boy."

"More cops?" Sal asked, hoisting her menu upward.

"Almost as bad."

As small a town as Santa Barbara was, Kordell hadn't seen his ex in months. It helps when you ban yourself from the gym, movie theaters, coffeehouse and beaches you frequented as a couple. Now, here was Toxic Tommy at the worst possible time.

He entered with his friend—a short, white man with black curly hair—and made a beeline for Kordell. Tommy's gym bod had moved up to the big leagues. The muscles on his dark chocolate biceps were almost shiny, especially against his bright yellow tank top. Kordell had the urge to say something dripping with sarcasm like, *I see the 'roids are paying off.* Or: *Does this mean you've been granted a full membership into the Bareback Circuit Boys Club?*

"We were just leaving," he said instead, standing up and throwing a buck on the table—a *faux* tip. "Nice not seeing you again. Let's not do it again sometime."

Sal and Jenna sat stunned until Kordell motioned for them to get up and get with the program.

"Hi, Toxic—er—Tommy," Sal said in her rush to vacate the table. "Bye, Tommy."

She didn't wait for a reply before heading for the back and Jenna followed suit after nodding hello. She had to at least acknowledge another black person in this small town. Kordell stayed behind. No harm in seeing how Tommy took the salvo just fired his way, as well as checking out this latest trick.

"Leaving on my account?" asked Tommy.

"Things to do, yadda, yadda, yadda." Kordell pretended to search for another bill to add to the tip.

"Elijah, this is Kordell," said Tommy. "Kordell, this is my friend, Elijah."

Kordell and Elijah nodded hello. The awkward expression on Elijah's face made it clear that the Jewish boy was Tommy's new toxic disposal dump and that he was keenly aware of the fact that Kordell had once held the position.

"Gotta go." Kordell started to leave, then paused. If he was going to be a good amateur investigator … "I'm trying to find out info about Project H.O.P.E. upstairs and two people who work there: Victor Pizarro and Brother John."

"Brother John?" Tommy said laughingly. "What is he, a frat boy?"

"Sorry I asked. Truly." Kordell started to walk away.

"I don't know a Brother John," Tommy added, "but I have met Victor."

"And?"

"Don't know much about him," said Tommy. "Just that they do some pretty intense New Age counseling."

"Where'd you hear this from?"

"Dude," said Tommy. "You should get out more. It's no secret they're into some pretty alternative stuff."

"I get out plenty, *dude*," said Kordell. "I just haven't been here."

"Have it your way." Tommy shrugged.

"And the Facility?" said Kordell. "Either of you heard of it?"

They both shook their heads.

"See ya."

"I'll call you to hang out sometime," said Tommy.

Kordell had already walked away and didn't bother responding to Tommy's bald-faced lie.

"Can my week get any worse—and do not answer that," he said when he reached the living room and found Sal and Jenna sitting on the blue velvet sofa.

"Heard you needed to go into de-tox," Arthur said, rejoining them with a tray containing their lunches.

"Sit," Jenna told Kordell as she indicated a yellow flyer on the coffee table.

"What's this?" Kordell sat and picked up the flyer. It was for a charity ball. Wear a huge wig, raise money for Santa Barbara AIDS orgs.

"Pay no mind to that." Jenna turned the paper over for him and handed him a pencil. "You've gotten yourself tangled in a wicked web. What you need to do is untangle it. Get it out in front of you so you can see things more clearly. Write."

Kordell regarded her as if she were the only one who understood him, then began making notes. First he put down names: Mario, Pizarro, Brother John, the Facility, H.O.P.E., Javy, Giovanni.

Sal and Jenna—and Arthur when he had a spare second—hovered over Kordell and around Kordell. They ate. They drew diagrams. They created wheels with spokes representing the different people and organizations involved. They put all the names in a circle and drew lines as if connecting the dots. They used the backs of more flyers. They ate more lunch, drank more coffee. And tried desperately to make sense of the bewildering web that had spun around all of their lives.

"Pizarro's connected to H.O.P.E. and the Facility, and knows Javier and Mario and preaches good mental health, but advocates touching little boys in restrooms."

"Mario hasn't heard of H.O.P.E. but has a vague memory of the Facility and knows Javier, Pizarro and Giovanni, though he barely remembers Pizarro and hadn't seen Giovanni for years until he saw him coming out of the Facility, which Pizarro …"

"Brother John knows Mario, Pizarro, the Facility and H.O.P.E., but …"

They used more backs of flyers, tore up more backs of flyers, and speculated on more possible connections, scenarios and entanglements.

"Giovanni knows his sons, though allegedly he hasn't seen them in years, and is connected in some way to the Facility; but how well does he know Pizarro? Brother John? Is he part of H.O.P.E.?"

At one point they passed around a bottle of Tylenol that Arthur retrieved from the kitchen. Another time, Toxic Tommy and Elijah passed by on their way to the restroom and snuck up on the unsus-

pecting foursome, who were planted on the couches, deep into their detective work.

"Thought you were in a hurry," Tommy whispered in Kordell's ear from behind.

Kordell startled, collected himself and stammered. "I am. I'm in a hurry doing stuff."

Tommy noticed the mess on the table; Kordell hastily gathered up the flyers.

"Whatchadoin'?" asked Tommy.

Kordell was at a loss.

"It's a game," said Jenna. "Kind of like a whodunit."

"We play it all the time," said Sal. "We have so much fun now, playing games and stuff."

"Woo, so much fun," said Arthur.

"How's it played?" asked Elijah.

"Look, if you don't mind," said Kordell, "it's way too complicated to explain right now."

"Massively complicated," said Arthur.

"Oh, boy," chimed Sal. "Complicated is not the word."

"Complicated?" Jenna scoffed. "More like impossible."

"I think they get that it's complicated." Kordell gave his friends a stern look, then turned back to Tommy and Elijah. "We're kinda anxious to keep playing, so if you don't mind."

"I meant it when I said I'll call you. As a friend," Tommy promised, and he and Elijah left.

"*Do* hold your breath." Kordell shuffled through the stack of flyers. "Where were we? Brother John works at the Facility or does he just know of it—oh, this *is* impossible." He flung the flyers toward the table. "I need to get to Mario in the Facility. That's the only way I'm gonna get anywhere."

"You could always call the cops." Sal held up her hands. "Just a suggestion."

"Okay, you two," said Jenna. "Let's take a break."

"Who wants cheesecake?" asked Arthur.

"I have a better idea." Kordell motioned toward their diagrams, which looked like hieroglyphics. "Let's just burn all this nonsense."

"Hush now, *chile*," said Jenna, after which Arthur sang:

"Things are gonna get easier."

"Speaking of breaks, Arthur." It was Koji, showing up again in the middle of their conversation. "Can I take mine now? I'm past due and I have a friend waiting." He indicated the café area, prompting Arthur to steal a glance and ask:

"Into older men are we?"

Koji averted Arthur's coy gaze.

"Take your fifteen," said Arthur. "You'll need it to deal with the lunch crowd."

Koji nodded in an overly grateful way, then untied his apron and headed for the café.

"Oh, and Yamo," Arthur said to him. "Make sure Jules knows you're on break, will ya?"

Kordell froze and came alive at the same time. Blood rushed to his head; his vision blurred. For several seconds, he was unable to focus, didn't need to, didn't want to. It was all happening a hundred miles an hour in his mind: the realization, the moment, the missing puzzle piece. He stood up just as Koji passed him on the way to the café. Koji regarded him and smiled, but Kordell was too deep in shock to acknowledge him.

"Paging Mr. Christie," Arthur said, but Kordell couldn't respond.

Koji Yamamoto was Yamo, the man who had entered Pizarro's house while Kordell and Mario had hid in the closet.

"McPherson. Yamo. No time. Company coming. Office."

Kordell hadn't dreamt of connecting the Anglo-sounding voice in Pizarro's bedroom with a man called Yamamoto, a common Japanese name, if there ever was one.

I almost fucked up, thanks to racial profiling.

Yamo entered the café area and sat at a table occupied by a dark-haired man whose back was all Kordell could see. Kordell moved forward to get a closer look. The two men were talking in a very friendly manner. This was definitely a pleasant meeting.

The man's profile came into view. Kordell recognized him, then slowly backed away. Giovanni Cervantes was having coffee with Koji Yamamoto. Yamo. Who'd been inside Pizarro's house. Giovanni.

Who was seen coming out of the Facility, where Mario had been returned to by Pizarro, who worked upstairs and to whom all roads seemed to lead.

Kordell's butt ran into something. It was a couch in the living room. He felt Sal and Jenna and Arthur in his periphery but couldn't take his eyes off the meeting of the two men.

"Yamo," he simply said.

"What about him?" It was Arthur, his breath inches from Kordell's ear.

"I should have known. Yamamoto. What do you know …"

"About Koji? Typical newbie. Wide-eyed, somewhat innocent to be in his thirties and from LA."

"What … you mean?"

"Too friendly sometimes," said Arthur. "Asks a lot of questions and talks to everybody, and I do mean everybody. Yammers on about H.O.P.E., too, like he's the damned chairmen of the PR department."

"Publicizing …"

"Huh?"

Kordell spun around and began shuffling through the flyers, looking for the ones he needed.

"You got something, baby?" asked Jenna.

"I don't …" His mind was moving too fast to speak. He didn't want to lose his train of thought, but instinct told him to look up. In the café, Yamo was pointing to the back hallway and Giovanni was getting up. "Where …" Kordell shuffled faster through the papers. "The one … the last one?"

"Here it is." Sal held up a sheet of paper.

Kordell grabbed it. "Can I hide?"

"In the kitchen," said Arthur. Kordell hightailed it behind the counter and into the kitchen, bracing himself against the first wall he saw to catch his breath.

"Shit, shit, shit," was all he could say at first. Arthur promptly entered and told the two Latinos cooking on the center island to take their cig breaks.

"A pen," Kordell said after they exited through the back door and he and Arthur were alone.

"I gotta check on the customers." Arthur fished a pen out of his shirt pocket and handed it over. "You okay?"

"Go." Kordell began writing. "H.O.P.E. is Koji, Pizarro and Brother John. The Facility is Pizarro, Brother John and Giovanni." He ran out of room on the paper. He scanned the room for more, saw a chalkboard on the wall. He raced over to it, erased some menu items with his forearm, then scribbled the names Giovanni and Yamo.

Yamo knows Giovanni who's tied to the Facility. Giovanni is a child molester. Pizarro, Brother John, molesters. All tied to the Facility.

"The Facility is all about child molesting?" he wondered aloud.

"That's a stretch," said a calm voice from behind.

Kordell swung around. It was Tommy, alone.

"What?" Kordell took the board down from the wall and hid his writing to his chest.

"Elijah had a better look at your *game* than I did," said Tommy. "I hope you're not seriously thinking of going there."

"I don't think I care what you think," said Kordell. "I haven't in a long time."

"You could call me every scumbag word ever invented and it would apply to me during the time we dated, but Kordell, you couldn't even father Sal's baby and now you're going to try to convince yourself you can turn straight?"

"Turn straight?" Kordell said laughingly as he lowered the chalkboard. "You think I want to turn straight?"

"I know about the Facility," said Tommy. "Elijah just told me about it."

Kordell stared him down with a tight-lipped poker face.

"He saw it written on your *game*," said Tommy.

Kordell didn't budge. Tommy became fed up and bolted out of the kitchen. Seconds later, he returned with a reluctant Elijah, dragging his Jewish boy toy by the arm.

"I've been to the Facility," Elijah said shamefully, as if forced to admit it on the witness stand. "But I only took the tour. No way did I actually do it."

Kordell feigned only mild interest.

"Go on," Tommy told Elijah.

"Believe me, you do not want to go there," said Elijah. "They strip search you, test you for party drugs—and that's just to take the tour. If you actually do the program, you can't tell anyone anything, just that you're going on a vacation, a vacation that'll cost you an arm and *two* legs."

"But think of all you can do with your NAMBLA discount card," said Kordell. To this, Tommy and Elijah stared at him blankly. "Or is chasing after the grade school set just part of the fun?"

"Kordell, quit bullshitting," said Tommy. "That's against everything those conversion mutants stand for."

"Conversion?" Then it dawned on Kordell. *Gay to straight.*

"Let's go." Tommy took Elijah by the arm. "The brutha can't admit …"

"No, wait," said Kordell. "I had no idea. I thought the Facility was something else. I thought it was connected to … maybe I should be more interested in Project H.O.P.E."

"I was at first." Elijah nodded toward their offices upstairs. "I went to counseling there for, like, twelve weeks, then Pizarro suggested—"

"So you do know Pizarro?"

"I didn't want to admit it before," said Elijah. "I never told Thomas about this. I never told anyone."

Thomas? Since when did Tommy become Thomas?

"I wasn't going to say anything because I figured you wouldn't get that far anyway," said Elijah. "Thomas said you're totally out and comfortable."

"That far?" said Kordell. "What do you mean?"

"To want to go straight," said Elijah. "H.O.P.E. doesn't recommend that to everyone. I was going through some Jewish guilt and coming out of addiction and thought maybe I should try clean and sober *and* straight."

"Who brought it up?" asked Kordell.

"I don't know." Elijah shrugged. "I guess I did. Come to think of it, Pizarro did."

"Pizarro was your counselor?" asked Kordell.

"He subbed one time," said Elijah. "The last time. He asked me if I'd ever considered it—trying to go straight—and I said yes."

"Did you see him at the Facility?" asked Kordell.

Elijah thought about it, then said, "Nah. Why would he be involved with them?"

"You said yes to turning straight?" Tommy asked his new boyfriend.

"I mean, we've all considered even the possibility of those places working, right?" said Elijah. "Who wouldn't want to snap their fingers and be accepted by the world?"

"Honey," said Tommy, "if you want to snap yo' fingers, you might as well just accept the gay boy within."

"Easy for you to say at forty," said Elijah. "Did you feel that way at twenty-six?"

He's only twenty-six?

"So you went to the Facility?" Kordell asked, getting back on track.

"Just for the tour, okay? It was basically two hours of them telling us how we can overcome evil. I bailed when I overheard this chanting—"

They were interrupted by the sound of someone coming. It was Arthur's big body balancing several trays of dirty dishes. "Sorry, boys, break's over." He nodded behind him to Koji, who was on his heels. "I've got tons of orders. Lunchtime."

"Maybe we'd better go," said Tommy.

"Is there anything else you can tell me?" Kordell asked as the two Latino kitchen workers returned through the back door.

"It's a chapter I'd rather delete from my life," said Elijah. "There's nothing else."

"Fat man with a hot plate coming through." Arthur blew by them with a tray and a bowl of steaming soup.

"Good luck, Kordell," said Tommy.

"I'm okay, thanks. Both of you, thanks." Kordell managed an appreciative smile. "If you wanna call, Thomas, call. As a friend."

Tommy gave him a friendly nod and left with Elijah.

"Good-looking men." Koji came up next to Kordell and

watched Tommy's big ass leaving. "Black men, I envy you."

"I wrote on the chalkboard," Kordell said warily. "I'm gonna go clean it off."

Kordell took the board and made his way to the restroom, figuring Giovanni to be long gone. He was right. He locked the door behind him (one of those single occupancy deals), erased the entire board with a wet paper towel and began writing once again.

KOJI (= GIOVANNI = PIZARRO = H.O.P.E. AND THE FACILITY) HYPES H.O.P.E. AT GAY COFFEE HOUSE.

H.O.P.E. SEES EMOTIONALLY TROUBLED GAY MEN.

PIZARRO LOSES INTEREST IN MY TROUBLES WHEN I SAY I WON'T GO STRAIGHT.

THE FACILITY = CONVERSION.

Next, he wrote down something Arthur had said yesterday, which seemed like eons ago:

GET US WHERE WE HANG OUT, RECRUIT THE NATIVES IN THEIR NATURAL HABITAT.

THE FACILITY (= PIZARRO) USES H.O.P.E. TO NAB POTENTIAL CONVERTS.

Kordell surveyed the board, then erased it once again, this time making sure all the evidence was completely gone. Undetectable, as it were.

The ultimate hypocrites, he thought. A gay-to-straight conversion house mixed up with men who moonlight as child molesters.

That still didn't explain how Mario fit in, but there was only way to find out.

He exited the restroom, replaced the board on the wall and caught up with his best male friend in the doorway to the kitchen.

"Arthur, I need some cash, lots of cash, my own cash. And I need you to go home and get me some ecstasy or hook me up with your connection."

"Get out. You are barking up the wrong tree. I haven't partied since Madonna's last tour."

"How much should I take to really get it in my system but still leave me functional?"

"Kordell, I don't know why you think I—"

"Cut the crap, Arthur, I know you haven't given it up completely and I don't have time."

Arthur hesitated, an admission if there ever was one. "Why do you need it? You don't want to drive my car on it, do you?"

"No time to explain, but I won't be needing your car anymore." He handed Arthur the keys. Arthur thought for a moment, looked him in the eyes and handed the keys back. Kordell was confused, but Arthur explained:

"You go and get it. I can't leave. Under my bed in the stowaway drawer with my sex toys."

"I'll leave your car in the driveway," said Kordell. "Tell Sal and Jenna I'll see them on Wednesday morning. With the truth."

"For the love of our friendship and your life, Kordell, do you swear that you know what you're doing?"

"I'm going to rehab." Kordell said, and then he was gone.

EIGHT

Kordell sat on the steps of the gazebo, rocking back and forth and cursing himself, Mario and the world for getting him into this. His heart was pounding like a woodpecker on steroids. His mouth felt like Death Valley. His clothes were drenched in sweat.

And the boys get off on this shit?

He didn't understand the joy of X during his party days, and he sure as hell didn't get it now. And thanks to some hardcore PR work on the part of his parents, he'd never had much use for recreational drugs anyway—until now.

Through the glaring afternoon sunlight, he saw a white minivan stopped at the edge of the park. Pizarro, the lone occupant, got out. Fuck him. Kordell was pissed, nervous, and on the verge of throwing up. On top of that, his vision was blurry as all hell, coming in and out of focus depending on the sway of the Tilt-A-Whirl in his skull.

The park wasn't as crowded as it had been a few hours ago. An Arab family was barbecuing and playing croquet near the sandy

playground. A few straight lovers lounged on blankets. No one else was within spitting distance of the gazebo except for Pizarro, who approached Kordell's backside.

"You're late," Kordell said without looking up. "You're no help; you can't even be on time."

"I came from the mountains," said Pizarro. "If you had agreed to see someone else, this could have—"

"There is no one else. Only the great Victor Pizarro can save my ass. Could have saved my ass." Kordell retrieved the Project H.O.P.E. business card from his pants pocket and tore it to pieces. It had been a chore reading the numbers, then dialing the phone. The buttons kept moving about.

"H.O.P.E.?" he had said on the hotline soon after the ecstasy kicked in. "This is a very wasted, very fucked-up homosexual who needs to speak to the number one guru, Victor Pizza, or is it Pizza Roll? No, Bizarro. I need to speak to Mr. Bizarro. What do you mean he's not available? Even to talk to a suicide coming soon to a theater near you? A suicide who's getting very … very … suicidal? No, I won't tell you where I am. But I'll give you a hint: I'm outdoors. Ha! I'm not telling anyone where I am unless it's Victor Calzone. Or is it Pepperoni? What? Whatever. Have her highness call me."

"You no longer want my help?" Pizarro asked, now that he'd finally shown up two fucking hours late.

Kordell nodded toward the Arab family. "What I want right now is to go over to those goat-herders and tell their little munchkins some very horrific stories about what will happen to them if they grow up to be faggots and dykes. And give them some very graphic visual AIDS, pun intended."

Pizarro knelt down until he was within inches of Kordell's face, then examined Kordell's eyes. "Do I smell poppers?"

Was there anything gayer than poppers? Was there anything more degenerate than poppers in the middle of the day?

"What else have you taken and how long ago?" asked Pizarro.

"Just my normal party favors." Kordell looked away. "Felt like shit after I bared my soul to you. Needed to lighten the mood and get started on the night's festivities a little earlier than usual."

Pizarro stood over him. "You want to get high or you want my help?"

"Depends on which minute of the day you want an answer."

"Now would be appropriate," said an impatient Pizarro.

A soccer ball landed on the gazebo and collided with Kordell's thigh. He jumped as if it were a rat, then seized the ball and angrily hurled it back to the Arab family.

"Right now," he said, "I could go for killing the evil gnome inside my brain who likes to suck dick and take a fat cock up the ass." He stood up and had to hold onto the railing for balance—no need to fake it. "I don't want to be asked if I'm a top or a bottom anymore. I want pussy and a picket fence and 2.2 children and the Rotary Club. What the fuck is the Rotary Club? Can they make me straight?"

"In my office you said you wouldn't turn straight if given the chance."

"What's the head of the Santa Barbara Gay Business Alliance supposed to say to that question? Geez."

"So you want to be … heterosexual?"

Don't seem too eager. Walk around a bit. Steady now.

"I want my headache to go bug somebody else." *Stumble for emphasis. There, didn't even have to try.* "Straight people don't do the crazed things we do, not the good Republican ones anyway. Why is that, Pizza Roll?"

"Why did you summon me here, Mr. Christie?"

Kordell held onto one of the gazebo's support beams as if he were on a boat threatening to toss him overboard. "You asked me if I want an *alternative,* alternative lifestyle. The answer is yes. How much does it cost?" He yanked balled-up wads of cash from his pants pockets. Dozens of bills spilled into the gazebo like scattered leaves. "This is all I could get for now."

"Have you lost your mind?" Pizarro didn't hesitate going after the dough. "You're in no condition … I'll hold onto this for safe-keeping. You'll be robbed or waste it on drugs before the day is over."

"I don't want to waste it." Kordell grew teary-eyed. Damn, he was a good actor. "I want to use it to change my life while I've got the guts."

"Guts for what?" Pizarro asked as he stashed the money in his leather jacket.

"Am I speaking Farsi here?" asked Kordell. "You said you have places you can recommend. For me to go straight. *Duh?*"

Pizarro paused, then circumnavigated Kordell. "Is this the drugs talking or the real you?"

"Does it matter?" Kordell glared at a young straight couple passing the gazebo. They were arm-in-arm and giddy, as if love conquered all. When they caught sight of the wigged-out black man, their smiles evaporated and fear took residence in their eyes. Kordell growled at them as if he were a jungle animal; they quickly looked away, their pace quickening. "Obviously *one* of me wants to lead a normal life," he said to Pizarro.

"Did you tell anyone you were coming here to the park?"

"Of course," said Kordell.

"Who?"

"You."

"Who else?" Pizarro was getting quite agitated. "Get serious."

"No one, dammit."

"Not even your fat friend?"

"Arthur? No." Kordell slowly turned to him and asked in a somber voice: "How do you know I have a fat friend?"

"The coffeehouse booth at Gay Pride." Pizarro stared at the Arab parents pushing their kids on the swing set in the distance. "I overheard you and your friend—the manager of the Mission, I believe—you were quite negative about gay life. Seems you were wondering if homosexuals, including yourself, had any reason to feel any kind of pride."

"You eavesdropped on a private conversation." Kordell feigned irritation. "I don't remember seeing you there."

"Of course, you don't," snapped Pizarro. "I'm not a buffed gym boy."

Got a point there. "So you already know how I feel," said Kordell. "You've known all along, when I met you, *before* I met you. And you didn't let on, even in your office."

Too pissed I stole Mario away from you, huh? Bastard.

"You have to be willing to do more than bitch and moan," said Pizarro. "You have to ask for help from the farthest reaches of your gut."

"*That's what I'm doing now!*" Kordell shouted. He was on a roll now. Pizarro had snooped around at Gay Pride—for his own depraved reasons, no doubt—and the child predator was about to pay for being nosy. "You need me to write it in the sky? I'm gonna die if I have to be a faggot one more day!"

Pizarro surveyed the others in the park and made sure they were all otherwise occupied before speaking:

"The place that comes to my mind is very strict in its policies and procedures."

"Go on." Kordell sat on the gazebo steps once again. The outburst had made him dizzy, igniting another round of sweats and chills.

"You can't tell anyone where you're going," said Pizarro. "They don't want family and friends interfering. They require you to tell everyone you're going on a vacation, alone."

"My friends and I are kinda on the outs right now," said Kordell. "My business is closed for repairs."

"Do you have a boyfriend?"

Kordell scoffed.

"This is highly irregular," said Pizarro. "They only take people at certain times. You become part of a class of students that evolves and graduates together. There's not another class starting for weeks."

"What do they do for faggots on the verge of a nervous breakdown?"

"As far as they're concerned, all faggots are on the verge of a nervous breakdown."

"Sign me up, I'm begging you."

"Next month—"

"I might not fucking care next month." Kordell let his head fall between his legs.

Pizarro stood stoically in the middle of the gazebo.

"I came to the wrong person." Kordell stood up. "Big help!" He stumbled and landed flat on his ass on the steps. "Give me my money back. I'll go find the best gay-to-straight business in the business on my own."

"They *are* the best," Pizarro snapped, offended that anyone could imagine otherwise.

"Then take me to them," Kordell said with equal vigor.

Pizarro stood directly over Kordell. "If I do, you put your fate in their hands, which is the same as putting your fate in my hands. If I take you there under these extraordinary circumstances, you are essentially signing your life over to me." He extended his hand to lift Kordell off the ground. "Do you understand?"

That hand, Pizarro's hand, looked larger than any man's hand Kordell had ever seen. Was it the drugs messing with his mind or the irrevocable leap he was about to take? Whatever the reason, that hand seemed gigantic as it loomed inches away from his face, waiting to crush his soul, eager to lift his trembling little body up and into Pizarro's massive monster-like mouth, which would then swallow him whole and, in time, spit him out a very different man.

But Kordell was intent on writing a very different script: the stable black businessman briefly infiltrates the house of twisted twinks hidden in the mountains and spirits his childhood friend away from their clutches. Outsmarting a bunch of conversion sissies would be a snap. He and Mario would be out of there by nightfall. From there, they would face their demons together. And whatever the outcome, Sal and Fredito would have all the answers they needed to begin the healing process long before baseball camp, which began in less than forty-eight hours.

Kordell reached out and grabbed the humongous hand before him. At the moment of contact, he felt dizzy. A beat later, he realized why: Pizarro had injected a syringe into his bicep. Kordell felt his body being pulled upward. Then silence and darkness engulfed his entire being.

"How long before it wears off?"

"Depends. But I maintain that as soon as he's able to walk and comprehend, he's good to go—straight, that is."

"It's that kind of haste and lack of precaution that could become our downfall."

"It's your brand of cowardice and lack of aggression that makes you powerless without a visionary like me."

"Shh … he's stirring."

Kordell moaned and fought to break out of the darkness. He turned to one side, then the other but couldn't wake up—just had to lay there, floating, hearing, only partially able to *listen*.

"He looks so troubled, so in need of what we have to offer," said one of the voices. This one sounded younger than the others. And vaguely familiar.

"You're too young to remember the old days, Brother John." That was Pizarro's voice. Yes, Pizarro talking to Brother John. Just like at the beach restroom. "Running a gay-to-straight conversion operation was a lot more barbaric back then. It took months, if not years, to do what we do now in a matter of weeks. We used torture chambers, deprivation tanks, electroshock therapy. And those were for the easiest cases. Ah, the good old days. Of course now, it's not quite as dramatic and visually stunning to watch the evil leap from their souls, but virtual technology does have its advantages; namely speed and cleanliness."

"Not to mention efficiency," said a third man.

"True." Pizarro again. "Back then, a tweaked-out faggot like this would have taken months of work. Now, he can rejoin society as a raging heterosexual in no time, *if* he isn't stubborn about it."

"I still have my reservations about his legitimacy," said the third man.

"The recreational drug test came back positive," said Brother John. "Ecstasy, and lots of it."

"Not to mention him reeking of poppers," said Pizarro. "I know a classic, self-loathing, addiction-prone homo when I see one. If you need a refresher, Clive, look in the mirror and imagine yourself fifteen years ago when I plucked you out of that little hole-in-the-wall bathhouse in Cleveland."

"I don't need to relive the past," said Clive, the name of the third man. "What about Mr. Christie's association with Cervantes—Mario, that is?"

"If there is anything to that," said Pizarro "what better way to keep an eye on both of them now?"

"Keep your enemies closer," said Brother John.

"Besides," added Pizarro, "this one owns a kiddie arcade. If he isn't legitimately trying to go hetero, he'll still be quite useful. Maybe even more so."

"Admit it, Victor," said Clive. "You're eager to try my new chip on him and you know it."

"Not necessarily." said Pizarro. "But what a challenge: converting a leader of the local gay community, a proud gay man, at least on the surface. Of course, deep inside, he's just like the self-hating twenty-somethings who come here. If he converts, it only further demonstrates the efficacy of our methods."

"If he doesn't?" asked Brother John.

"Perhaps the chip *can* begin its journey outside of the lab," said Pizarro. "And, one day in the distant future, they'll name schools and parks after us."

"There's that cockiness you wear so well," said Clive. "I *knew* you were thinking of the chip when you brought him here."

"And if I was?"

"What if he's an undercover activist or investigative journalist?" asked Clive. "We're about due for another pretender, you know."

"Yes, and look what happened to the last one," said Pizarro. "Poor soul took his own life."

"Does their father—" Brother John began, but Pizarro interrupted.

"Still thinks it was suicide and that the dead son was a closet case."

"And the remaining twin?" asked Brother John. "Mr. Mario?"

"Still quite an asset," said Pizarro.

Kordell's upper body twitched as if rising from the dead. His eyes remained closed and he mumbled something that seemed to be in direct response to what was being said. Then he collapsed again. Something other than his own willpower was running the show.

Some time much later—or, at least it *seemed* much later—Kordell's fog began to clear. He was on his back when he opened his eyes, but his limbs felt trapped, his waist immobilized, his weight ... weightless. His contact lenses were dry as hell. He blinked sever-

al times, then yawned repeatedly to lubricate his eyes.

A white room came into focus, then abruptly spun around in a smooth but swift motion. His stomach heaved, trying but failing to throw up. He was now facedown. Only there was nothing underneath. He tried to raise up but felt restraints on his arms and legs.

"Jerk like that again and you'll be covered in your own blood."

It was Pizarro's voice from somewhere behind him. Kordell remained motionless except for his head, which panned the room. Soon it hit him: he was suspended in midair, spread-eagle on what looked like one of those gyroscope contraptions he'd seen at street fairs and the beach. He was also butt naked. He felt a tingle just inside his right thigh, precariously close to his balls. He let out a gasp—a small one so as not to move too much.

"You might want to breathe," said Pizarro.

"Where am I?"

"This is part of your intake: returning you to the state you were in when your mother gave birth to you. Smooth as a baby. For your rebirth."

You're shaving me.

Kordell meant to say it aloud but was glad he didn't. He felt a cool breeze on his head, then realized that he was now bald. He brought his chin down to his chest. Gone were the curly black hairs that were normally between his pecs. His pubes felt … gone. The area itched like mad, yet he couldn't reach it and sure as hell wasn't going to ask Pizarro to scratch.

"Uncomfortable?" asked Pizarro. "We're almost finished."

"What did you shoot me up with?"

"Something to ease your transition to true manhood. Nothing as harmful as the drugs you take voluntarily."

"So you're part of—" *don't use the term* the Facility; *you're not supposed to know that name* "—this conversion deal?"

"This conversion deal is called the Facility and there's no need to worry about my responsibilities."

"Isn't your work here, whether it's resident barber or whatever, some kind of conflict of interest with H.O.P.E.?"

"I give people what they truly want," said Pizarro. "Where's the conflict?"

"Do the people you counsel at H.O.P.E. realize you're also part of a conversion operation?"

No answer. What sane answer could an insane person possibly give?

Kordell surveyed the room. They were alone, but there was a large glass pane on the wall—a one-way mirror no doubt. He could just barely see Pizarro underneath him, wearing surgical gloves and brandishing an old-fashioned razor. Right near Kordell's dick and balls!

"Don't people have to sign some sort of waiver before you start this?" he asked warily.

"You already did."

Kordell vaguely remembered a gathering in the lobby, now that Pizarro had mentioned it. And ... yes, a strip search! But the phone ... Arthur's cell phone ... where? ... palm tree? ... yes! Kordell had managed to stash the phone in the soil of a massive ceramic pot in the lobby. The palm tree plant. And now that he thought about it ... Kordell realized his ass was a little sore, too ... fuck.

"What about my history, medical, sexual, mental?" he asked.

"You're gay-identified," said Pizarro, "that's all we need to know."

The razor made its way around Kordell's balls, which were hanging like nuts on a tree. They were also stretched downward, thanks to Pizarro's latex-gloved hand.

"You know," Kordell began, "some gay men would find this very erotic and stimulating."

"Are you among them?"

Kordell didn't answer. "Are you gay-identified?" he asked instead.

"Used to be," said Pizarro. "I was one of the first gay men to move into the Castro way back when. The police and gangs of homo-phobic boys beat up me and my friends more than once. The neigh-borhood did not want fags there at all."

"Didn't that make you angry?"

"It made me move back home to Petrolia, a little nothing town way up north. My mother had disowned me when I told her I was one of you; but she took me back with open arms when I renounced gay life. She even gave me the money to start my first gay-to-straight support group and left me a sizeable estate to continue my work."

"I suppose your father—"

"Long dead," Pizarro said without the slightest trace of emotion. "Long before all my worthwhile endeavors."

"You're head of H.O.P.E. ... and this place," Kordell realized and said. Just then, the gyroscope rotated so that he was on his side, facing a stark white wall.

"After your treatment is over, you won't remember that little tidbit," Pizarro said as he shaved the crack of Kordell's ass.

"You can't erase people's minds; it's not possible."

"It's better that way, lets me go about doing what I need to do. The important thing is that, when you're done here, you'll go home and throw out all your club drugs, dildoes, gay porn videos, bareback party invites and little pieces of paper with tricks' phone numbers who you never intended to call anyway."

"I don't do—"

"You'll begin your search for a beautiful female who will accept you as a former fag, regardless of your HIV status—see, we don't even need to know that."

The gyroscope whirled Kordell around again, backward this time. When it came to a stop, he was facing the ceiling again, wondering if it he should have just taken the nickel tour like Tommy's new boyfriend.

"As you embark on your straight life," Pizarro went on, "of course, you'll know you've been to the Facility, and you might even recommend it to others, but you won't remember all the specifics. Above all else, you will be the man that you always wanted to be. The man society wants you to be. And you'll be happy. I'll be happy. Your parents will be happy. And the world will be a much better place."

"So you're the shit when it comes to going gay to straight?"

And being head child molester on the side.

"If, by your common ghetto vernacular, you mean the best, the

answer is 'of course.' Since going digital years ago, we've had the most astonishing success rate of any conversion group in the world, including the Middle East, where their methods are far more barbaric. We have no equal, just competitors whom we buy and swallow up."

"Digital?"

"You'll see," said Pizarro. "And rest assured, you'll be cured."

"What happens with your failures?"

"You needn't be afraid of returning to the outside world as someone who enjoys watching vulgar trash like *Will and Grace* and *Queer As Folk*. I can practically guarantee success."

"But what if the great Victor Pizarro fails?"

"You'd be better advised to spend these last few minutes before your training in quiet contemplation. Your life is about to change in profound ways."

The gyroscope began moving again, this time stopping when Kordell was upright, inches away from Pizarro's face.

"No worries," said Pizarro. "No one comes in here a productive homosexual. And no one leaves out of here a productive homosexual."

NINE

"We'll bypass the lobby since you've been there and done that."

Like a proud university president, Pizarro gave Kordell a personal tour of the Facility, taking him down long fluorescent hallways and rambling on about things that went in and out of Kordell's ear. The building's interior resembled something out of *Star Trek,* right down to the smoked glass doors that vanished into the walls instead of swinging open. The floors, equipment and furniture were all bathed in silver, white, and lime green. Everything was shiny to the point of being slick—not a speck of dust on the furniture or a smudge on the glass, which was everywhere. The place looked like one big high-tech mental hospital.

The tour started with the sleeping quarters, which consisted of dozens of bunk beds in a long gray room resembling an army barracks. Walking past the empty beds, Kordell wanted to make a comment about the arrangement being titillating to gay men; but then he noticed the miniature video cameras hanging from the ceiling like little black spiders and killed the joke. The subsequent cocky smile on Pizarro's face did not escape Kordell's notice.

Next they visited a hallway featuring identical glass doors on either side. "The Individual Counseling Chambers," Pizarro explained. "Let us visit an observation room." He stared at the retinal scanning panel adjacent to one of the doors. A blue laser reached out and studied his eye. A split second later, the LCD display above the box read ACCESS GRANTED and the glass door slid open. "Shall we?" Pizarro waited for Kordell to enter first.

The observation room was no bigger than a large rectangular closet. A large, one-way mirror covered one wall, revealing one of Pizarro's counseling chambers on the other side. The chamber reminded Kordell of a doctor's examining room, albeit a very high-tech one. Bright vertical stripes of green light covered the walls from floor to ceiling. A Latino in a white lab coat was sitting on a steel stool, making notations on a tiny handheld computer. Next to him, a bald white man lay at a forty-five degree angle in a metal reclining table that was equipped with levers, knobs and odd shaped gadgets.

"Why is he blindfolded?" asked Kordell.

"Look closer," said Pizarro.

Kordell approached the mirror until his breath fogged up the window. What he had thought was a blindfold was some sort of thick plastic mask ... no, it was ... a pair of virtual goggles. They were purple and smaller than any goggles he'd ever seen, even the tiny ones competitive swimmers wear.

"He's being programmed?" Kordell whispered in astonishment.

"He's being reconditioned to live the kind of lifestyle he really wants to live." Pizarro's voice came to within an inch of Kordell's ear. "The kind of lifestyle *you* want to live."

"So this is how you do it." Kordell swallowed to rid himself of the lump in his throat.

"We have a very aggressive approach when it comes to using technology," said Pizarro. "The Facility is known as the Microsoft of the conversion therapy world."

"Does Bill Gates know about this?"

"Let the tour continue." Pizarro didn't seem the least bit amused.

A corridor identical to the last one was their next stop, only

Pizarro said that this hall contained the Group Counseling Chambers. Once again, they ducked inside an observation room and watched through a one-way mirror. On the other side, six soon-to-be-former gay men lay on metal tables arranged in a semi-circle. They were all wearing the same purple goggles and presumably having the same virtual experience.

What are they doing, watching a football game and making lurid comments about the cheerleaders' pussies?

Kordell kept that one to himself. Good thing, too, because Pizarro was taking things much too seriously, as if he were presenting the place to potential investors or the Pope, who would then tap Pizarro's head with a sword, making him a living saint. St. Pizza Roll.

They visited a lecture hall, the cafeteria and a non-denominational chapel. They looked in on a recreation room featuring big screen TVs showing team sports and the competitive games heterosexual men play: poker, pool, darts (never mind that both pool and darts were staples at many a gay bar). Outdoors, they peeked in on the Contemplation Gardens, where men could take walks, jog through wooded trails, mow the lawn or sit and ponder their sexual journey.

I hope you've got cameras in the bushes. Otherwise the Contemplation Gardens will become the Suck-and-Fuck Gardens, just like every other woodsy cruise area in the world.

As they toured, Kordell saw staffers (all men) in white lab coats or white scrubs, and students (Pizarro's term for them) dressed in green scrubs and white slippers. The students walked like zombies. Gone was every follicle of hair. Also absent was any color in their faces. Black, white, brown, yellow, red—every hue of humankind was there, but unless they were extremely light or dark, the "students" all blended into one sad shade of gray.

Another thing missing were the knowing looks Kordell was so used to from gay men: the widening of the eyes, the lightning quick evaluation of one another as potential sexual conquests. That instinct had already been zapped out of these dead men walking, which was made even more shocking by the fact that most of them had the potential to be lookers in the real world. Kordell had expect-

ed the Facility's patients to be weaklings, nerds, geeks—the kind of men who avoided mainstream gay bars because they didn't feel "beautiful" enough. Instead, he saw a mix of gym rats, queens, bears (shaved, granted), butch guys *and* geeks. Most of them appeared to be near the "young and questioning" age, but there were also men in their thirties and forties.

The demographic was quite varied with one very notable exception: there was no half-Latino, half-Native American stud anywhere in sight. Kordell had the urge to ask Pizarro about Mario, but knew it wasn't such a good idea. Better not to seem eager in any way, shape or form.

As the tour wore on, so did Kordell. The X was loosening its grip on him, but he still felt sluggish. And extremely parched. At one point, he stopped at a water fountain near the intersection of two hallways. He drank from it for quite some time, unaware that Pizarro had walked ahead and rounded the corner. When Kordell finished quenching his thirst, he found himself alone—a good time to backtrack and look for Mario.

At the end of the corridor, he came to a steel door labeled AREA 2. It was the only non-glass door Kordell remembered seeing on the entire tour. He tried to open it with his eyeball, but, of course, the display above the retinal scanning panel flashed ACCESS DENIED. He looked up at the security cameras watching his every move, then knocked on the door.

"Area off limits," said an effeminate voice from behind. A short, pudgy man wearing a dark suit had come from out of the blue.

"I'm new," Kordell stammered.

"Where are you supposed to be?" asked the man. His mannerisms were quite fey and reminded Kordell of Truman Capote, the old writer/celebrity/*grande dame* from years ago.

"With me, Clive." Pizarro emerged from a sliding glass door.

Clive. One of the men in that first room—when I was out cold. The doubting Thomas. Cautious queen.

"I stopped for a drink of water." Kordell shrugged. "Got lost."

Satisfied that the new student was in the proper hands, Clive disappeared behind yet another sliding glass door.

"What's Area 2?" asked Kordell.

"Research and development." Pizarro led him out of the hall-way. "Called that because only two members of the staff are allowed in there. Ever."

"You and …"

Pizarro let out a smug laugh. "It's no secret, but why bombard you with so much on your first day? It's time for your initial session. In the Physical Therapy Chambers."

"I thought only my mind needs working on," said Kordell.

"As a gay man, your body is controlling your mind." Pizarro rounded the corner and opened the first door he came to. "Our brand of physical therapy will change that completely."

"Your brand?" Kordell entered the chamber, immediately taking note of the large padded examining table.

"It's no accident our little tour ends here," said Pizarro. "The next step in your journey is a sort of personal cleansing."

"Of?"

"You'll see." Pizarro indicated the tall Oriental dressing screen in the corner. "That is the changing area. When you've finished dis-robing—entirely—make yourself comfortable on the table and one of our attendants will be in to help you."

"But—"

"Have no fear, Mr. Christie. Everyone I've hired is very compe-tent at what they do. It's been a pleasure personally admitting you to the Facility, but other duties call."

"But, Mr. Pizarro—"

"Now, now. Trust." Pizarro held Kordell's chin between his fingers. "Welcome and enjoy your journey to wellness and heterosexuality."

Quickly and deftly, Pizarro slipped through the *Star Trek* door, which slid shut before Kordell had a chance to utter another word.

Kordell lay naked on his back on the padded table. Was that another one-way mirror on the ceiling? He scanned the room, searching for more mirrors and cameras. Found none, but that did-n't mean they weren't there.

Physical therapy. What the fuck am I in for now?

Another lab coat came into the room—an Asian man, not nearly as handsome as Koji Yamamoto.

I'm just as bad as everyone else. Why did I have to compare him to another Asian? Is this what people do when they see me, then another black man?

The Asian lab coat muttered something indecipherable, then began putting Velcro restraints on Kordell's wrists and ankles.

Spread-eagle at the Facility for the second time today.

The Asian lab coat spoke again.

"How's that?" asked Kordell.

The accent was too thick to understand. Was he even speaking English?

"What's going to happen now?" asked Kordell. "To me? *Me?*"

"Body cleansing." Finally, discernable words. "Last time you think of men in that way and come to them."

"Where are they coming from?" asked Kordell. "Come to who? I'd like to know what this is all about before I—"

Some sort of apparatus began descending from the ceiling. It was metallic or steel and the size of a football. At the bottom of it was some sort of opening.

They're going to cut out my heart, Kordell thought; but as the device came closer, he realized it was aiming for a different, equally precious organ.

"What are you going to do to my—*Jesus Christ*—"

Just then, the Asian lab coat jabbed a needle into his right bicep.

"What was *that?*" Kordell nodded toward the syringe exiting his body.

"Silence." The Asian lab coat started toward the door.

"What *was* that?" Kordell pleaded.

"Better than Viagra." The Asian lab coat punched a display panel next to the door and slipped into the hall. "I leave you now. In dark. Come back when you cleansed."

"Hold on a sec. What did you do to me?" Kordell yelled, but the door slid shut, leaving him alone. Just before the lights dimmed—casting the room in total darkness—Kordell caught a glimpse of the strange device as it clamped down on his dick.

The feeling was incredible—in a good way—and the ecstasy in his system wasn't the sole cause. Inside the steel football was some sort of gel-like material that warmed his cock like the best mouth or ass he'd ever felt. His dick sprouted up through the gel, which gave way and encased his manhood. The contraption began vibrating, then spinning around, its speed gradually increasing. It was the best, the most intense, the most heavenly feeling his cock had even known, better than the best blowjob anyone had ever given him, better than the hottest, tightest, most moist and silky smooth ass he'd ever been inside. His cock was rock hard, jism swelling and simmering, but not for long.

He let out a primal scream. His body jerked and twisted violently, threatening to tear apart the restraints. He was powerless to stop the maddening sensations racing over every inch of his big fat dick. His hands, his screams, his pleas couldn't help him. He came and came. He tried to stay still and minimize the movement of his penis. Didn't work. The machine kept spinning and gyrating. He was in the midst of his best orgasm ever and he was powerless to do anything about it.

He told himself to breathe. He was reminded of the times in his life when he'd come close to this kind of orgasm but backed away from the intensity, holding his partner's head over his dick so as not to cause further sensation, burying his ejaculating cock deep into some guy's ass and remaining motionless to avoid further feeling in his dick, jerking himself off to climax but keeping his fist below his cockhead to dull the effect.

But there was no dulling the effect now. The machine kept milking him and he kept cumming and cumming. He swore a heart attack was imminent and that he was about to die; albeit, die a happy man. But he remained very much alive, maybe more so than ever before.

Mercifully, the sensation swirling throughout his entire body began to dissipate. The strange steel football with the gel inside seemed to sense this and began to slow down, but not to the point of completely stopping. It began massaging him, soothing him. His verbalizations slowed and morphed into much calmer "ohs" and "ahs" and "oh, God's." He was even able to feel the streams of sweat run-

ning over his forehead, his stomach, his groin area. They cleansed me all right, he thought, equating cleansing with draining, thinking of the hundreds of men who'd drained him before, but never like this. Was this how it was supposed to be with those men? Sex partners from his past flashed through his mind and he felt blood rushing to his head—the one with the brain inside. Then he realized that the blood had already made its way to his other head—the one his brain visited on such a regular basis. He was fully erect again. The machine sensed this and began swirling and gyrating as it had before.

"Oh, God," he repeated over and over, not sure if he was saying it out of anticipation or fear or both. The fact that he knew what was coming made him crave it even more, despite the fact that cumming would put him on the verge of cardiac arrest once again. "Oh, God, oh, God." His hips were bucking upwards toward the steel football. He was fucking the thing. He wanted it, had to feel this again. The gel wasn't just warm this time; it was on fire. He fucked and bucked, hips attacking upwards, dick in control.

Rule, cock. It's all yours. My life is yours. Take over, take charge, take full command. Be a man. Be a fucking God-damned animal who can't—get—enough—cock—and ass—and sex—and men—and fucking—and getting fucked—getting fucked—I wanna get fucked—and fuck—and fuck—and fuck—and—

"Ahhhhh, oh, God, oh, God, ahhhh, help me, God, help me, God, fuck me, God, fuck me!"

This orgasm was only a shade less intense than the last. He collapsed, his mind scrambled eggs, his body spent. Even as a teenager, he wasn't sure if he'd ever had back-to-back orgasms in such a short time. As his breathing subsided, he realized that he was still at the Facility. All that it represented came flooding back to him. He wondered if Mario had been subjected to this "physical therapy." Subjected, he thought sarcastically, as if any man wouldn't want to subject himself to this.

He imagined Mario on the blue-padded table, the cum from his big brown uncut cock blowing a hole through the other end of the football. Mario's penis has been minuscule when they were kids, so

much so that it was far from a turn-on. But now, surely Mario was the possessor of a massive tree trunk of a cock. How Mario must love brandishing that manly piece of meat in his hand.

Kordell eyed the steel football. It was beginning to gyrate again. Why? Was it sensing ... yes, it felt the stirrings within his dick and was obliging him.

Oh, God, this is supposed to make me turn straight?

In a matter of milliseconds, he was just as hard as before. The machine kicked into full gear, spinning, whirling, whizzing.

Soon after, he came again.

Kordell was amazed and bewildered. He scanned his sweat-drenched body, especially his gut, which was in the crunch position and feeling quite cramped. His legs were stiff; so was his dick. His head fell back onto the table. He had expected the Asian lab coat to come get him after the second orgasm, but it was clear that wasn't part of the plan.

All the sex you can eat.

The steel football started up again, working away on his cock. This time, the sensation was much less sexual and much more mechanical, reminding him of another scenario.

Sex clubs, late night, you've been there for what seems like hours, grabbing and sampling as much flesh as you can—it's all about quantity, not quality, which is why cumming is neither a big deal nor or a Holy Grail. But, after being there for hours, whether you've cum or not, you're spent, sated, ready to breathe some fresh air, clear your head and clean up your sticky, funky body. Normal thinking says you're done. But it's a weekend night and the place is still charged with testosterone and gluttony. Hell, tons of guys have passed through the doors while you've been sucking and fucking away. You haven't even sampled them yet. You don't leave. You go for more, not because you want it or need it, but because it's there and you hate the idea of missing out on one single opportunity to suck on a massive piece of meat, lick some muscled pecs, or get another cock up your ass to break your record.

Tommy. Driving down to LA every weekend to be part of that scene.

Kordell's mind was overcome with images of his ex fucking him

with that painfully huge dick. How did Kordell manage to take it over and over?

The steel football was whirling away. He *wanted* it to keep spinning, reveled in the feeling of the gel soaked with his cum, massaging itself back into his shaft.

Fucking sex. Fucking sex. What gay man in their right mind could give up sex with other men. Fucking hot men, fucking who-cares-if-they're-hot men, fucking men will do anything and anybody, fucking men, I love fucking men and men fucking me!

Another orgasm. This one almost hurt. Afterwards, his dick refused to go down. The cum inside the machine was plentiful, warm and moist. He even caught a whiff of it. Instinctively, he tried not to inhale it.

What if it turns me on?

Then he began to realize.

They want me to be turned on. And get off. And keep getting off. Until I can't anymore. Until the very thought makes me want to vomit.

Suddenly, the apparatus, the table, the room that momentarily took him to unprecedented heights—all of it made him feel trapped. His body tensed up, as if on the other side of mirror on the ceiling, somebody was laughing and saying: *gotcha.*

He vowed not to think another sexual thought. But his dick inside the football was as hard as it had been during the first orgasm. In fact, he'd been nonstop rock hard since the Asian lab coat shot him in the bicep with some drug that was "better than Viagra."

Oh, shit.

The machine felt more heat and began spinning again.

Fuck.

His dick was aching now with pain and pleasure. It felt as if a steel rod had been inserted like a catheter into his penis. He was being jacked off against his will, milked by a machine, raped and drained of every ounce of seed within. He thought about screaming aloud, but didn't. Was the sensation too intoxicating? Was he determined to beat them at their own game?

He came again, and this time felt more pain than pleasure. His dick was sore, chafed, going numb.

I can't cum again. No matter what, I cannot cum again.

How do JO addicts do this? The ones that claim to wank so many times an hour, a day, a week?

The visual made the steel rod inside his shaft grow steelier. The football picked up on this and increased its speed.

Shit.

"Not again!"

He tried to relax, remember why he was in the place. But did prisoners of war relax while drops of water plopped on their forehead for hours at a time? Did Mafia thugs breathe easily while their thumbs were in vise grips?

He came again. And stayed hard.

He was so sore, he wanted to cut off his penis.

The thought aroused him, gave the rod inside his penis a reason to become even steelier.

He could only think of sex, and whatever he thought about, no matter how arousing or disgusting, the hard-on would not go away, the machine would not stop spinning and his guts would not stop emptying.

At times, he lost consciousness. Other times, his orgasms were more like dry heaves. He was sure his dick looked like raw red meat inside the machine. He never wanted to use it again, not on men, not on women, not even for taking a piss. He wanted to be a Vietnam vet whose manhood had been blown to pieces and was scattered all over some rice field. He wanted to feel numb, not all this life-draining pain. Sex was pain. Men were pain. Except for some thankfully rare occasions when STDs got the best of him, men had only been emotional pain for the most part. But now, he knew the real truth: men, their actions and their extremities, were nothing *but* pain, emotional, physical, spiritual.

He drowned in the realization, glad to be submerged in nothingness.

Feel nothing. Feel nothing to survive, he told himself, trying to will the sexual life out of him as the steel football kept spinning and spinning and spinning.

TEN

"Lift it up. If you got the strength to."

"Huh?"

"I said you gots to lift yo' tray up if you want some."

Kordell looked down at the dull green serving tray and its contents: an empty white plate, silverware, a napkin, a straw. An old black man in a hairnet stood directly in front of him. A serving line and a glass countertop separated them. Dinner, Kordell realized, remembering the Asian lab coat's last words in the physical therapy room:

"You very exhausted now, we know. Time for energy."

It took an extraordinary amount of concentration for Kordell to land the tray on the glass countertop. His nuts weren't the only part of him that was spent: his hands were shaking, his arms limp, his legs wobbly.

A lump of—what was it? Mashed potatoes? Slop?—landed square in the middle of his plate.

"Newbie food," said the old black man with a smile and a nod before turning his gaze to the next man in line. Kordell looked at his

own right pec. A pink dot had been Velcroed on his green scrub top.
Pink equals newbie … okay.

The food looked neither appetizing nor edible, but Kordell did-
n't care. He was ready to devour it if it gave him the strength to find
Mario and get out of this hellhole alive. He moved down the serving
line; other servers added toast, chocolate pudding and ice water to
his tray. There was no cashier at the end of the line. Like a luxury
cruise, everything was prepaid—not counting the blood and life they
sucked out of you by the hour.

He panned the room. The cafeteria was a more posh version of
something one might see in high school. The teachers' lounge perhaps. The lights were bright, the tables rectangular, each large
enough for eight future straight men.

Where to sit?

It was the same dilemma he'd faced daily in junior high and
high school. Where did he fit in amongst guys who were taught to
abhor faggots?

An empty table on the outskirts of the room caught his eye.
Fine. Mario was MIA and Kordell planned to use what little energy
he possessed for chewing and swallowing anyway. He walked past
the other tables, trying not to allow his raw, sensitive cock to come
in contact with his clothing. Other men noticed him but didn't make
the kind of wide-eyed contact interested parties made to one another. For once, the lack of interest wasn't because he was black or did-
n't possess six-pack abs. This shit was really working on them.

He saw colored dots on each man's scrub, pink for the newbies,
and green and blue, which represented things he was clueless about.
At each table, at least one man was dressed in white scrubs. Staffers.
Each table had a camp counselor present in case the boys decided to
be boys.

He sat at his lonely table, back to the world, and began using his
fingers to scoop the mashed potatoey slop into his mouth. The ration
was tasteless crap and filet mignon at the same time. Instantly, he felt
his blood sugar rising, so much so that he decided to wipe off his
fingers and use the fork on his tray.

When the tremor in his head subsided, he took a moment to

glance around the room. There was very little talking amongst the other students. It might as well have been a cafeteria at a funeral parlor. And not one face was familiar. Was this the only dinnertime? The only cafeteria? If so, where was Mario and what was he having?

Some of the men walked as if they were sore from penile surgery—victims of the steel football, no doubt. He also saw more than one man walking with an opposite sort of discomfort, as if their assholes, not their cocks, had been subjected to something mechanical. That particular walk was the walk of frat boys after Hell Week. Kordell remembered it well.

Some of the camp counselors began eyeing him, so he turned around and faced his food. The slop was looking and tasting progressively worse with each bite, but he knew he had to force it down. In his periphery, he saw a few bodies joining him at the table. None of them had Mario's dark brown skin, so he avoided direct eye contact. What do you say to men who've chosen to "be cured" of cocksucking, butt-pirating and having a manly man's ass squatting over your face?

Abruptly, he wanted to jab his fork into his forearm to prevent arousal in his loins. He grimaced—as if the steel football could read his mind and emerge from the floor beneath him. He brought the glass of ice water to his forehead, then his cheek. He closed his eyes and tried to think of graves, graveyards and dead kittens.

"The first day is always the toughest," said a voice right next to him.

"Huh?"

"You'll get your blue dot in no time, I'm sure," said the same voice.

Kordell looked to his side and saw Koji Yamamoto.

"Yamo," Kordell murmured, keeping the glass on his face.

"You remember me," Koji said with a lilt in his voice.

"Duh? We only met a few hours ago."

Koji laughed shyly.

"Why do I want a blue dot?" asked Kordell. "Will it mean I get real food?"

"Not as good as the greens, but it is a hundred times better than

the mush; although the mush is fortified with every essential vitamin and mineral. A blue dot means you've given up gay life and are now learning to be straight."

"Like a baby boy getting a blue bib."

"Exactly," said Koji. "And green dots are those almost ready for re-entry back into society."

Kordell looked at the big hamburger on Koji's plate. Succulent, juicy, fatty cheese draped the sides of the patty of succulent, juicy, fatty beef. The bun was a soft supple Kaiser roll, garnished with fresh lettuce and tomatoes. It looked like the kind of burger prepared for magazine ads.

"Spare me the infomercial for now, okay?" he said to Koji. "Unless you're going to have mercy on a newbie and give me some of that thick, juicy piece of meat." He gasped at his unintentional double entendre and grabbed his fork, ready to stab his arm should his dick revive.

"I can't feed you." Koji laughed. "I'd lose my job."

"What is your job anyway?" asked Kordell.

"Counselor-in-training. Each client has a counselor that acts like a caseworker. I wanted to be yours, but I'm not quite ready for my own cases yet. And besides, Mr. Pizarro is your counselor, which is a very rare thing."

Kordell's right eyebrow raised halfway to his hairline. "Why did you want to be mine?"

"You need my help." Koji drew a little closer, barely concealing a spooky grin. "More than you think."

Kordell was reminded of the time when he was a freshman in college and a young black girl approached him on the steps of the library and struck up a friendly conversation. Five minutes into this "friendly conversation," she mentioned that she was a member of the Moonie cult and invited him to a meeting. Five minutes and ten seconds into that same "friendly conversation," he was outta there.

He blanched, drew back from Koji's intense stare and muttered, "I'm going to go now … to get some more mush … and pudding." Then he stood up and looked at the others at the table for the first time.

Poor fucked-up souls.

He headed for the serving line, wondering what it would take to bribe a server into some real food. In the next beat, he started to make an inside joke, a sexual one, of course. Then he remembered his chafed penis and killed the thought.

With a little more fuel in his brain, he saw that there were two serving lines, each one mirroring the other at the front of the cafeteria. He headed for the one he hadn't visited before, plotting to hide his pink dot in an effort to score some better food. When he reached the serving line, he coughed, then began scratching his chest to cover up the dot.

"Cheeseburger, please," he said with the perfect blend of confidence and casualness. The server was a Latino with dark skin. His back was to Kordell and he was talking to a co-worker farther down the line as he scooped up a hamburger patty with his spatula. Kordell's mouth watered; he could taste success. But just then, the Latino turned around.

Well, well, the perverted gang's all here.

Kordell recognized him instantly, then collected himself and put on a poker face, baiting the man's memory skills.

"The Christie boy? From Oxnard?" said Giovanni Cervantes. "Do you remember me, I'm—"

"I remember you, Mr. Cervantes," Kordell said without emotion.

"Glad to see you here. Well, you know, I'm not glad to see you turned out confused, but I'm glad to know you've chosen to turn your life around."

As if Kordell were a heroin addict or serial murderer. Or child molester.

Fucker.

"That's what I'm here for," Kordell said. "To get better and be a real man." All expression drained from his face, then he added: "Just like you."

Giovanni blanched ever so slightly, unable to hide the fact that he was at a loss for words. Another patient joined Kordell in line. He was a tall, thin black man in his early twenties. Giovanni turned to

him, noted his blue dot and served him the cheeseburger that had been meant for Kordell.

"So you're the cook?" Kordell said after the man left. "*A* cook."

"Server, janitor, handyman," said Giovanni, "whatever needs fixing, cleaning or doing."

Kordell stared at him blankly.

"You probably heard stories about me from your youth," Giovanni said, "but I only do the Lord's work now. I only wish I could've helped Javy get right before he sliced his wrists. Did you hear?"

Kordell remained mute, which Giovanni took for a yes.

"Thank God that won't happen to Mario now."

"What is Mario's story these days?" Kordell asked, feigning mild curiosity.

As an answer, Giovanni stepped sideways, revealing his only surviving son, who was sitting very casually in a chair in the kitchen, eating a bag of potato chips.

Kordell kept silent for a beat, fearing what might come out of his mouth.

It was Mario who spoke first:

"There he is again."

"Again?" said Giovanni.

"Ran into him this weekend when I went AWOL," Mario explained. "How you doing, K? I'd get up, but I'm maxing and relaxing. You understand."

"No problem," Kordell said, reining in his shock. He was also trying to figure out how to grit his teeth and mouth the words *let's the get hell outta here* without the father noticing.

"So you leaving the wild life behind, huh?" asked Mario.

"Only way to fly," said Kordell.

"When'd you get here?"

"Today," said Kordell. "This morning, this afternoon. I dunno. My mind's a little f'ed up, right now. How about yours?"

"He's coming along," Giovanni answered for his son. "Doing some very fine work to get his life right."

Kordell eyed Giovanni, then Mario and said, "You are, huh?"

Mario nodded.

"Mario?" Kordell began, wanting more out of this exchange. Mario sensed this and Kordell could tell that Mario was also trying to communicate beyond the small talk. But before either one of them could offer up anything more, they heard another man's voice.

"Let father and son have their reunion." It was Pizarro, coming up behind Kordell and scaring the shit out of him.

"Reunion?" asked Kordell.

"They haven't spent much time together in recent years. You know how families can be torn apart." Pizarro put his hand on Kordell and patted his shoulder—a physical attempt to extract him from the scene. "More food?"

Kordell had no choice. This wasn't the time or place to play Rambo. That moment will come, Kordell promised himself. He didn't do X and have the cum sucked out of the far reaches of his soul to let these self-righteous perverts get the best of him.

"Why all the personal attention from the head honcho?" Kordell asked as he walked down the fluorescent green hallway. "I feel like the teacher's pet. You sure all the other boys won't start resenting me?"

Pizarro laughed a smug laugh. "You didn't come in with a scheduled class. To assign you to a regular counselor would disrupt things."

"You must have thought me in very dire straits."

"I know an emergency when I see one." Pizarro stopped in front of a glass door and gained access through the retinal scanning panel.

An Individual Counseling Chamber, Kordell realized as he crossed the threshold. Bright, vertical stripes of green light covered the walls from floor to ceiling. One of those strange metal tables lay in the center of the room, the sight of which prompted a nervous twitch on Kordell's face.

"*That* was physical therapy," Pizarro said, sensing his fear. "This is psychological therapy."

"What happens here?"

"You'll see." Pizarro went over to and began messing with an LCD display that looked like a thin picture frame on the wall.

"You guys got a suggestion box?" asked Kordell. "Because nobody around here offers much in the way of explanations and I'm not sure how comfortable I am with that."

"We find that the mind is much more open to the Facility experience if one is not bogged down with details." Pizarro indicated a door behind Kordell. "If you'll be so kind as to disrobe, put on the garment you find, then lay back and *chill*—I believe that's the proper the slang term—Yuri will be in to further assist you."

"Chill. Right. Ha, ha, very funny," said Kordell. "As if anyone could chill after that *physical* therapy."

A few minutes later, Kordell was alone and dressed in what looked and felt like a silver spacesuit. The metal table was surprisingly comfortable and warm, as if it weren't metal at all. And whatever was in store for him in this room, he was thankful that his sore penis was covered and, apparently, a non-participant in this event.

He was actually starting to feel better physically. Whatever was in the newbie mush had vanquished his feelings of hypoglycemia and the X high had taken a sharp nosedive. Still, it had been a long-assed day, one that started with him and Mario waking up in the woods outside this place after sleeping on the ground all night.

The door slid open. In walked Yuri, a bald, dark-skinned man in his forties. He was wearing the white lab coat and nodded but didn't speak. He headed for the LCD panel on the wall and began manipulating the controls.

"How long does this last?" asked Kordell.

Silence from Yuri.

"Longer or shorter than a three-minute egg?" asked Kordell.

More silence from Yuri.

"Tough facility," said Kordell.

Yuri's booming voice muttered several sentences, but he was definitely not using English. Maybe Russian. Maybe Martian. Definitely not English.

"Ex-squeeze me?" said Kordell.

Yuri fronted him and repeated himself. He was holding a small pair of purple goggles—the virtual goggles. He moved to put them on Kordell.

"Tell me something," Kordell said as the goggles came over the crown of his head. "Do none of youse lab coats purposely not speak English so you don't have to answer our questions?"

"Asshole," came from Yuri in his thick Martian accent.

"So it's true!" With the goggles on, Kordell's world cut to black. "Just don't touch my winkie," he pleaded.

Yuri said something in broken English, but the only word Kordell understood was "movie." Or was it "music?" Had to be "music," Kordell decided as easy-listening elevator tunes began streaming in his ears from speakers that were somehow inside the goggles. Nice, Kordell thought. Long day, heavy meal, might as well catch some Zs instead of their virtual freak show.

Some time later, hundreds of tiny TV screens appeared before his eyes, each one playing something different. No sound came from them, just images of people, places and animals. The "big picture" of all these screens made it impossible to make out any single image, so Kordell decided to "zoom" in on a few. His eyes went toward the right side of the collage of screens.

Lucy and Ethel in front of a conveyor belt in a chocolate factory.

A white man with white hair reading the news in black and white.

A woman washing her hair and having an orgasm caused by her shampoo.

Home video of a black mom pulling a cake from the oven while her kids dance around the kitchen all excited.

A blurry streak flashed before Kordell's eyes. He was in another area of the "big picture" of hundreds of screens and paused to scan the images here.

Boxing. A slo-mo shot of a man's jaw being knocked to the side of his face, blood and sweat flying through the air like particles in space.

An Asian boy playing with a puppy on a front step.

Wrestlers—the fake, professional kind—hitting one another over the head with metal chairs.

He stayed with the wrestlers, just as he did while channel surf-

ing at home. How he loved their gladiator-sized bodies all glistening with sweat and practically naked. The shots of their asses alone. Just a second or two on this channel, he thought; before the dreaded stirring of the loins and a painful, raw hard-on.

Suddenly he was in the video. *In* the video. He was watching himself on the screen. A huge, beefy white wrestler with a blond Mohawk smashed Kordell's head with a two-by-four. Fake, nothing; it hurt like hell. Suddenly Kordell's point of view went from watching the screen to being in the ring. The wrestler pulled down his red tights, exposing his massive dick amidst red, wiry pubic hair. Kordell looked down at it, then lifted his head up just in time to see brass knuckles landing on his nose. It hurt, but not as bad as it should have, and not nearly as bad as the anticipation of it.

I'm dreaming, he said to himself. Dreaming of sweaty pro wrestlers pummeling me with their massive bodies. Not today.

He didn't want to feel anything associated with pain, not from a chokehold or his dick, which was stirring from its restful state.

He left that "channel" and surfed over to birds nesting on a nature show. Mother feeding babies a worm. How sweet. What cute little creatures, so fragile, so in need. He stayed in the tree—yes, he realized, he was perched on a skinny little branch—until the aftereffects of the WWF were but a memory. Then he decided to move on in this incredible dreamscape where he could surf a plethora of images.

He flew by racing cars, boys playing with toy soldiers and girls playing basketball. He saw a rap concert and descended like an angel onto the stage. A very short black man sporting a red warm-up suit handed him the mic. The crowd erupted as if the main act had just arrived. Kordell started rapping. The crowd went off. They were all women. They threw their panties on stage. He was the king of the rap world.

King of the world. The phrase made him think of Leonardo DiCaprio and Kate Winslet in *Titanic*. And just like that, as if his very thoughts could conjure up whatever he wanted, Kordell saw a screen that contained an image of himself with the buxom actress from the blockbuster of the 1990s. Kordell and Kate were on the bow of the

great ship, naked, limbs wrapped around each other, having passionate vertical sex.

Sex with Kate Winslet?

The Titanic was flying. The iceberg hurled toward his face at light speed. He braced himself for impact. White streaks passed underneath his eyelids. Excruciating pain was about to invade his world. He couldn't wake up—he was that tired from the day—but he could banish Kate and her iceberg. He did and the pain went away immediately.

He was floating in the ocean now, a warm tropical ocean. Gone was the ill-fated ship, the big block of ice and the fear. He drifted up onto an island filled with palm trees and a black supermodel with hair down to her ass. She was naked except for some strategically-placed fig leaves. She struck a seductive pose and welcomed him to their island paradise with a tropical drink in a half-coconut.

He felt thirsty. He accepted the drink, took a sip, then had the urge to pour the rest over her smooth, chocolate body. What the hell. It was a dream after all. She loved it; she moaned. He licked her shoulder, then, fearing the possibility of a hard on, stopped. He hugged her. It was an awkward, overly dramatic hug, one a gangly kid might give. But she seemed to accept it just fine; indeed, she hugged him back like a mother, a sister, a girl who didn't mind that he had no experience being this intimate with a woman.

A huge yet gentle wave rolled in from the ocean, so high that the water washed over their heads, showering them in warmth. He hugged his black supermodel a little tighter. It was the most sensuous feeling Kordell had ever felt, in real life or in a dream.

I could definitely fall in love with women and forget the pigs that are men.

His eyes sprang open. He tried to sit upright but lost his balance. It was then that he realized that the reclining metal table had reclined so much that his head was almost touching the floor and his feet were high in the air. Yet some sort of gravitational force prevented him from falling. He took off the goggles and glanced around the room. He was alone. Had they been fucking with his mind? Or did he simply fall asleep and the dreams were the product of suggestion?

"Hey!" he shouted out of panic. "Somebody!"

His upper body began to levitate, his lower body descending. The frigging table was moving, and still some gravitational pull kept Kordell locked in place. Just as he reached an upright position—completely upright, as in one hundred percent vertical—Kordell saw Yuri's bald head in front of him.

"Shit!" Kordell cried out.

"What wrong?" Yuri said in his gruff voice.

"I want to see Pizarro. Pizarro. Boss. Now."

Yuri flashed a knowing, cocky smile and left the room.

Kordell tried to talk himself out of the fear that they could play with his mind that easily. He removed the goggles from his forehead and examined them. Nothing out of the ordinary, just two panes of purple glass. Certainly nothing that could have programmed beefy wrestlers, buxom actresses and fine black supermodels in his head, right?

It's just the day, this creepy haunted house and whatever hallucinogens they pumped into my system, he told himself. Ultimately, they can't fuck with my mind. They'll never turn me straight. Give up male booty?

He laughed at the thought, but made sure he didn't imagine a male posterior on account of the steel football.

"Something wrong, Mr. Christie?"

It was Pizarro, emerging from behind.

"Nuttin', honey," Kordell said with a cocky smile.

Pizarro was not amused.

Frisco, a burly white student, dabbed at a tear lodged in the corner of his eye. Once composed, he clutched the handkerchief in his fist, glanced around the support group and continued:

"My big sis wanted a baby sister so bad, when I was born, Pops told her *I* was a girl. I swear, I have these faint memories of the first months of my life, and Ginny—that's my sister—is showing me how to play with Malibu Barbie. And whenever we watched the animated classics together, we'd both spend hours afterwards pretending to be the heroine. Is it any wonder I was confused before coming here?"

You needn't be confused, Kordell thought, looking at the five o'clock shadow creeping up over Frisco's entire body. You're a big ol' hairy girl.

"When did your father tell your sister she had a baby brother?" a young Arab man asked the big ol' hairy girl.

"My thirtieth birthday, if you ask me." Frisco shrugged. "By the way, I'm thirty-one."

Laughter rippled through the room. The support group was made up of eight students, all of whom were seated in chairs arranged in a semi-circle. Presiding over them was a facilitator with a short blond crew cut. Before the session, he had introduced himself to Kordell—the newcomer—as Brother John. Kordell didn't bother informing Brother John that no introduction was needed, that Kordell had already seen him encouraging Mario's attempt to get to know underage boys in beach restrooms. Instead, Kordell simply shook Brother John's sweaty hand and was taken aback by the young man's ultra-smooth skin. In some other context, Brother John would actually be attractive. In West Hollywood, he'd be the one porno directors recruited for video stardom. The Power Bottom. Kordell must have been staring at him a little too intently while Frisco, the big ol' hairy girl, shared with the group.

"How about you, Kordell?" Brother John said when Frisco paused. "Anything you'd like to share, like your own personal confusion in your youth?"

Kordell surveyed the vacant faces around him. Souls being wrested away from rightful owners. Men who'd rather follow other men over a cliff instead of figure out the world for themselves.

"I was molested," he said matter-of-factly. A lie but good bait. "Anyone here suffer the same fate?"

The room went still.

"C'mon," Kordell went on. "You can't tell me this isn't par for the course here."

No one made eye contact with him, except Brother John. It was then that Kordell took note of the one-way mirror on one of the walls—so natural around here, he almost overlooked it.

"We don't allow molestation to be an excuse for homosexuality," said Brother John.

"I'm not saying it is," said Kordell. "But you have to admit—"

"Why don't we move on," said Brother John. "Mr. Christie is new. He's got a lot to learn. Apparently."

"I have a nifty share," said a young black man in his early twenties. "In my virtual session today, I married Mariah Carey and we had triplets."

The group erupted in envious "oos" and "ahs."

"And I stayed in that world and was happy for two whole hours!" said the young black man. "No distractions, *no* thoughts of, well, you all know my past weakness for blond surfers—anyway, me and Miss Mariah—sorry, Mrs. Waters—that's my last name, Waters —we were doing just fine. She even sung me a ballad."

Brother John and the other students broke out in a small round of applause while Kordell sat frozen in his chair, stunned to realize that his dreams—the WWF, the Titanic, the supermodel—weren't dreams at all, that this conversion house was equipped with far more weapons than he envisioned as he goaded Pizarro into accepting him as a student on the gazebo steps.

But how?

"All for today." Brother John stood up. "Now it's … free time!"

Happily, the men filed out, their noise and commotion bringing Kordell back to reality, as it were.

"What's free time?" he asked the young black man as they exited the room.

"Fresh air in the Contemplation Gardens."

"One more thing," said Kordell. "Why the *ixnay* on the molestation talk?"

The young black man's face grew nervous. He looked around to make sure no one was within earshot.

"Don't do it again," he whispered, then couldn't get away from Kordell fast enough.

Free time—a misnomer if there ever was one—was one measly hour in the great outdoors before some ridiculously early bedtime. Then it was off to the barracks for a paltry six hours of sleep, to be followed by more lies and programming at daybreak.

Kordell sat alone on a stone bench, staring at the ghosts in green scrubs who had surrendered their lives to the evil Pizarro. The large, open-air patio was a hum of testosterone-filled activity. Men were arm wrestling, thumbing through *Hustler* magazines, playing poker and shooting craps. In one corner, five men were making use of Microsoft's new RealLife Hologram 4-D technology. Thanks to the new software, three Victoria's Secret underwear models stood atop a patio table, shaking their tits, sticking out their asses and looking very lifelike, as long as you didn't try to reach out and touch them. In another area of the patio, a group of men guzzled beer while watching a baseball game on a miniature TV, the kind people brought to tailgate parties. To Kordell, the whole thing resembled a living museum exhibit: the accepted activities of the hetero ape as performed by the American male homosexual.

"Enjoying your free time?" Koji asked as he sat on the bench, uninvited, of course.

Kordell said nothing. He didn't need a cult-following space cadet hanging around. What he needed was a moment alone to figure out the best way to find Mario and get out of here by nightfall. Fredito's baseball trip was T minus thirty-six hours away. Kordell's nerves were on an even shorter fuse.

"You can join them if you'd like." Koji indicated the men taking turns arm wrestling each other. Two frail college-age kids were up against one another. Neither one could move the other's arm even an inch.

"I'm better off processing all that's happening to me," said Kordell. "Alone."

"Big changes?" asked Koji.

Kordell didn't answer.

"Do you really want to be here?" asked Koji.

"Why would you ask such a thing?"

"Your energy is very negative. It says to me: I have a hidden agenda."

"Your energy meter needs a tune-up," said Kordell. "Aren't all newbies nervous?"

"I apologize then."

"I mean," Kordell went on in his own defense, "the security is just one of the things that gives this place a creepy, Orwellian touch. Cameras around every corner, retinal scanners. There's no escaping Big Straight Brother."

Koji laughed a sympathetic laugh. "Except in construction zones."

Kordell didn't recall seeing any construction zones and dismissed the comment.

"Tell me about the revved-up Speedo goggles," he asked. "How do they do what they do?"

"Amazing, isn't it, how far virtual technology has come."

"How far has it come?" asked Kordell.

"You had a virtual session? Oh, man. We did, too, during training. The eSuit is the key. That and your mind."

"What's my mind got to do with it? And what the hell is an eSuit?"

"Sensory-based virtual technology doesn't take you anywhere you don't want to go," Koji explained. "The Cray XR Image Server contains literally billions of moving images. Combine that with a VT 3000 Über Computer with 178 terabytes of storage and you've got almost every morsel of culture known to the western world inside those tiny little goggles. The images fuel your imagination. Where you go is up to what your body tells the eSuit, which can make you happy or sad, depending on your body's vibes and what you're supposed to be liking and not liking on screen. Oh, yeah, and the metal table, it's far from just a table."

"What do you mean?"

"It takes you where you want to go," said Koji, "like a space-age travel agent."

"I specifically remember *not* booking a trip on the Titanic with Kate Winslet."

Koji laughed. "The technology guides you, sure, based on your cultural profile. But I bet if you were turned off by Kate's big boobs, something bad happened to you."

Kordell refused to tell him about the iceberg smacking him in the face.

"That was your mind creating that," said Koji, "not the computer."

"I still don't understand."

"Think of it like smoking pot and your mind goes off on wild free association trips. Only with sensory-based virtual technology, you don't need to inhale. Plus you feel it so much more."

"This place has got bells and whistles beyond anything I expected," Kordell said warily. He eyed the men ogling the three Victoria's Secret models, who were now strutting around the patio table in a circle.

"This is the future, man," said Koji. "They don't tell you everything in those PC magazines. Hell, even they might not be up on it. But we are. And so is the military."

A cheer erupted from the group watching the sporting event on the television, prompting Kordell to wonder if the game was real or something cooked up in a microprocessor.

"With all the gizmos here," he said, "I feel like if I slip up, they're gonna shackle me or re-introduce me to the steel football or something."

Koji chuckled, then came to within inches of Kordell's face and said, "The solution is simple, my friend: don't slip up."

I've had enough of you. Forever.

"Think I'll take a stroll to stretch my legs." Kordell rose up and excused himself from this very handsome but very strange Japanese man.

The gardens beyond the patio were quiet, even though they were full of students sitting, standing, walking, contemplating. Kordell made eye contact with the men he passed and wondered: do any of you know Mario? Why isn't he ever present at anything?

He debated talking to some of the men, to find out what they knew, whom they knew. But he felt isolated from them, as if he had little in common with them, as if they saw him as an outsider and wanted to keep their distance. Then it occurred to him: this wasn't all that different from the atmosphere in a gay bar: no one talking or trying to make a connection, Kordell feeling like the pudgy black man no one was interested in approaching or being approached by.

He made his way toward the wooded area on the other side of the gardens and strolled down a long pathway lined with tall shrubbery. If there was cruising going on, it would be here. Not that he was in the mood to wake up his thankfully unconscious penis. It was just another sarcastic thought, which he quickly jettisoned from his mind.

He made a pact with himself: for the duration of this nightmare, he would, under no circumstances, think about, joke about, or even remotely wonder about anything relating to homosexual sex. Straight sex he could deal with. That wouldn't make his dick hard. True, they wanted him to replace thoughts of gay sex with images of cocks penetrating pussies and men's faces planted in women's breasts. He'd give them this. They'd won this pitiful, fruitless battle for the duration. But when he got out …

He looked down the pathway. Up ahead, a brown-skinned man ducked into the woods on the right. Seconds later, a brown-skinned hand motioned him to come hither. Kordell made sure the coast was clear and scurried down the pathway. Finally, the chance to catch up with—

He came face to face, not with a man, but a naked ass. A naked, brown-skinned ass, not belonging to Mario but another Latino who was bent over and ready.

"Fuck me," said the Latino, not bothering to look at Kordell.

"You're not serious." Kordell held up his hands to form a force field to keep the image at bay. Was this a test? A trap? "We'll get caught. I don't want this."

The Latino turned around. He was very skinny and had a pock-marked face. His eyes were ripe with some kind of desperation or drug.

"Fuck now." He was jacking off. *"Por favor.* Quickly."

Kordell heard rustling in a nearby bush. His panic multiplied.

"Get away from me!" He sprint-walked back down the pathway, his head spinning from the idea that this kind of scene was taking place at the Facility. And in wooded areas, back alleys, bookstores and bathhouses all over the world at that exact same moment.

They'd do it in the mud if they had to.

Later that night, in the sleeping quarters, Kordell was still thinking about this bizarre encounter as he climbed into the top bunk of his bunk bed. Dozens of men flanked him on either side and the same arrangement mirrored them on the opposite side of the long corridor. Seemingly every twisted fag he'd seen today was sleeping in this room. Except the crazed Latino bottom. And the staffers. And Mario.

Reluctantly, Kordell had resigned himself to the fact that he was in for one overnight stay in this house of horrors. Getting to Mario was proving to be more than he bargained for. He certainly hadn't expected the drugs and the steel football, not to mention the other high-tech barriers and the resolve of Pizarro and his men. But he needed the rest anyway, to clear his mind completely from the X and everything else that had transpired, to rest up for their Rambo-esque getaway, to deal with whatever awaited them after their escape.

"Goodnight, men," said the bald white man who was the last staffer to leave the room. "Remember, straight dreams."

The glass door slid shut behind him and a computer belted out three loud beeps. They were locked in for the night. The only place they were allowed to wander in the moonlight was the single-occupancy bathroom at the end of the room (it too was watched by Big Straight Brother).

Kordell lay on his back, discouraged, unsure of his game plan come morning. As exhausted as he was, he couldn't sleep. The idea that, all in the span of one day, he'd taken drugs, been drugged, shaved completely, jacked off to the point of nausea and programmed with virtual hetero propaganda—it all left his senses just a bit overwhelmed. Plus, he was scared that if he did drift off, he'd start dreaming of Kate Winslet and black supermodels again.

So he just lay there, arms above his shoulders, head resting on his hands.

Soon, he noticed an odd sort of humming in the room, a muted, melodic whisper that became more and more audible. Someone was chanting something over and over, their voice too low to understand. Eventually, another voice joined in, then another and another, all in perfect synchronization. The voices mutated into

more and more voices until it seemed as though Kordell was the only one in the room not chanting. It was then that Kordell realized what they were saying:

"The devil inside, the devil inside; every little homo has the devil inside.

The devil inside, the devil inside; every little homo has the devil inside."

It was ... so similar to ...

They had appropriated the old INXS pop song from the late '80s that had nothing to do with gays. They had claimed it, bastardized it, were drumming it into these poor men's heads, had drummed it into Mario's head, which is why he had tried to spit out the phrase during his most heightened bouts of confusion.

Or did Mario volunteer to have the concept drummed into his head? Was he like Pizarro, Brother John, and Koji—involved in this mindfuck on a management level?

Kordell tried to banish the thought and trust his intuition about Mario; but with everything he'd been through in the last twenty-fours hours, he was having a hard time knowing what to believe. Indeed, he was having a hard time concentrating on anything but the hypnotic chanting of his fellow students.

"The devil inside, the devil inside; every little homo has the devil inside.

The devil inside, the devil inside; every little homo has the devil inside."

ELEVEN

S ometime in the middle of the night, Kordell fell into a deep
sleep. And thanks to the power of suggestion, he dreamed of
being straight.

He was married to Whitney Houston, who had long ago
kicked bad boy Bobby Brown to the curb. Kordell and Whitney and
their four little black babies were causing chaos in an expensive hotel
lobby. She was blowing grade-A coke in the faces of nosy reporters;
he was tipping over plush sofas, angry at her for wasting their stash
and disgusted with reporters who never left them alone. But they
were straight. And being straight meant being happy. Even the most
miserable straight life was better than the most allegedly happy gay
life. Being straight meant you were whole and right with Nature, no
matter how fucked up your straight life was.

He reached this epiphany as a cold hand rocked him gently.

"It's me," said a voice that had been trying to awaken him for
some time. "Koji. Yamo."

"Morning?" Kordell stammered.

"No," Koji whispered. "Special duty."

Kordell needed rest, even if it meant straight dreams; but he

sensed that this wasn't just some whim on Yamo's part, that Kordell was about to become acquainted with another part of his journey to true manhood. In any case, he was too weak and tired to fight. Obediently, he climbed down from the top bunk and followed Koji through the barracks.

"The fun never stops here," Koji said once they were in the hallway.

Kordell returned a stare that said he couldn't care less.

"Tough hallway." Koji escorted him through the dimly lit corridors of the Facility and Kordell couldn't shake the feeling that he was being led through a morgue.

"Remember that musical group Men at Work?" Koji asked at one point.

Kordell didn't answer.

Eventually, they came to a set of double glass doors, which slid open—after Koji's retina cleared security—and revealed the Contemplation Gardens. The patio was dark, the night air chilly. They walked along a concrete pathway near the exterior of the grounds and heard humming machinery and muffled chatter on the other side of a tall adobe wall. There were also lights, huge, towering lights on stilts that illuminated the area over the wall like a Hollywood movie set.

They stopped at a gate. Once again, Koji cleared security and they crossed the threshold onto what loomed like a large parking lot swarming with activity. Dozens of students were dressed in gray jumpsuits. They were hammering, sawing, rolling wheelbarrows, carrying two-by-fours.

"Men do construction," Koji said with a silly grin. He retrieved a jumpsuit from a bin and offered it to Kordell, who didn't take it at first. "It's yours," Koji explained. "We build things at night. It's my week to supervise. I thought you could use the fresh air."

Kordell looked at him as if this were a joke on some hidden video show.

"Come help me do the ceiling." Koji made his way down a set of steps that disappeared into a large opening in the ground. A tunnel. Like a subway entrance.

Instead of following, Kordell stood there momentarily, stunned by the concentration and dedication of his fellow students. Hairdressers with jackhammers. Circuit boys turned welders. There were even holo-gram figures of sexy women strutting by for the men to whistle at.

It was all too much for his groggy senses. Warily, he slipped the gray jumpsuit over his pajamas and headed for the tunnel, which was wide and made more than one turn. All throughout its corridors, gay-to-straight worker bees busied themselves painting, plastering and hammering, their dutiful efforts forcing Kordell to step around scaffolding, equipment and paint buckets.

Koji was atop a ladder deep within the interior, applying white, donut-like fixtures on the ceiling. "Good," he said upon seeing Kordell. "Just keep handing me those."

Kordell saw a bucket full of the fixtures at his feet and began handing them to Koji as needed.

"Secret passageway?" Kordell whispered while eyeing three men painting a nearby wall.

"Your typical expansion," said Koji. "In business, you're contin-ually growing or you're continually shrinking."

"But why a tunnel?"

"Not everybody likes to, or should, come through the front door." Koji grabbed the fixture in Kordell's hands, but Kordell didn't let go.

"Why are you here, Koji?" he asked while the fixture remained in both their hands.

"Same reason as you," said Koji. "I want to see the world become a better place with better people."

Kordell let go of the fixture. "Why did you wake my ass up? Just to get me to shuffle these widgets to you?"

"Why don't you like me?" Koji's attention returned to the ceiling.

"I'm being programmed not to like *any* men, am I not?" Kordell's tone was snide, like a triumphant smart-ass. A smirk wiped across his face. He was rather proud of that one.

"Why don't you go deeper into the tunnel," Koji said without looking at him. "See if you can find a more useful purpose for your time since my presence repulses you."

"Whatever." Kordell walked away like a petulant child who'd just been dismissed. He wandered past his fellow students, making sarcastic comments to himself, comparing these macho men to the Village People. Eventually, he came to a black velvet curtain designed to prevent further exploration.

Why not?

No one was paying attention to him, so he peeked around the curtain and saw a sliding glass door, on which was a sign:

AREA 2. HIGH SECURITY ACCESS ONLY.

Not only was there a retinal scanning panel, but there was also a thumbprint box.

How paranoid is that?

Kordell walked away in search of more accessible territory. But a few steps later, he stopped, remembering his conversation with Koji earlier in the day.

"There's no escaping Big Straight Brother," Kordell had said.

"Except in construction zones," Koji had replied laughingly.

Kordell glanced around at the other students in the tunnel. They were busy being obedient slaves. He backtracked, then drew back the black velvet curtain. As he did, a young white student sweeping the floor took note of him.

"Shut-eye," Kordell announced and slipped behind the curtain.

After manually opening the door, he found himself in a long red hallway full of sliding glass doors, not too dissimilar from the long green hallways in the rest of the place. Except in this hallway, every door was open, every room empty. Some rooms had metal examining tables, others strange wires and straps hanging from the ceiling. Security cameras hung like vultures from the ceiling, but they were covered with plastics bags—new toys as yet unwrapped.

He passed a dozen empty rooms; then, to his right, he saw a body on one of the metal examining tables. At first, it frightened him. Then he realized that the body belonged to Mario. He was wearing an eSuit and seemed so peaceful: hands clasped together on his stomach, purple virtual goggles covering his face. Kordell crept into the room and stood above his childhood friend.

"Mario," he called out softly. No answer. He said it two more

times and still no response. He removed Mario's goggles, but Mario's eyes remained fixed on the ceiling. Kordell said Mario's name a fourth time. No answer. He examined the goggles, then decided to put them on to see what garbage they were spewing.

The instant they were on his face, Kordell staggered. Thousands of little TV screens appeared, instead of the hundreds he'd seen in his own session. The screens were everywhere—above, below, behind him. He whipped around and almost lost his balance. He wanted to yank off the goggles but didn't. He tried unsuccessfully to make out some of the scenes, then remembered that he had to zero in on them.

Little boys. Shirtless in a sandbox.

Little boys. Taking a nap in a daycare.

Little boys. Typing on a computer keyboard.

Little boys. Swimming in a community pool.

The swim instructor was a man Kordell's age. The instructor *was* Kordell. Kordell's arm reached out to help one of the boys learn the backstroke—no, not the backstroke. Kordell reached for the boy's—

He let out a loud gasp, wrenched the goggles from his face and flung them against the wall.

"Don't break them," came from Mario, who was still staring straight ahead. "If they are removed for anything more than a ten-minute bathroom break, my teachers will come check on me."

"Then that gives us ten minutes plus the time it takes for them to get here." Kordell quickly retrieved the goggles and inspected them. "Not broken." He paused, taking in the sight of Mario. "Who are these teachers?"

"Pizarro," said Mario. "And Brother John."

"What's going on, Mario? Do you know who I am?"

"I am going through the finishing touches of my evolution."

"Into what?"

"Pure evil." Mario's gaze remained fixed on the ceiling. "Evil that preys on the innocent. Some have to be sacrificed. This is war."

"Sacrificed to who? To what? What kind of evil do you think you are? Just because you might be gay or bi?"

"Those who cannot be changed into productive heterosexuals

shall be used to teach the world that homosexuality must be eliminated at all costs." Mario began trembling. "Pizarro is programming
me to become parents', popes' and politicians' greatest living exhibit of why homosexuality is wrong."

"Child predators," said Kordell. "You want this?"

"I'm too afraid of suicide."

"How … how?"

"I ran away and missed my final exams and graduation with my
class."

"There are others?"

"Eight in my class," said Mario, "but once I am done with my
training, I will not remember them or Pizarro or coming to the
Facility."

"I don't understand, Mario."

"Listen to me, homie." There was urgency in Mario's monoto-
ne voice. He tried to look at Kordell, but wasn't able to move his
neck. "I have clarity now only because I am in a session. As soon as
it is over, things get screwy in my brain."

"How?"

"Maybe a flaw in the system, maybe why Pizarro is working on
some new method, some chip, which is much worse. Or better,
depending on your perspective. But forget that right now. Let me
talk. Little time."

"Go."

"Hold my hand," said Mario.

"What?"

"Do it."

Kordell grabbed Mario's hand; it was hot and moist.

"This is *me* talking," Mario said, his hand squeezing Kordell's.
"Not the shit they're putting in me. You feel me?"

"I feel you."

"This may not come out coherent, but … the older I get, the
more I think about being with men. My bisexual side was coming on
in a big way. I wanted to do some research. I want a family, kids,
maybe a wife, maybe a live-in girlfriend. But I also want to be with
men, maybe even have a boyfriend. I searched the 'net for answers.

Why am I bi? Am I gay? What makes a person gay? No one to talk to. I brought it up to my girlfriend and that was the beginning of the end of our relationship."

"Your last girlfriend."

"I found the website for H.O.P.E., made appointment, saw counselor. Couple of times. Not Pizarro. Never saw him there."

"But that's why Sal saw you at the Mission," said Kordell.

"Maybe stopped for a Snapple; I remember that now. Anyway. Someone at H.O.P.E. told me about the Facility. I came here for a tour. Nothing wrong with taking a tour, hear their side of things. I had lunch with the tour guide in the cafeteria. I saw my father working in the kitchen. I fainted."

"Just like on the mountain top."

"When I woke up, I was in a room, a chamber. My father and Pizarro and others were over me—"

"Who? Brother John? Koji?"

"Don't know a Koji."

"Yamo?" asked Kordell. "Yamamoto?"

Mario shook his head, his eyes still locked on the ceiling. "Gotta keep talking. Found out my father had been in jail for molesting— but not with Javy. Only my *familia* knows about Javy. Even Pizarro is clueless. *Papi* was having sex with a minor in Lompoc and got caught. After jail, Pizarro found him and took him in. Pizarro turned him straight. They told me they wanted to do the same for me."

"So you said yes?"

"I said maybe. A part of you always wants to please your father, no matter how much damage he's done. Plus, I think I was drugged."

The room fell silent until Mario went on:

"I enrolled. One night, *Papi* brought me to the kitchen for some extra food. I was a newbie, hungry as hell. *Papi* fed me, then tried to molest. I snapped, wanted to kill him—all the anger. Big mess. Staff came in. I told them they ripped me off, drugged me; I hadn't con- sented, gonna bring in police. *Papi* said I was mental, told them I was mental as a kid. Fucking lie. Men grabbed me. Fight. Kitchen all bloody. I woke up in Area 2. I'm just like Daddy now. Daddy is my idol."

"And what about Javier? How did he—"

"They took me and my class on a hike. I escaped, called Javy. He came up here to get me. They set him up. Corrupting a minor charges. They're very resourceful. Brother John killed my brother and made it look like suicide from shame."

"Does your father know this?"

"He thinks Javier killed himself because he was a pervert. I want to kill Brother John. Evil has the freedom to be evil in all kinds of ways."

Kordell listened for footsteps; he heard none but knew time was running out. "That's what you really want? To be evil?"

"I try to escape, tried at Gay Pride where Pizarro took me for field training."

"Field training?"

"I had all kinds of instruments on me, up me, to measure my reaction to gay men. I escaped, ditched the sensors, but I was so fucked up in the head, I didn't call the cops or hide the fuck out." His face twitched, remembering some terrible pain. "Every time I escape, they catch me. Virtual torture, drugs. Goggles—they are my only source of relief. I feel okay in them. I must. I am."

Kordell looked at the goggles on the floor, then the eSuit Mario was wearing, the one that gave him warm fuzzies for thinking of corrupting children.

"You don't want to do this … do you?"

"A part inside me believes I'm evil," said Mario. "Wanting to be with men is not right. That is my reality. I'm not a real man. But I see you. I see others, like at Pride. I don't see you as evil. Maybe I am a man. There's a part of me that knows this, but it gets blurry more and more. Soon I will only know evil and I will relish it."

"What will that make you do?"

"Maim little boys and make sure I'm caught someday. Then I will ramble on about things, like how a voice or a cartoon or song told me to rape and kill. No one will believe me, but it really will be a cartoon or song. One I saw here in the goggles. Only I won't remember the goggles, just the messages."

"Mario, how can you say all this now and not get up and get the hell out of here?"

"I fucked up my training during my escapes. But don't worry. When they're through with Mario Cervantes, only the devil will still be inside. Everyone, homie, has the devil inside."

Kordell, can I see your dick?

You sure can, little boy. I'm so glad you asked. Look how much bigger it is than your own little wiener. Go ahead touch it. You're mine now, my pretty.

"Mario, I have to go, but tell me: do you want out of this?"

"You're my angel. You know I do. They're coming."

"Then let's go, pronto!"

"Go where?" asked Mario.

Kordell thought about it. It was the middle of the night; they were in the middle of nowhere. The only sure way out was through the tunnel and an army of homo-hating homos was holed up throughout.

"Can you hold on, Mario? We can do this, but at the right time."

"I can hold on if you can, homie."

"Like Schwarzenegger, I will be back." Kordell turned to leave.

"Homie?"

"Yes, Mario?"

"The goggles."

Kordell realized the spectacles were still in his hands. Reluctantly, he moved to put them on Mario, but stopped short. Instead, he seized a pair of foot-long tweezers on a cart in the corner of the room.

"Sorry, Pizarro, but I'm gonna have to interrupt this program."

Kordell used the tweezers to scratch up the goggles' inner lenses.

"You might have to look at Sicko TV for a little while longer," he told Mario, "but with any luck, the images will be a little less potent now."

"Hurry," said Mario. "Go."

Kordell slipped the goggles over his friend's head, feeling as if the action was tantamount to molesting him. Again.

"I promise you, Mario, I will not let you down."

There was no time to wait for a response. Kordell stepped into the hallway, looked both ways, saw that it was clear and hurried out of Area 2.

A young man's voice permeated Kordell's sleep: "I told you, sir, he said he was going to get some …"

A curtain ripped open.

"… rest."

Kordell awoke. Standing over him were Koji and the young white student who'd seen Kordell slip behind the black velvet curtain. Kordell sat up against the door to Area 2 and shot them a guilty expression that said: you caught me, sleeping on the job.

"I know, I know," he mumbled. "Back to work."

"You don't have to," said Koji. "It's morning already."

TWELVE

aywatch. Every single one of the hundreds of screens in the virtual goggles featured beautiful white girls in red bathing suits. They were running in slow motion toward the camera and Kordell swore they were calling his name.

Where are the smooth, chiseled lifeguard boys *when you need them?*

Like magic, male lifeguards replaced the females. They too were running in slo-mo.

"Rescue me!" Kordell sang out like the old Madonna song.

He was determined to repel further brainwashing and corruption of his soul. He was also hell-bent on earning the classification "helpless homosexual" in order to be banished to Area 2, where Mario was stashed away. Kordell wasn't sure of his plan once inside the off-limits, predator training quarters, but time was running out. It was now Tuesday; Fredito was headed to baseball camp tomorrow; Kordell had promised Sal some sort of resolution by the crack of dawn Wednesday.

He marveled at the *Baywatch* hard bodies running toward him. "Is that a red buoy in your hand or are y'all glad to see me?"

The buoys morphed into sharks that swam toward Kordell. Furious ocean waves swallowed him whole. He was drowning in a sea of hungry great whites.

"Whoa … dude!" he cried out laughingly. "Exit, stage right."

Like a superhero, his feet turned into fins and he out-swam the sharks, swerving around them, dodging their attempts to take a chunk out of him.

"Life is a cartoon. Whoopee!"

He popped up through the surface of the ocean and began surfing. The male lifeguards reappeared and threw spears at him. His body—his real one—twitched with pain. Sharp objects hit him in the gut, the leg, his right eye, his left eye.

"*Fuck!*"

He reached for his face, but felt glass instead of flesh. He yanked off the goggles and saw blurry figures towering over his horizontal body. When his vision cleared, he recognized Pizarro and Brother John, their faces solemn and disappointed.

"Having a difficult time this morning?" asked Pizarro.

"So *you* were jabbing my body." Kordell looked around the room for props.

"If something was attacking you," said Pizarro, "it was your own conscience for not gravitating toward images that give you the most comfort."

"The *Baywatch* boys do way more for me than fish, what can I say?"

"Indeed," said a fey voice from another part of the room.

"He's not the first to resist, Clive," said Pizarro.

Clive—the pudgy, cautious queen who appeared to be third in command—came into view and said, "He'd be better off leaving the Facility now and starting from the beginning with the next class."

Kordell knew he needed to be careful around this loose cannon. Clive didn't share Pizarro's cockiness about the program; his perception of Kordell was unclouded by maniacal ego.

"Yo!" Kordell said with a hint of ghetto in his voice. "If you had some black honeys in the *Baywatch* scenes, maybe a brutha wouldn't think about men."

"The male lifeguards were all white," said Brother John.

"White guys I can deal with," said Kordell. "And I have. White chicks? No dice. If I'm gonna do white, it's got to be dudes. Surely you're not suggesting I marry outside of my race."

Pizarro, Brother John and Clive remained silent.

"Re-program." Kordell snapped his fingers high in the air. "More sistas for da bruthas in da joint." He tried to get up, but Pizarro held him in check with a bony finger to the shoulder and said:

"Brother John, dial up Janet Jackson for our African-American friend and set the eSuit on high. He's going to need a strong dose to make up for lost time."

Brother John attended to the LCD display panel on the wall. Clive beamed a smug, approving smile. And Pizarro had a look on his face that said, "Check."

"Today," Pizarro began from the pulpit, "two newbies will graduate to blue dot status and six men wearing blue dots will receive their green dots, becoming one step closer to graduation."

"Ooos" and "ahhs" filled the auditorium. The students sat upright in their stadium-style seats, some holding hands for good luck.

"First the newbies," said Pizarro.

"Not holding my breath," Kordell said from his spot in the very last row. The man next to him—a young black man—overheard and rolled his eyes with disdain.

"Henry Donaldson," announced Pizarro. Several rows below, a tall, skinny white man jumped up and screamed as if he'd just won the Miss America pageant. Once he saw Pizarro's disapproval, he butched it up and tried to strut like a manly man toward the stage. He failed. Miserably. Brother John handed Pizarro a blue dot, which he Velcroed on Henry Donaldson, after which there was applause from the audience as the nelly queen returned to his seat. Pizarro then called another name and another man only slightly less fem went up and received his blue dot.

"They do this every morning?" Kordell asked the young black man next to him.

"Shh," was his answer.

"Where have you been?" came from a row below them.

"In the real world," said Kordell. "Meeting real men with great big—"

"Shh," came from several men around him. This caught the attention of Pizarro and the staffers, who were all sitting in the front row. Onstage, Clive whispered something to Brother John, and Kordell slumped down in his chair, looking like a bored high school delinquent at a career day assembly.

"And now for the blue dots who will move up to green," Pizarro said, prompting more stirring and anticipation.

"So these guys don't need Viagra and a cast-iron stomach to screw chicks?" Kordell asked the men around him, receiving an even harsher round of shushes in return. The young black man next to Kordell got up and moved to another seat, prompting even more commotion.

"Mr. Christie," said Pizarro. "Is there something you'd like to share with your fellow patients?"

"I thought you said we were *students*," said Kordell.

"Stand up, please," said Pizarro. "We should all hear what you have to share."

Kordell stood up. "I was just wondering if these guys no longer need Viagra to be inside a woman."

A collective hush came over the room.

"Viagra?" asked Pizarro.

"Yeah, you know"—Kordell thrust his hips forward as if he were fucking—"to *badda bing, badda boom.*"

The hush morphed into murmurs.

"Students, quiet!" Pizarro eyed Kordell with a confident sneer, as if he relished this little challenge to his supreme authority. "Who would like to answer the newcomer's question?"

A young man, who would normally be a hairy bear cub were it not for the total body shave, stood up. "When you are right with Nature, you need no medication."

Another black man stood up and spoke with a Jamaican accent: "When you have rid yourself of all the clutter in your mind that

made you think you were attracted to men, you will have feelings toward the ladies to spare, *mon.*"

Their decrees were met with murmurs of approval and even a smattering of applause.

"Yeah," said Kordell, "but I know a lot of you guys are total bottoms—*were* total bottoms, excuse me—and throwing your legs up in the air and being on the receiving end of a nice, fat cock is all you know. Are you sure you can, you know, stick it to a woman? A pink, wet vagina? It's not like a guy, you know. It smells different. It's got that furry bush around it, and if they don't trim it, whoa! Watch out—"

"Mr. Christie, are you quite finished?" asked Pizarro.

"Your goal," Kordell began, "*our* goal for being here is to remove all evil from our bodies and minds so that we can be husbands and fathers to a bunch of screaming babies, right?"

Pizarro remained silent, his arms folded, his lips pursed.

"I ask you," Kordell continued, "how can I get rid of my evil if I still have these questions and don't ask them?"

"The time for questioning is over," said Brother John, prompting more murmurs of approval.

"Brother John is right as usual," said Pizarro. "You—everyone in this room has been questioning their sexuality all their lives, wondering if they were normal, if they could fit into society the right way."

"We don't have questions here," said Clive. "We have answers. You came here for answers; answers are what you get."

The volume of approving murmurs rose even higher, this time accompanied by a smattering of amens.

"But what if I still have questions?" Kordell shouted over the ruckus. "I mean, how in the fuck am I ever going to give up dick? I love dick!"

A scandalous, collective gasp.

"More than dick," said Kordell, "I love ass!"

Some men were visibly shaken, others mortified, like great-grandmothers hearing this kind of talk for the very first time.

"A real *man's* ass." Kordell cupped his hands as if he were grab-

bing a massive, baseball catcher's butt. "Big, meaty, round mounds of masculinity. Ass and dick. Oh, God, I love ass and dick!"

The auditorium erupted with yelling and screaming. Screaming ex-queens. Several staffers bum-rushed Kordell; others held angry students in check, preventing them from enacting their own brand of justice. Pizarro and Clive were arguing on stage. Brother John begged the room for calm, but didn't get it. And Kordell swore he saw some men covering up hard-ons.

"What's wrong with honesty?" he yelled.

The room was more chaotic than a Russian parliamentary meeting. Two staffers grabbed him and gave him a rough escort through the aisle and down the steps.

"A chick can strap on all she wants!" He was being ejected and refused to shut up. "It'll never be the same as a live, hard, fleshy cock! How can you give up cock? How can anyone give up cock? Can you really give up cock?"

The two staffers shoved him through the doorway like bouncers. One of them was Koji Yamamoto. The other one—a Latino—closed the doors behind them, muting the chaos in the auditorium behind smoked glass.

"You just bought yourself some serious physical therapy time," said the Latino, who was bald and muscular. And very handsome.

"You trying to commit suicide?" asked Koji.

"Trying to be real," said Kordell. "Something none of you are doing."

The doors slid open and Clive joined them. "Handle this?"

"Under control," said Koji.

"You know what to do," said Clive. His bouncers nodded. "I've got to help Victor." He rejoined the mayhem, closing the doors behind him.

"Anyone ever tell you that you look like Mr. Clean?" Kordell asked the Latino.

Ignoring him, Koji and Mr. Clean grabbed him by his arms and led him down hall.

"Look, fellas," Kordell pleaded, "I've been drugged, whacked off to within a inch of my sanity and bombarded with *Baywatch*. No

doubt I'm not the first homo to crack in here."

"What you did in there was beyond egregious," said Mr. Clean. Kordell started to speak, but Mr. Clean shook his fist and said, "Can it!"

They walked without further debate to a hallway that Kordell immediately recognized as the physical therapy area. And if he had any doubt he was about to have another date with the steel football, it was erased when an ear-piercing scream came from one of the other rooms farther down the hall.

"Wait here," Mr. Clean said, then went to investigate the source of the shriek.

"Not very smart, are you?" Koji said once they were alone.

"Right now, I feel like a genius compared to these nitwits," said Kordell.

"At least these nitwits won't have sore nuts like you and that poor sap."

Mr. Clean reappeared with the Latino who had begged for Kordell's dick in the Contemplation Gardens. He looked as spent as a circuit boy the morning after a White Party. He could hardly walk, and drool covered his chin; that is, until he vomited all over the front of his green scrubs.

"Not again," Mr. Clean said, then turned to Koji. "I'll take care of this one. You handle the newcomer."

Koji agreed and led Kordell into his own torture chamber.

"Shit," Kordell said once the door was closed behind him, the full implications of his rebellion now more apparent.

"Should've thought about that," said Koji.

"You're not really going to do this to me, eh, Yamo, buddy?"

Koji got up in Kordell's face and whispered, "Keep your voice down."

"I could resist, you know, fight you," Kordell whispered back.

"Black belt. Besides," —Koji brandished a syringe between their faces— "I was supposed to inject this the minute we grabbed you."

"Why didn't you?" Kordell asked, still feeling cocky. Koji shoved him backward; Kordell fell onto the padded table.

"Let's just say I feel for you," said Koji.

"I would have never guessed."

"You misunderstand," Koji said as he quickly secured the Velcro restraints around Kordell's limbs. "Even though you're right on that count, too."

"Riddles," said Kordell.

"I pity your approach." Koji went over to the LCD panel on the wall, messed with the display, then returned to the table and spoke in a normal voice. "But then again, you're an amateur."

"Say what?"

"I wouldn't have gone about it the same way," said Koji. "I would have been a little more judicious, recognized friends who are trying to help, not hurt."

"The only friend I have in here is—"

"Shut up." Koji went over to the panel again, checked it but didn't touch it. "I've only got a few seconds before I need to realize I made a mistake and accidentally shut off the audio to the room. Can't be too careful, don't know who's listening or watching."

Kordell started to look at the mirror on the ceiling.

"*Do not* look that way." Koji said emphatically.

Kordell froze.

"Geez, amateurs," said Koji.

Kordell started to speak, but Koji put a hand to Kordell's mouth.

"I can tell you this," said Koji. "You think I'm a dumb, deferential Asian, right?"

Kordell's guilt was implied by his silence.

"Understand something," Koji came to within inches of Kordell's face. "I hate dumb, deferential Asians." Then he dashed over to the panel.

"You mean you're—"

"Silly me," Koji interrupted. "I accidentally pushed the wrong … there. The audio should be working just fine now."

"You're not going to really put me through this football again, are you?" Kordell asked, his eyes pleading with this new version of Yamo.

"Pizarro won't mind if I put it on low setting," said Koji.

"Since when do Pizarro's minions call the shots around here?"

It was Brother John, standing in the doorway. "Only the highest doses for the doubters."

Kordell gulped. Brother John walked over to the panel and corrected the settings.

"Have you given him his shot?" he asked Koji.

"Not yet, sir," said Koji. "I wasn't sure if he should get the tranquilizer or the sexual drive medication."

"Give him both." Brother John shrugged. "He'll survive. Maybe."

Koji had no choice. His eyes said so as he held Kordell's bicep, then shot him up, once with a tranquilizer, then with the drug that was like giving *Viagra* Viagra.

"Enjoy hell," said Brother John. It was the last thing Kordell heard before the lights went out and the steel football descended from the ceiling.

THIRTEEN

Kordell screamed until his lungs stung and his throat was sore, then he screamed some more—gut-rattling cries of ecstasy, agony, glory and devastation. He never knew testicles could ache to the point where you actually *wanted* them to fall off. He was also sure he'd have no penis once he stood up. But he didn't give a damn. The steel football was having its way with him; his mind was delirious with rebellion and whatever drugs had been injected into his system. At one point, he sang the Hallelujah Chorus, bucking and writhing, simultaneously in heaven and hell. Angels and devils danced within. He was more alive than he ever thought possible. He was also dead, or wished he were. It was strange. It was confusing. It was a slice of dementia. Whatever he felt, he let it out verbally and that made it bearable.

When the mechanical JO machine finally came to a halt, he opened his eyes and saw a disgusted Pizarro standing over him. Brother John was also in the room, messing with the display panel on the wall. Clive was there, too, a safe distance away from the freakazoid.

"Don't stop it," Kordell begged, knowing that would get their

goat. "Don't stop, Daddy. More, more, more. Give me more, Daddy, please!"

Seconds later, he staggered out of the physical therapy room on Brother John's arms. Pizarro and Clive stayed behind, but he could hear Pizarro saying:

"Maybe the scorn of his fellow homos will do him some good."

It was lunchtime; Kordell was late. When he reached the entrance to the cafeteria, all motion within ceased.

"I'll be watching you," Brother John said, pushing him forward. "Don't even think about another outburst."

Kordell would have to walk this walk alone. He limped down the aisle in the middle of the room, all eyes glued on the delinquent pervert. Some looked on with fear, some with pity, some with contempt. A true believer in his position would have felt nothing but shame at that instant; and even though he was an impostor, he still experienced a strange sense of alienation that perplexed him.

I've probably tricked with some of these men. Or tricked with men who've tricked with these men. Or tricked with men who've tricked with men who've ...

Making light didn't work. Being here was the polar opposite of Gay Pride, the thing he allegedly celebrated just days before. He felt sick and sad for these men and for the kind of world that created them. He was all the more determined to walk out of here a man free of society's branding and dictates. And to save Mario from whatever demons he possessed, demons that Kordell may have caused when they were kids. But first he needed sustenance to restore the life "physical therapy" had wrenched out of him.

He reached the serving line to find Giovanni Cervantes already holding a ladle full of mush, glorious mush. Brother John approached and said, "Get your slop and have a seat." Then he moved away. Mustn't get too close to the pariah.

Kordell eyed Giovanni, trying to find a shred of decency in the eyes of a man who went from molesting children to working in a gay-to-straight conversion factory.

"You approve of what they're doing to your son?" Kordell asked.

"Mario came here of his own free will," said Giovanni.

"Is he still here of his own free will?"

Confusion washed over Giovanni's face. He doesn't know about Area 2, Kordell decided. Or he's a damn good poker player.

"What about your other son?" Kordell checked the immediate vicinity to make sure they were alone. "I suppose you don't know what I know about Javier's death."

"Educate me," Giovanni said, his eyes still mistrustful.

"Food," Kordell demanded. "Real food. Hide it underneath."

"How do I know you don't lie?"

"How do you know I won't *not* lie?"

Giovanni thought for a moment, then loaded Kordell's tray with corn, carrots, green beans and a hamburger patty. Afterwards he covered the food with a good helping of mush.

"Ask them how your son died," said Kordell. "Check with the coroner if you have to."

Giovanni started to speak, but a short Asian student approached the serving line, abruptly ending their conversation. Kordell turned and walked away. Giovanni could follow up on his own, maybe trust his cronies a little less. Sowing suspicion and mistrust had to be a good thing, one way or another.

Kordell walked like a condemned man back down the middle aisle. As he passed each table, heads turned away in ripples. Even Koji Yamamoto looked away, his message the same as the other men: don't come near me. Kordell parked himself at an empty table. Men at nearby tables moved away, deciding lunch was over. Only one man remained at the adjacent table, the Latino who had wanted to get fucked in the woods and who had also been subjected to physical therapy this morning.

"What's your name?" Kordell mumbled.

"Sabatino." His eyes were still wide, desperate, needy.

Kordell looked away. Time to eat and regain the strength and conviction this nuthouse had stolen from him.

"We need to determine," Pizarro began as he paced the floor behind his cherry wood desk, "just how serious you are about changing your lifestyle."

"I wouldn't be here if I weren't serious," Kordell said from the chair in front of the desk.

"Our concern is you may be too far gone," said Clive, who was, once again, a safe distance away in the corner. "That you're too sucked under by the gay lifestyle to be effectively reformed."

"Sucked under?" Kordell chuckled, but Pizarro and Clive didn't see the humor. "Ah, come on, guys, the analogies you use, shaving guys, whacking them off—you really think these men don't find this stuff homoerotic?"

"Not if you want to re-think how you perceive these things," said Clive. "You're here to learn not to homoeroticize every little innuendo and slice of culture, don't you understand that? Or is your brain too twisted and filthy to turn back now?"

"Here's something I don't mean in an erotic way," said Kordell. *"Fuck you!* How's that?"

"Back to your corners, both of you." Pizarro demanded. "There's no such thing as going too far down the path of the wrong. At least not anymore."

"Victor, no!" Clive's expression went from angry to apprehensive. "We're far from ready for that."

"For what?" asked Kordell.

"None of your damned business!" A layer of sweat appeared on Clive's brow.

Pizarro held up a hand to silence Clive, then sat on the desk in front of Kordell and said, "It's true that your psyche might be extremely entrenched in the homosexual gutter. After all, you are older than most of our students and you've been out for quite some time. Let's face it: you may be a self-loathing, drug-abusing queer, but you never were the ideal candidate for our program."

"Victor, I'm begging you, please—"

"Clive, leave us," Pizarro said while staring at Kordell.

It took him a couple of fits and starts, but Clive followed his boss's orders.

"Sometimes he forgets that he works for me," Pizarro said when they were alone. "And that I rescued him from a life as pitiful as yours many, many years ago."

"You got some deal for me he doesn't approve of?" asked Kordell.

"There are no deals here at the Facility." Pizarro rose up and circumnavigated the desk until he was sitting in the chair behind it. Above his head was a plaque:

NO ONE COMES IN A PRODUCTIVE HOMOSEXUAL. NO ONE LEAVES OUT A PRODUCTIVE HOMOSEXUAL.

Kordell had heard it before, but where?

Ah, yes, while being shaved on the gyroscope.

"You signed a consent form stating that you would accept whatever assistance we offer," said Pizarro. "Unfortunately, your resistance and your party drugs are impeding your evolution."

"Don't forget your drugs on top of my drugs," said Kordell.

Pizarro drew an impatient breath through his pursed lips. Once he collected himself, he said, "You will not leave here the same little faggot you came here as."

"That's what I'm counting on," Kordell said with an equally stern expression.

"You can resist." Pizarro leaned forward. "But you can't run, you can't hide and you can't get past security and rejoin the outside world until I say so. Now" —he settled back in his chair, the fingertips of his hands meeting to form a tent— "you can do this the easy way and become something you know you want to become. Or you can do this the hard way. And I don't think you want the hard way."

"That what Mario had to do, learn his lessons the hard way?"

Mention of Mario gave Pizarro a start, until Kordell continued in an unassuming tone:

"I assume this is where you were 'mentoring' him and I haven't seen him around with the other students. And judging by how he was acting in Santa Barbara, he was obviously resisting your efforts."

"Mario is no concern to you anymore," said Pizarro. "Besides, there is more than just one … hard way."

"A steel dildo instead of a steel football?"

"Technology that's quite painless actually," Pizarro said with a smug grin. "Though as you can see by sissy Clive's reaction, it is technology capable of invoking fear in the meek."

Something other than what Mario is going through? What else does this man have up his sleeve? What could make Clive so nervous?

Kordell shuddered. To hide his own jitters, he stood and put on the same stoic mask he used whenever he found himself in a ghetto.

"I'm missing my support group session," he said without emotion.

With a flick of the wrist, Pizarro dismissed him. But that didn't stop Kordell from wearing his ghetto mask until he was on the other side of the sliding glass door.

The support group had chosen to meet in the Contemplation Gardens as a reward for two of its members graduating to green dot status. The men were sitting in a tight circle on the lawn, all holding hands and listening intently to the teary-eyed mulatto student who was sharing. He was the first to spot Kordell approaching and stopped mid-share. A beat later, the rest of the group turned and discovered Kordell, who subsequently received yet another round of disdainful stares.

"Come on, guys," said Kordell. "What is this, high school? I'm not going to have a chance to be prom king now?"

"That's enough for today, men." Brother John, the facilitator, stood up. "Congrats again to the two who evolved one step closer to true manhood."

The lemmings stood and applauded.

"And tomorrow morning," Brother John said while giving Kordell a cold stare, "I move that we welcome our strayed brother back into the fold with open, supportive arms."

Kordell broke out in mock applause; he was the only one.

"Tough garden," said Kordell.

Brother John and the others passed by without a word.

"I could've sworn I used Right Guard this morning," said Kordell. "Isn't it the deodorant of real men?"

No response. They left Kordell alone on the lawn. Out of his periphery, he saw that Koji had observed the entire exchange from the patio. Kordell quickly turned away, as if to render himself invisible. Too late. He could feel the Japanese enigma advancing on him.

"Your joking is not winning you any friends." said Koji.

"I'm not here to win friends."

"I know."

Kordell eyed him curiously. Koji returned a confident half-smile and started walking around the perimeter of the lawn; Kordell followed.

"Harder to be overheard." Koji nodded toward an Arab student mowing the grass, then went on: "I know you're here to spring your friend from the joint, which is noble of you, but take me very seriously when I say: exercise extreme caution."

"I'm sure I don't know what—"

Koji stopped in his tracks. "You wanna waste time or you wanna talk?"

"You're not gonna rat on me?" asked Kordell.

"What you're doing is kinda cute. Stupid, but cute." Koji paused. "*You're* kinda cute."

"Thanks, but I don't need another date with the jack-off machine."

"I'm trying to get you to understand that we're on the same team, my amateur black rebel." Koji started walking again; Kordell did the same and said:

"So now I'm supposed to believe you're what—the cops, the FBI, the CIA, Homeland Security?"

"I couldn't tell you if I was," said Koji. "Trust no one in here."

"*No one*?" asked Kordell.

"Okay, trust no one except me," said Koji.

Kordell snickered like a smart-ass.

"Who do you think arranged your little reunion with your confused Hispanic friend last night?" asked Koji.

"I figured that out already, thank you very much." Kordell paused, then repeated with earnest: "Thank you very much."

"No sweat." Koji pointed to the shrubbery as if they were discussing the gardens. "Learn anything during your little field trip?"

"They're fucking up his mind, way more than they're fucking up mine and everybody else's. He's in virtual training to be a child predator."

"I *knew* it, dammit."

"How?"

The Arab and the lawnmower came so close, shards of grass pelted their faces, prompting them to change locales.

"They think they cover their tracks by pushing the delete key on people's memories," Koji said as they walked along the pathway to the woods, pretending to admire the palm trees while keeping an eye on the men just out of earshot. "Six molesters in custody throughout the West might have been brainwashed here. All of them acknowledge looking into conversion therapy ops, but all of them changed their minds about going through with it. We wouldn't have known that much until a shrink studying sex offenders in Denver connected the dots. Every gay-to-straight insane asylum in the country is being checked out, but I had a hunch about this place since the day it came across my computer screen."

A tall, lanky man with a tray of iced teas caught up with them and offered Koji a tall drink—sucking up to the staff, no doubt. The only thing he offered Kordell was a cold shoulder. Koji shooed the kiss-ass away, then led Kordell to a small pond of large goldfish.

"I knew my hunch was right," Koji said. "But we need more to go on. Kordell, I need you in that area."

"For what?"

"Whatever you can get your hands on and get to me. Running a conversion house is not illegal, but whatever they're doing in there is. I bet my life and my job on it. I need proof, evidence, witnesses. Your friend might be too far gone to help, but if you can get back into Area 2, get me something solid to go on, and escape through the unsecured tunnel entrance—"

"You used me last night," Kordell realized and said.

"What happened to *thank you very much?*"

"I don't—what is—what were you doing at the Mission meeting Mario's father?"

"We don't have time for this." Koji scanned the gardens in his periphery.

Kordell remained mute as a way of standing firm.

"Okay," Koji sighed. "Long story short: I 'accidentally' lost some

keys to get Giovanni to meet me away from watchful eyes. To see if he had any worthwhile info, which he didn't. Area 2 is off-limits to all but Pizarro and Brother John. Letting you in is win-win."

"So the professional needs help from the amateur black rebel."

"Touché. Look at the little fishies like they mean something to you. How close are you to convincing Pizarro you're a hopeless homo?"

"You said trust no one," said Kordell. "I'm not trusting you. Totally. Yet."

"What do you need, a big kiss on those beautiful full lips of yours?"

"Somehow I think you'd like that." Kordell looked him dead in the eye.

Koji returned the favor. "Would you?"

Kordell didn't answer. This was all a bit overwhelming. Fighting on his own to save Mario (and himself) was one thing. Sure it was daunting, but at least he knew the difference between the good guys and the bad guys.

"I left a cell phone in the lobby in one of those big plants," he said, "the one closest to the desk. Get it for me. I'll feel a lot better if I'm within arm's reach of 911. You get me that phone and I'll give you whatever I find."

"I know you don't know me" —Koji's big black eyes *seemed* sincere. And adorable— "but I promise you this: if something happens, picture the cavalry coming in with me leading the charge."

My very own samurai warrior. Hope he's got some of those big-ass swords.

"I need the cell," said Kordell. "I promised to make a call tomorrow. In less than twenty-four hours."

"To the kid's mom?"

Kordell did a double take. "Anything you don't know?"

"Plenty," said Koji, "which is why I need you and you need me."

"Get me the phone."

"The lobby is full of distractions every afternoon." Koji eyed his watch. "The receptionist is busy welcoming tours and taking deliveries and cig breaks. You've got free time now to think about your sins against Nature. Meet me behind the tool shed in ten minutes."

"The tool shed?" Kordell glanced over at the small aluminum shack wedged between the lawn and the woods. "Isn't that a little close? And obvious?"

"The more conspicuous, the less suspicious."

"What?"

"Go with me on this," said Koji. "Ten minutes, fifteen tops. You'll have your phone—oh, shit—you can't keep it on you. The scrubs."

"I'll do what smugglers do," said Kordell.

"I'll get you a plastic bag from the kitchen, too."

"Thank you very much."

"That's cool of you, keeping your promise to your friend. I like that about you." Koji glanced around, his face apprehensive. "We've been talking too long." He turned to leave.

"Yamo?" said Kordell.

Koji swung back around.

"You got my back?" Kordell asked.

"I got your back," said his samurai warrior.

Kordell managed a smile, one that promised Koji an open mind and heart. When Koji was out of sight, Kordell made his way to the woods. He hadn't gone more than a few steps on the main trail when he ran into Sabatino, who didn't seem startled or surprised.

"Fuck me now?" The Latino with the pockmarked face looked drugged, wild, desperately in need of cock up his hole—the drug he really wanted.

"You're bullshitting," said Kordell. "You don't want a fat black cock. You want a woman's pussy and babies for your *familia*."

"No, no. I need it." He turned around and took down his scrubs to entice Kordell. For a little man, Sabatino had one plump brown ass. And it was talented, too. He bent over, exposed his hole and gently pushed out his bowels. His entire inner hole came blossoming into full view. On the outside of his body. "You need it, *que no?*"

"Put that back in there!" a horrified Kordell said of the guts sticking out of Sabatino's ass. "My God, talk about making a guy want to go straight! How do you do that? Never mind! I don't wanna know. I do *not* want to know." He looked around to make sure they

hadn't been seen, then an idea came to him. "Wait a minute. The tool shed. You know where that is?"

"You fuck me there?"

"Behind it in ten minutes, okay? No sooner. Ten minutes *exactamundo*."

"You give it to me?"

"And how."

"No condom, right? I want your cum."

"Any way you want it. Now go, we must be careful."

"I have poppers."

"Ten minutes. Go."

Quivering with excitement, Sabatino dashed away.

Kordell tried to banish the image of the insides of an ass pushed all the way out and concentrate on the plan he'd just laid in motion: get the phone, hide it in the crack of his butt, then get caught *almost* having sex with Sabatino.

Hello, Area 2; goodbye, Pizarro.

One side of the tool shed was hidden from view from the rest of the Contemplation Gardens. Only someone lurking in the woods beyond would be able to see anything, and even then, the tall trees and thick shrubbery provided substantial cover.

Kordell waited for Koji and took a leak next to the shed. Afterwards, he decided to use the time to examine his shriveled penis. It didn't *look* any different, but, of course, it *felt* different, as if no amount of Viagra or Bobby Blake porn videos could awaken his manhood from its steel football-induced coma. His meat would be meatless for weeks, which was okay by him, because one thing this whole ordeal had made more salient was the complicated nature of sex and sexuality in today's world, made even more complicated by being gay, what you did or were exposed to as a child, men and their animal-like ways, head games, dating games, STDs ...

And this Latino fool wants me to shoot up his ass?

Kordell looked around for Koji, then Sabatino, but it wasn't quite time for either one to show up. He left his dick hanging limp in the wind and thought:

Barebacking. The new national gay pastime. Anonymous raw fucking, sometimes literally, sometimes slightly less literally (when you meet him at a bar before you head to the nearest dark hole).

AIDS. That now-manageable dis-*ease*, or so everyone so desperately wanted to believe. Pop a few pills, party like it's 1979. What death? What suffering? What frail men hobbling down the street looking like skin and bones?

Circuit parties. Sex parties. Gym bodies. PNP. K. X. G. Tina. Crystal. BB. m4m4anything/everything. Sex. Sex. Sex. Did we mention sex? With as many people as possible. You can have a lover. You can be single. Doesn't matter. You will still have sex with animals you don't know, don't wanna know and don't give a damn about. And never will.

It's all about sex. It's always been all about sex. It will always be all about sex. God's blessing and curse, but why does it feel like a curse except during those very few seconds when you're actually enjoying it without thinking of what you might be catching from him or giving to him or swapping with him, thinking of how you have no idea who this person is, what this person is, if you'll even recognize this person in one month, one week, one day, one hour.

Or maybe this hot encounter is the start of The Real Deal. Oh, God, yes, it feels so good. He feels so good. He looks so hot and he must think I'm hot enough, too. Otherwise, he wouldn't be licking my ass like that, sucking my dick with such passion, kissing my pecs so fiercely. If only we could do this over and over, and get to know each other and find out we're just as simpatico in every other way as we are right now with his mouth feeling so good all over my dick, which he obviously loves.

This moment he loves my dick. He loves me. Loves part of me. My dick. He loves my dick. I love his ass, the way it feels in my hands. The way it's gonna feel on my tongue in just a few seconds, after I take another hit of poppers and that mind-blowing wave rushes over me.

I have to pull him off my dick so I can taste his ass and channel all my energy into my tongue, turning it into a lightning rod that sends shockwaves throughout his entire body. I can't wait for him to

moan so intensely from my surprise attack, so intensely he'll want me to eat him forever, every night, until he is a part of me and I am a part of him.

But forever only lasts as long as The Moment. He'll part. I'll part. We may or may not cum. Cumming takes the edge off, lessens the heat the male animal needs for prowling. And we males need to prowl. There are always other animals lurking in the jungle, behind the next tree stump, over the next ridge, in the next cave, behind the tool shed. Other males to size up, sniff up, fuck up and be fucked up by. Not just physically, but mentally, too, because what all this "getting in touch with the animal side of man" does is fuck with the mind, the spirit, the soul that needs so much more to subsist on.

But we men—we gay men especially—we only feed ourselves meat, no vegetables, no fruit, no fiber, no vitamins, no minerals. Just meat. True carnivores. Living for meat and meat alone. Even this so-called changing of sexual orientation is about meat: denying yourself the meat you crave, replacing it with nutrients that are of no value to you because your body doesn't recognize foreign substances like pussy and wobbly tits.

Gay men. Straight men. Most men. All society. Feeding on a diet out of balance, from too much sex to not enough sex, from living a "gay lifestyle" to living a "straight lifestyle."

What the hell is either one?

"I'm not going to be able to get hard enough to fuck you," Kordell finally said out loud as he pried Sabatino's mouth off his cock. "You can suck me all you want and I can play with your incredibly talented ass for eternity, but it just ain't gonna happen. Too many drugs in my system."

The same lie he'd told countless times in sex clubs when, just like now, he couldn't live in the moment because the "before" and "after" weighed too heavily on his mind.

"Please," Sabatino begged, putting Kordell's hand back on his ass, which was very wet with Kordell's spit and sweat.

Kordell peeked around the edge of the tool shed. Koji was late. Or had Sabatino been early? Or did Kordell screw everything up,

including the timing of his plan? Did he play with Sabatino's ass because he was setting himself up to be caught, or because he was a freak for ass and had wanted it?

Where the fuck was Yamo? Who the fuck invented poppers?

"Fuck me now!" Sabatino cried like a toddler begging for candy in the checkout line.

"No! I mean … wait!" Kordell pulled up his scrubs and tiptoed through the woods adjacent to the gardens, ducking behind the tall shrubbery that bordered the two landscapes. Sabatino followed, grabbing at the elastic waist of Kordell's pants.

"I need black dick."

"I said not yet."

"You promised. Give me now."

Kordell walked faster, Sabatino held on tighter, first on his knees, then on his stomach, not caring that he was being dragged through the dirt. Kordell yanked away with all his might, hoping to rid himself of the desperate bottom. It worked. Kordell stumbled free, but lost his balance and went falling into the shrubs. As he collided with twigs and leaves, he felt a breeze. *He* was free of Sabatino, but his pants weren't. Just before Kordell disappeared into the bushes, he caught a glimpse of Sabatino on the ground, clutching Kordell's scrubs.

Kordell could do nothing to stop his fall and the bushes weren't strong enough to hold him. He fell into and through them and wound up on his naked ass on the lawn on the other side. In full view of a good chunk of the Contemplation Gardens, which was packed with both students and staffers.

Most of the faces staring back at him wore expressions that said they weren't surprised. Kordell hurried to right himself, then looked into the bushes in the name of reclaiming his pants. But Sabatino was using them as kneepads. His plump brown ass was on all fours, butt waiting for Kordell.

"Fuck now?" Sabatino pleaded.

Kordell turned and saw them coming: six angry staffers led by Brother John. Sabatino must have seen the fear in Kordell's eyes, for he abandoned his quest for dick and ran deeper into the woods.

Brother John and the staffers closed in on Kordell, the lone sex offender remaining.

Hastily, Kordell scanned their faces. Koji was not among them. Koji was nowhere in sight. Neither was the cell phone that was Kordell's link to the outside world.

FOURTEEN

The gurney raced down long green hallways, barely slowing for corners and obstacles. Brother John, Clive and an Asian lab coat sprint-walked alongside the stretcher, propelling it forward like pallbearers on speed. Kordell was strapped down and woozy from an injection of some kind of drug, but he could still see the faces of his fellow students appearing and disappearing above him. Their eyes were ripe with fear for him, as if they knew that, whatever his fate, it was much worse than theirs.

Kordell tried to speak, say something rebel-like, but he couldn't. His mouth was stuffed with … a sock? A ball gag? They turned a corner, went through a set of double doors. The heads of fearful students vanished. Lights blinked on and off. Darkness, then light, repeating every other second. As the pattern kept recurring, he realized it was caused by Brother John's large head hovering over him, obliterating the ceiling lights, then revealing them again. It only served to further disorient Kordell.

They stopped for a second. Kordell heard computer beeps, then the now-familiar *whoosh* of the building's *Star Trek* doors. They started moving again. The walls turned red. Area 2. He tried calling

out for Mario, but realized that even if the obstruction weren't in his mouth, he didn't have the stamina to do it. The gurney was moving faster now; he wanted to throw up.

Concentrate.

His head fell to the side. For a split second, they passed something familiar, then it was gone, behind them. Part of his brain processed it: it had been an open room, *the* open room, where Mario was lying on a table, being programmed. He counted the doorways. Two, three, four … seven. Eight?

The racecar gurney slowed to a crawl, then turned again, sending vomit spiraling upward in his system. He held it in check, then forced it back down. Tasted like mush.

They had entered a room. Pizarro was there, waiting in a white lab coat. He tapped a syringe, then held it to the light. The syringe ejaculated, shooting out a big wad of green cum. Brother John and the Asian transferred Kordell from the gurney to a metal reclining table. In the process, they freed his limbs and Kordell snatched the ball gag from his mouth.

"I thought only two people were allowed in Area 2," he promptly said. Ever the smart aleck.

"You've presented us with an emergency." Pizarro motioned toward the door and Clive and the Asian lab coat promptly left. "We've never had someone as stubborn as you, but that's about to change."

"Oh, goody, more drugs?" asked Kordell.

Pizarro looked to Brother John on the other side of the table. Brother John fetched an object out of his lab coat and held it up for Pizarro's inspection. It was a smart card, a digital data storage device the size of a postage stamp.

"The other one," said Pizarro.

Brother John retrieved a different card and inserted it into a slot near the LCD display on the wall.

"What's on that?" asked Kordell.

"Desperate measures for desperate men." Brother John punched the touch screen display with haste and precision, as if he'd manned the controls countless times.

Kordell started to speak, but Pizarro silenced him with two gentle but sticky fingers to Kordell's mouth. Next Pizarro used those same sticky fingers to part Kordell's eyelids and ply him with eye drops.

"In case you decide to doze," Pizarro explained.

Next came the goggles, and in a matter of seconds, Kordell was immersed in darkness. A needle invaded a vein in his arm. He wanted to resist, but couldn't.

That's what I'll tell the officers when I'm arrested for child molestation.

I wanted to resist, but couldn't.

A crackling voice on a two-way radio sifted through the blur.

"Victor, we need you STAT. Mr. Yamamoto has uncovered another possible security breach."

"On my way," said Pizarro. "You'll be okay, Brother John?"

"Of course."

"Shall I strap him down?"

"And interfere with his hands?" said Brother John. "Besides, the drugs."

"Fine then."

Footsteps left the room, followed by silence.

Yamo. Emergency. Helping me out? Setting me up? Chance to escape? Only chance? What about the phone? Middle of nowhere. Can't call Sal. Tomorrow. Freddy. Poor Freddy. Poor Uncle Kord.

The infinite-ring circus of predator images appeared in his eyes and circled his head like vultures. Little boys everywhere. Naked at the beach. In Thai brothels. On bright-colored swing sets. In classrooms. After school. Carry along a cute little brown puppy and get them walking home from school.

"Can you help me find this little doggie's home?"

He smelled fresh cut grass, saw little boys playing Little League soccer.

"You love little boys. Thank heaven for little boys. The men you love to suck, fuck and have sex with were once little boys. You crave little boys. Society needs boundaries that define acceptable behavior. You are outside that boundary. You always have been outside

that boundary. Now: show society what those outside the boundaries are capable of. It's time to give your gift to society. You are ... a gift giver."

He had some phlegm in his throat. He began breathing in short, erratic bursts, then quietly, purposefully gagged on the phlegm. He tried to close his eyes but couldn't. The eye drops had dilated his pupils and rendered his eyelid muscles useless. The freak show continued.

Keep breathing, choking, breathing.

He heard the shifting of Brother John's body, moving about restlessly somewhere near Kordell's head.

I'm drowning. Come save me little brother.

Kordell stopped breathing altogether. His body was deathly still. The images flickered in his brain—Dahmer, Gacy, Cunanan, heroes all. He smelled strawberry-scented soap hovering directly over him. Peach fuzz from Brother John's pretty boy face tickled his nose.

Kordell's right hand reached up and found hair. He grabbed at the golden locks. Too short. He went for the throat. Got it. He used his other hand to snatch off the goggles, then doubled his grip around Brother John's neck. Kordell hurled himself off the table, but instantly felt a wave of vertigo that sent them both crashing to the ground. They wrestled for control, grabbing at each other's throats, rolling over one another, pulling faces, limbs, clothing, anything they could. Brother John was half Kordell's size, but Kordell was drugged, making it an even match.

At one point, Brother John broke free and hurried to the LCD panel, presumably to push a panic button. Kordell lunged at him and pulled him down to the ground as Brother John's fingers fell short of their intended destination. The move seemed to signal to Brother John that he was defeated, that even a big black man who was drugged could handle a 5'2" white boy like him. Kordell rolled them over so that he was on top.

"You broke my neck!" cried Brother John.

"Shut the fuck up if you want that to be the only thing I break."

"They'll come for me. Those goggles can't be off more than ten minutes. You're a dead man and I'm going to be the one to kill you."

"Where is it?" Kordell wrestled the lab coat off Brother John and felt inside the pockets.

"I don't know what you're talking about, you lunatic." Brother John had given up fighting. He was too busy attending to his neck and the blood running from his mouth.

"The smart card," said Kordell. "The one you didn't put in the panel."

"Stupid fool, Victor has it."

Kordell re-checked the pockets, then glanced around the room. Nothing.

"Move back," he ordered Brother John. "Now!"

Brother John backed up against the gurney. Kordell used the lab coat to tie him to it.

"You'll never win," Brother John yelled. "Security!"

Kordell reached for the ball gag on the counter—the same one that had been used on him—and put it around Brother John's head and into his mouth. Next Kordell rushed over to the LCD panel and pushed every button in every combination possible. But the smart card refused to eject. He slipped off one of Brother John's hard-soled shoes and, like a thief trying to make quick work of an ATM machine, he attacked the panel with the heel. After a few tries, the smart card slot widened. He picked at the card with his fingers, but they were too unsteady from the drugs. He was also having trouble seeing. With his pupils dilated, his eyes were sensitive to the light, his vision blurred. He pressed his mouth against the slot, gripped the card with his teeth and yanked as hard as he could. He staggered backward halfway across the room, his aching front teeth gripping the smart card.

He slipped the card into his right slipper, took one last look at Brother John, then scooped up the goggles on the floor. There was a small digital display on the outside, something he'd never noticed before. It read 5:49 and was counting down. To give himself more time, he decided to put the goggles back on. The images bombarded him again, but his dilated eyes actually felt better in this *dark,* dark world.

He staggered into the hallway, feeling nausea from the drugs

and the predator images. His body also ached from the struggle; he'd pulled something in his chest. He held onto the walls, counting the openings that were doorways. Mario's would be the seventh one.

Suddenly he had doubts. Was he going the right way? He swung around. The images in his brain all spun with him, but at a faster rate. He lost his balance and went crashing to the floor. He wanted to take the goggles off, just for a second, but between his dilated eyes and the timer, he knew it was best if he didn't. He tried to ignore the thousands of images of naked little boys raging in his vision like a hurricane with each shift of his head.

Trust your intuition.

He stuck with his original direction. Mario would be coming up in the next room or the next one after that.

Please God, let him be there.

He felt another surge of queasiness at the next door. A sign? He felt his way inside.

"Mario? Are you here? Speak to me. It's Kordell … Mario."

His pleas were met with silence. He turned 180 degrees in a panic, arms outstretched. He felt an examining table, but accidentally kicked it away. He started for it, but realized that if it was light enough to kick …

He felt his way back out of the room and continued down the hall, back sliding against the wall for balance. When he got to the next door, he took the goggles off and saw Mario, resting peacefully on the table, wearing his own set of predator headgear. Kordell hurried over and ripped them off, blinding Mario with the light.

"No!" Mario cried, covering his eyes.

"We're getting out of here, now or never!"

Mario understood the severity in Kordell's voice and leapt up. But he too felt a wave of nausea and staggered backward. Kordell caught him and kept him from falling back onto the table; then Kordell himself stumbled forward.

"You, too?" Mario asked, noticing Kordell's enlarged pupils.

"We can do this together."

"Take the goggles," said Mario.

"The more the merrier."

They peeked out in the hallway. Empty. They took off, staggering but buoyed by their mutual determination to survive this house of horrors with their minds intact.

"You've got enough to put these sickos away?" asked Mario.

"With the help of this Koji guy." Kordell looked at the clock on his goggles as he walked. The timer had been reset, but that was two minutes ago. They were now down to eight minutes. "Just a little ways to the exit. Then it's the outside world and we're home free. Forever. You and me, Mario, we can do it."

"I wasn't a star athlete for nothing, homie."

"Let's go Yellowjackets, come on. You can do it. We can do it."

They heard a noise behind them, echoing from the far reaches of the hallway. The source may have been pipes creaking or heavy metal shifting, but Mario doubled his speed, only to look back seconds later and discover Kordell slumped against the wall, puking.

"Am I gonna have to carry your ass?" Mario asked, rejoining him.

Kordell fell to one knee, soiling the scrubs with his own vomit.

"I'm not leaving here without you," said Mario.

"Just let me … catch my …" Kordell stood up with Mario's help. " … breath."

They took off again and rounded a corner just as they heard more noise behind them. Pushing onward, they came to the glass door leading to the tunnel under construction. They crept up to it, barely breathing. Mario looked to Kordell to see if this was the right door. Kordell gave Mario an anxious thumbs up. Mario then put a finger to his lips to signal "quiet" while he tried to pry the door open with his fingers. It didn't budge.

Mario kicked the door with his heel, shattering the smoked glass and rendering his right slipper blood-soaked. Next, he cleared away more glass with his elbow, not caring about the blood running down his arm.

"Let's go," he said when there was enough room to slither through. "Careful."

If anyone had been in earshot, the jig was up. They wormed their way through the broken door, Mario first, then Kordell, who

sliced his bicep on a shard of glass. "Fuck it, I'm fine," he said to Mario, and they raced through the tunnel, tipping over buckets, ladders and anything they came across in the name of providing obstacles for anyone chasing them. The dim lighting helped their sensitive eyes. The idea of freedom fueled their drive.

"We can do this, Mario. Just get outside."

They heard voices, then that *whoosh* wafting through the tunnel. Someone had opened the broken door and was after them. They put up more barriers in the form of wheelbarrows and two-by-fours.

"What if someone's waiting for us at the other end?" Mario asked as they ran.

"With any luck, it'll be Koji who's trying to help us. If you see a Japanese guy, he might be on our side. I hope."

They heard voices again, something about getting through the barriers Kordell and Mario had erected. They charged ahead until they saw something they hadn't expected to see.

"There was no fork in the tunnel last night!" said Kordell.

"Which way?" pleaded Mario.

Angry noise echoed throughout the tunnel, growing closer and closer. Obstacles made of two-by-fours, wheelbarrows and ladders were being deconstructed. Kordell grabbed his head and squeezed it, as if trying to force out the knowledge that would get them out of this.

"Pick a tunnel," he said.

"What?" cried Mario.

"Pick a direction. What do your instincts tell you?"

"Me? Think back to last night," said Mario. They looked at each other with blank faces, then Mario pointed to the left and said: "This way."

But at the same time, Kordell pointed to the right and said: "This way."

"Shit!" said Mario.

"You're right," said Kordell. "I've done this before." He took the pair of goggles he was holding and threw them a few feet down the hallway on the left, a decoy for whoever was following them. "This way."

They took off through the tunnel on the right. Kordell didn't recognized much, but he wasn't trying. They had sealed their fate: the tunnel would pan out and bring freedom or be a bust and lead them right back into the arms of the sex Nazis.

Farther down, Mario looked on the verge of hyperventilating or regurgitating as he stopped to rest against the wall.

"Save yourself," he said between gasps to Kordell, who was several feet ahead. "Come back and get me."

"That's what I'm doing now." Kordell doubled back to Mario.

"I can't."

"Yes, you can. This is your angel talking. Get off your ass and move!"

Mario took a good look at Kordell, then found the strength. They both took off again, running until they saw sunlight around the edges of a large metal door.

"We were right." Kordell grabbed Mario and hurried them both to the door. "There's stairs on the other side that lead to—"

"Can we get it open?" asked Mario.

"Angels can do anything." Kordell knew that it would be unlocked, according to Koji, but kicked it open for dramatic effect anyway. The door swung open, flooding them with daylight. Hastily, they shielded their sensitive eyes and ascended the concrete steps, relieved and giddy about their first glimpse of the outside world in what had only been days, but felt like a very long time.

But it didn't take long to realize that freedom was going to be short-lived.

Near the top of the steps, their eyes adjusted enough to see what was waiting for them on an incline in the distance: men, at least twenty of them, all dressed in white lab coats, lined up in a semi-circle that blocked any potential escape route. Between the bright sun and Kordell and Mario's dilated pupils, the figures loomed like black shadows standing at attention, looking down from the slight upgrade upon which they stood.

Kordell and Mario froze, trying to believe their eyes or their minds were playing tricks on them, that this was some product of the drugs and their imaginations gone corrupt from all the virtual brain-

washing. But in reality, they knew the men were no mirage, that what they saw before them was real: stoic, faceless men. Soldiers in the battle against homosexuality. Captors of two bloodied escapees.

When Kordell woke, he found himself naked, hanging horizontally in midair and staring up at a stark white ceiling. He wasn't on the shaving gyroscope, however—whatever was holding him wasn't swaying or moving. His arms were perpendicular to his body, his legs tied together, his lifeless penis exposed. Dozens of thin padded cables descended from the ceiling and wrapped around his body, holding him in strategic areas—the head, the neck, the shoulders, the elbows, the wrists, the chest, the waist, the legs, the ankles, the groin. He was weightless. He still felt woozy, but didn't have the urge to vomit anymore. Had they pumped his stomach?

Earlier, outside the tunnel, he and Mario had stood back to back and watched helplessly as Pizarro's automatons closed in. Neither he nor Mario had possessed the strength to fight one man, let alone a couple dozen. Half the lab coats had grabbed Mario; the other half, Kordell. Immediately, the two prisoners were blindfolded and whisked away. Kordell knew they had been taken in separate directions because he heard Mario calling his name in vain. Too weak to resist and too drugged to have complete control of his own body, Kordell had passed out shortly thereafter. Only the heated exchange taking place just below him had brought him back to life.

"If you try this, I quit." It was Clive. No need to see their faces. Kordell knew these voices all too well.

"Is that a threat?" Pizarro said, followed by the sound of slow footsteps.

"No. Not a threat." Clive's voice was trembling. "You know I'd never—I just meant that—"

"By all means, spit it out. Get it out of your system. Shouldn't he, Brother John?"

"Victor knows best," said Brother John. "We cannot have this evil black man ruin all our work, years of work."

"But …" Clive stopped himself.

"Speak, dammit," said Pizarro.

"The EVL chip is not ready," said Clive. "It's too risky. We have no idea what it will do when tested on a human. Chimps are one thing and, yes, we do need to take care of the impostor, but ..."

"But what?" asked Pizarro. "You'd rather Brother John kill again?"

"Brother John could do that." It was Brother John who said it.

"Not now," said Pizarro. "It's too soon and not convenient. And we don't dare move him out of the Facility to do it."

"But is the chip the answer?" asked Clive. "The second iteration of the chip, no less? You promised we'd do four betas before even considering human tests. And besides, the body needs to be free of drugs. His system is loaded, not only with what we've given him, but who knows what he was hooked on before he came here."

"He does have a point," said Brother John. "The subject's system is as impure as any half-naked faggot at a Chicago leather convention. Isn't that one of the reasons you haven't tried the EVL on Mario, the drugs we've given him?"

"Mario's virtual training is nearly complete," said Pizarro. "There's no need to use him as a guinea pig when he'll be out on the streets molesting in a matter of hours. Look at it this way: when we create undercover cells and send them out to implant the patrons of gay bars, bathhouses and sex parties, those queens will be just as high as this one."

"It is true we planned to test the chip on sober gay men first," said Brother John.

"Please, Victor," said Clive. "Don't let your ego be your guide this time. Let me continue developing the EVL so we can run an accurate field test on drug-free men, then we can move on to the tweakers."

"I could easily bump this nigger off myself, Victor," said Brother John. "It'd be my pleasure after what the fucker did to me."

"Both of you," shouted Pizarro, "enough!"

Kordell held his breath. For several moments, the room remained still. Then Pizarro spoke, seemingly to himself more than his lackeys.

"We have a chance to do something truly revolutionary and great. *I* have the chance to do something truly revolutionary and

great. I've seen the conversion movement go from séances and baptisms to virtual reality that produces *better, lasting* results. But the world still doesn't believe that homosexuality can be cured—the gay world that is, that sick, twisted, immoral crime against nature. To think I was once one of them. To think that now I have the chance to make a lasting contribution to society, to be mentioned in the same breath as the great scientists and psychologists. Nothing can stop genius, nothing!"

Kordell heard footsteps ascending steps. Then he saw Pizarro's face hovering above his own.

"Mr. Christie has been sent to us as a gift from God." Pizarro eyed him with affection and gratitude. "We mustn't misuse God's gifts."

Kordell tried to speak, but his esophagus was full of phlegm.

"You're probably wondering what all the commotion below is about," said Pizarro. "Well, it's about you. Time to let you and Mario return to the world outside."

Kordell cleared his throat. "Do I get to hear the catch?"

"Victor!" warned Clive from below.

"It's all right, Clive. If our dear little friend Chippie works properly"—Pizarro help up a tiny silver object the size of a grain of rice—"and I'm sure he will, Mr. Christie's memory will be devoid of every single incident that transpired in our little neck of the woods."

"What is that?" Kordell asked as the object reflected off the ceiling lights and shined in his eyes.

"Your future," said Pizarro. "You might as well know, and I might as well enjoy the pleasure of you knowing. This is my greatest innovation to date: the EVL chip. Once inside your neck, you will become acquainted with the devil that you truly are. You will show that devil to the world and the world will know that you are pure evil, to be legislated against, sequestered from our children, barred from political office and positions of authority. Evil that will ultimately need to be destroyed for mankind to survive. This chip will make you the ultimate pariah in society. When you wake up tomorrow morning, you will embark on a journey that will make Jeffrey Dahmer and John Wayne Gacy, and even Mario Cervantes, seem like Peter Pan compared to you."

"Only a warped zealot would think he could erase homosexuality from the planet," said Kordell.

"My plan is not a short-term one, silly boy. Of course, I realize the older, more hardcore homos can't or won't change. That's why we've found ways for you to make yourselves useful. Believe me, nothing can stop us heterosexuals overcoming perverted evil."

Kordell's stomach turned; his head went light. Heterosexuals Overcoming Perverted Evil. Project H.O.P.E. None of it—not a single ounce of it—was ever about helping gays.

"You would sacrifice innocent kids," he stammered, "have gay men molest and murder and cause all kinds of grief and pain … for what? Some Right Wing agenda? How sick is that?"

"There was a time when the world understood that homosexuality was a sickness that led to many of society's ills. You're not too young to remember that thing called The Closet."

"Which plenty of people are still in and persecuting themselves on a daily basis, including kids committing suicide."

"Don't try to cheer me up," said Pizarro. "The '60s, so-called gay rights, your parades and TV shows—you ruined the balance of Nature and made the world think it's okay for fags to demand rights, political office, special laws. There's nothing special about you perverts. You lie. You surround yourselves with filthy orgies. You spread disease and are proud of it. You corrupt children, break their hearts and abuse their spirits. You force them to become ugly creatures, evil little boys who don't have a fighting chance."

"Is that what you are, Victor, an evil little boy? Who corrupted your spirit? An uncle, a friend, an older brother? A neighbor?"

Pizarro's eyes glazed over.

"Is that why no one here is allowed to mention molestation?" asked Kordell. "Whoever he was, he was a sick man who shouldn't have touched you. He stole something from you, your innocence. Tell me about it. Let me help. Others can help."

Pizarro turned to Kordell and regarded him as if for the very first time. His tender gaze wandered over Kordell's face, then body.

"You will have the distinction of being my first EVL patient." He caressed Kordell's cheek. "Someday, long after your insidious ram-

page has been discovered and you've been executed and buried and homosexuality is a crime punishable by execution, I'll be sure to put your name on a plaque in my office, who knows, maybe the Oval Office. See how much meaning your life will have? All beginning tomorrow."

Tomorrow. Fredito. Sal. My word.

"What are you going to do?" Kordell tried unsuccessfully to free himself from the cables.

"Merely give you a little present that will allow you to fully immerse yourself in the vile gutter that is homosexuality." Pizarro shrugged. "You yourself acknowledged that your world was vile."

"What?"

"At Gay Pride when I overheard you bashing gay life to your fat friend. And I quote: 'What do we have to be proud of? Circuit parties? Bareback websites? X? K? Tina? A bunch of gay characters on network television?' Your words, Mr. Christie, not mine. Now you can truly wallow in your depravity."

"That's not what I meant," Kordell cried.

Pizarro laughed. "No retractions now, I'm afraid. Time for you to do what gay creatures do best: molest, destroy, maim."

"Innocent kids?"

"After you corrupt them, you'll murder them. No sense handing down the legacy of abuse and shame to another generation."

"I'm begging you—"

"You won't remember a thing about the Facility." Pizarro's voice was full of serenity and conviction. "You'll just be someone who's been evil from the start."

Tears welled up in Kordell's eyes. "Think about the kids, Pizarro."

"You mean the angels," Pizarro said calmly.

"What?" cried Kordell.

"The kids are all angels helping us fight the devil inside mankind."

"What you're doing is way more depraved than anything I was bashing!"

"Enough debate."

"You're a madman!" Kordell lurched forward with his head—the only mobile part of his body—and spit in Pizarro's face.

Pizarro used a handkerchief to patiently wipe the saliva from his eyes and nose, then he doused the cloth with something from a bottle. Next he put the cloth over Kordell's nose and mouth.

Kordell tried to fight but was helpless. The ether kicked in; his mind began to float. He refused to look at the man who was trying to destroy his very existence. Instead he stared at the ceiling; but he could still hear Pizarro's last words:

"You have that quite wrong, Mr. Christie. *You* are the madman."

FIFTEEN

The sound of ocean waves washing against the shore began to crawl into Kordell's subconscious, nudging him awake. It wasn't too difficult a task; although he was in a deep sleep, his body was uncomfortable. Hard to get a good night's rest sleeping in—

The fact that he was sleeping in the driver's seat of an automobile did more to wake him than any alarm clock. He hadn't slept in a car in ... ever. And it was *his* car, too, his navy blue SUV. He looked to his right, where Mario Cervantes was sitting in the passenger seat.

Mario from the old neighborhood down in Oxnard ... and Gay Pride ... and ... the boy I molested years ago, my first recruit ... original sin.

"Hey, homie." Judging by Mario's groggy voice, he'd only beaten Kordell awake by a few seconds.

"How do you feel?" asked Kordell.

"Like I been sleeping in a car too damned long."

"How long is that?"

Not finding the answer in each other's bewildered faces, they looked beyond the windshield and saw that they were in a parking

lot facing a broad stretch of beach the size of several football fields. Not far from the car, a trash can sat crooked in the sand like the Leaning Tower of Pisa. On the can's side, the name of the beach was stenciled in white paint: El Destino.

"Do I know this place?" asked Kordell. "When did you and I run into each other?"

"Don't you remember the festival, homie?" asked Mario. "How wasted did you get?"

"Yeah, I remember Pride. We met at Liquid."

"And hung out at the beach, and cruised back to—-"

"Batter Up, my business, where we played ... everything."

"Air hockey, hoops, foosball." Mario laughed. "We blasted the music and were dancing and ... fuck, homie, you know how to party!"

"I do? Dancing? Music?"

"Par-tay!" said Mario. Kordell looked down at his body. He was wearing the same white T-shirt and jeans from the night of Gay Pride, but he had no idea why a large bandage was on his right bicep. He peeled it back and saw a long scar, still fresh and red and—now that he thought about it—sore. Something had sliced his arm, a knife or piece of glass perhaps. Or maybe he scraped it on barbed wire. He reattached the bandage and noticed that Mario had a similar dressing on his elbow.

"Do you know how you cut ..." Kordell started to ask, but trailed off as Mario shook his head. "How the fuck we did get here?"

This one stumped Mario, too. The way he was looking at their surroundings—the beach, the curve of the mountains along the coast to the north—Kordell could tell that Mario wasn't familiar with this area either.

"Do we know what day it is?" Mario asked.

"The morning after?" ventured Kordell.

"I don't think so." Mario rubbed his eyes, then his temples. "I'm kinda sure it isn't. I have a hunch anyway."

Kordell pulled down the sun visor, hoping to find his cell phone, which could tell them the time of day. It wasn't there. He looked through the sunroof. The sun hovered high above to the

north and east. It was early in the day, but not too early. The parking lot was three-quarters full, the beach alive with families, girls in bikinis, volleyball games, Frisbees sailing through the air.

"We've been on something," Kordell said wearily. "What did we take?"

"I'm not sure, man, but I think it's more like what didn't we take."

"But I don't really do—" Kordell closed his eyes. Some event he didn't recognize flashed behind his eyelids. There was white, lots of it. And voices:

"Right eye. Look straight ahead. Now up to the ceiling. To the right … left … now down … to the right … the left … Good. Now the left eye …"

"What time is it?" It was Kordell doing the asking as a small but bright light probed his left eye.

"Six in the morning," said a man's voice. *"You slept like a hibernating bear. I wasn't sure we should wake you, but you have much to do today."*

"Fuck, man," Kordell said aloud to Mario. "I haven't partied since … I don't know … my twenties?"

"My new party bud." Mario gave him a playful punch on the shoulder. "I love you, man."

To deflect the sudden rush of embarrassment, Kordell smiled and glanced downward. Papers were scattered all over the floor of the car. Photos. Snapshots on white paper, as if they had been downloaded, then printed out.

"What's all that?" asked Mario.

Kordell picked up the photos. They were of naked young boys, most of them black and Latino. Each boy was tied up, some on beds, some in chairs. Only the boys could be seen, but hairy adult arms came from the side of the photos, each one performing some act: spanking little boy asses, pinching little boy tits with pliers and clamps, stuffing little boy mouths with butt plugs and ball-gags.

"Those yours?" they both asked almost simultaneously.

"I don't remember these being part of our par-tay," said Kordell.

"But then again, what *do* you remember?" asked Mario.

Kordell searched his brain. "The arcade and the fun. And games. Then … blank."

"Same here."

Kordell let the photos fall in his lap; his neck gave way and his head came to stop on the headrest.

Who am I?

Sure, he remembered most of his life—the business, Arthur, Sal, his family, his last boyfriend, Toxic Tommy—but something was missing. *Chunks* were missing. It was like the time when he was crash-dieting, eating nothing but one Lean Cuisine frozen entrée a day. One afternoon, he stood up too fast. Next thing he knew, he woke up on the floor next to his bed. After a few moments of processing, he realized he'd fainted and had to slowly reassemble the moments of his life just before the fall. Now, sitting in the SUV, things weren't all that different, except the time spent passed out seemed much longer and thus there was more to remember. Only he couldn't remember. He could only feel, live in the moment. Even the past that he was cognizant of seemed to hold little meaning.

"We got a lot in common, eh, homie?" Mario nodded toward the photos in Kordell's lap.

"What do you mean?" asked Kordell.

"You know what I mean," said Mario.

Kordell turned his head sideways on the headrest and eyed Mario. "How do you know if I know what you mean?"

Mario snickered and punched him again. "Don't worry 'bout it, man. We'll get along just fine, you and me. We obviously talked about it last night, and … whatever else we did about it."

Kordell shot him a blank stare.

"You know what I mean." Mario flashed a confident grin, then began singing: "Thank heaven for little boys."

"I know." Kordell returned a sly smile. "I just didn't wanna say it out loud."

"Homie, if you and me can't talk about lil' boys, together—all honest and shit—we're screwed."

How creepy and depraved. I feel creepy. Creepy. Creepy. Creepy.

You're gay. Gay equals creepy. Equals sick equals deviant equals sick, sick, sick. This is your license to be ill.

"Remember that smelly gym teacher with the big gut back in high school?" asked Kordell. "He was still there when you came up, I think."

"Mr. Finkman."

"Yeah, we used to call him Funkman 'cause he didn't believe in deodorant and smelled like a burnt rubber."

"Funky Finkman." Mario chuckled.

"We called him Funkman when I was there. Anyway, Funkman, AKA, Funky Finkman used to always say: 'Don't tell me about it, show me about it.' As stupid as it sounds, I still believe it. Talk is cheap."

"Let's stop talking then and walk the walk."

Without waiting for an answer, Mario got out of the car, slammed the door shut and marched down the beach. Kordell scampered after him, but as he walked, he felt something very foreign in his ass. Had Mario fucked him? Did Kordell have to take a dump? Maybe he felt the urge to shit sometime during their partying and was too high to do anything about it. He looked behind him for a trail of feces. Nothing was falling out. The seat of his pants didn't feel wet either. Too embarrassed, he decided to play it off for now.

He caught up with Mario and they carved their way through the blankets and beachgoers around them: a heavyset white man lying directly on top of his equally heavyset white girlfriend; three young girls using their toy shovels to bury their father under a heap of sand; four shirtless men in their twenties tossing a football to one another; and, of course, plenty of lifeless bodies already settled in for a day of sun worshipping. Kordell and Mario ignored them all, walking instead as if they had some predetermined destination in mind.

We've done this before, Kordell realized. *Walking down State Street, me keeping up with Mario, not knowing where we're going.*

The night of Gay Pride ... the morning after Gay Pride.

"Freddy!" Kordell said with a rush of panic. "Sal's kid!"

"Huh?" said Mario.

"Freddy. Fredito. You remember meeting anyone by that name? Fredito?"

"What's he look like?" Mario stopped walking. His face turned contemplative, his eyes narrowed. "Did we party with him?"

"You think we did?" asked Kordell. A lot was unclear in his mind, but he was worried about his best friend Sal and her boy Fredito. Had they done something to him? With him? Fredito was like a nephew to him.

He's molesting Fredito. My God, what have I done?

"Nope," Mario said decisively. "Haven't done or met any Fredito."

Kordell didn't feel the relief he had expected to feel. Instead, he felt like vomiting, collapsing, dying.

"Whoa, dude, you cool?" Mario reached out to steady him, but was interrupted by the sight of two boys running by on their way to the water. They were white with brown hair and lean, shirtless torsos bronzed by the summer sun. From the momentary glimpse of their faces, Kordell could tell they were brothers, one older, one younger, maybe five to seven years apart. The oldest was in his mid-teens, his tag-along little bro a younger carbon copy.

"*That's* why we ended up at the beach, buddy." Mario's gaze followed the boys as they purposely bumped shoulders and swatted at the top of each other's head. "I would love to grab a piece of *dat.*"

"Which one?"

"You have to ask?" Mario scoffed, then walked away in the opposite direction.

Nothing like their hairless little butts. Maybe some peach fuzz on them so when you ram your massive adult cock inside, you'll feel a tickling on your belly. Massive adult cock that erupts with the virus like lava from Mt. Etna.

Kordell staggered in place. He longed for something to lean against, but Mario had walked over to the children's play area and was carefully examining the chrome on a sliding board, looking at it with the curiosity of an alien creature seeing shiny metal for the very first time. Not far from Mario, a middle-aged man was pushing his middle-aged wife on a swing. Kordell labored forward, the sand harder to traverse than before. When he reached the play area, the middle-aged couple froze. Between the Latino giving the sliding

board a trance-like once-over and his black friend staggering over to him, the couple's fear of all things urban got the best of them. In a matter of seconds, they were gone.

"Can you smell it?" Kordell asked Mario.

"What? Oh, no. I can't. My sense of smell has never been that great." Mario walked away and sat on one of the swings. Kordell stayed behind and slowly lowered his face to the shiny metal sliding board. Then he kissed it.

Slide down into my arms, little fellers. So Uncle Kord can butcher your legs off.

He looked at the lumpy figures of the middle-aged couple getting farther and farther away.

That's what they think of you: murderer, pervert, faggot nigger with AIDS who has no use in society. Die, faggot. Take a few little boys with you to prove you are the evil you know you are.

If it runs through your mind it must be true—

It is not true—

I do not want to kill little boys. I do not want to kill or hurt anyone. I only want to love—

Just like you loved little Mario when he was a little boy sliding down sliding boards like this one?

"Kordell!"

Kordell opened his eyes to see that he was hanging onto the sliding board to keep from falling. Vertigo again. Like when he was crash-dieting. Had they eaten anything?

"What's wrong with you, nigga?" Mario indicated the swing adjacent to his. "Sit yo' ass down over here."

Mario never talked this way before—

Before what?

Kordell did as he was told. Mario nodded to the middle-aged couple, now hand-in-hand at the water's edge, and said:

"I asked Mom and Pops what day it was. It's fucking Wednesday. Can you believe that shit?"

"Gay Pride was Saturday. What did we do with Sunday, Monday and Tuesday?"

Mario shrugged and laughed. "I just hope it was all good."

"How can it be good if we don't remember it?" Kordell stared at the ground. Mario started swinging and asked:

"How do I know I can trust you?"

"Right back at you, amigo." Kordell started rocking back and forth in his swing.

"We're gonna have to take this slow," said Mario. "This being buddies into boys."

"Slow is for sissies," said Kordell. When there was no response, he added: "Okay, slow it is."

Mario's swing came to a stop. "But not that slow."

"Let's just take it as it comes," said Kordell.

"Cumming is good," said Mario.

"Especially when it's up some little boy's ass."

"Speaking of ..." Mario nodded behind Kordell. Two young boys were headed for the restroom in the distance.

One for each.

Mario got up and headed for the restroom, not waiting for his newfound partner to follow. Kordell also rose up, but something that felt like a piece of shit fell down the right leg of his jeans. When it hit his ankle, he knew it was too hard to be a turd. He looked around, decided he wasn't being watched and bent over to retrieve the object, not looking at it until it was in his hands, discreetly in front of his waist.

A cell phone. His friend Arthur's Nokia. It had been wedged between his butt cheeks in Saran Wrap. Thank God Arthur had bought a small enough phone.

Small enough for what? For who? For why?

To call Koji. Koji who? Yamo. Sal. Call Sal. That's it, Sal. You'll know what to say, just do it, dumb ass faggot nigger. Nigger faggot. Do it.

He staggered backward from the barrage of epithets, then slid the phone into his right pocket and looked around again.

Who the hell is you looking for, nigger faggot? More boys? Aren't the ones Mario is heading toward enough for now? Look at him, not much farther to go. Better catch up and get yours—

I am not a nigger faggot—

Do you or do you not like sex with other males?
Are you or are you not of African-American descent?

He stumbled to a trash can in the sand and put his head inside as if he were about to throw up. But he didn't throw up—hadn't intended to. He pulled the phone from his pocket and—head still in the trash can—dialed the phone.

"Del Rio residence." That boy. That dear, sweet boy. Like a nephew.

I love Fredito. Don't I?

"Salina Del Rio, please." Kordell deepened his voice to disguise it.

"Uncle Kord?" Fredito had been answering that phone and recognizing Kordell's voice since the boy was four years old. You can't fool kids. Fucking kids. Fuck kids.

"Can't talk right now, Fredito," Kordell said. "Speak to your mother now. Me. I need to speak to your mother."

Don't say another word to this child.

"Uncle Kord, today I'm going to baseball—"

"*Freddie!* Put your mother on *now!*" Kordell peeked out of the trash can. No one. Still safe. Was it drug-induced paranoia or was he right to expect company? "Wait, Fredito, don't go yet … Fredito … how are you? Tell me you're all right."

But Fredito was already gone, replaced by noises from the Del Rio household: footsteps on hardwood floors, muffled speech, bodies in motion. The trash can reeked of rotted food, potato salad, dried beer, dog shit. I can throw up on a whim, he thought.

"Kordell, where are you?" A female's voice. Sal's voice. "What's going on?"

"Sal. I'm calling you like I said I would. I remember this. I said I would call you, made a promise. To clear up the confusion."

About what?

Horrid images flooded his senses. Dark brown hands around Fredito. A dead man that looked like Mario on a bloody bathroom floor. Mad writings on a chalkboard. Cute Japanese ass. Cute Japanese smile. Thin man. Gaunt face. Pizza Roll.

You want to molest every little boy you see. St. Dahmer. St. Gacy.

Become a saint. Higher than the Pope. You are a saint. St. Kordell de Christie.

A multitude of lives that he had led collided in his head: facades, lies, closets, masks. He regurgitated, spraying the sides of the trash can but somehow sparing the phone.

"Kordell? Speak up. I can barely hear you. You sound like you're in a tunnel."

Sal's voice. His best friend who trusted him, loved him, had given him time to sort out the molestation of her son—

That's it! Fredito was molested. Molested? Attempted? Almost? It's the thought that counts and maims and is good for a beginner.

"I'm calling from the inside of a garbage can, Sal."

He was gasping, choking on his own breath and the shock. Mario and/or Kordell had touched Fredito, recruited him into their satanic world. A world with a population of ...

"A garbage can?" It was Sal again. "You're kidding, right? Have you found anything out? What can you tell me?"

"I'm not kidding, a garbage can." He knocked the phone three times against the inside of the can. "Did you hear that?"

Satan rules hell and I am in hell. Mario and I ... touched by Satan ... devil inside ... every single one of us ...

The smell of death invaded his nostrils. Dead flesh in the trash can.

Somebody's killed something. Animal or human. Human is animal. Human is worse than animal, maiming, killing, corrupting, brainwashing, stealing, brainwashing, abusing, brainwashing. Virtual brainwashing—

Virtual brainwashing? What a crock of shit! You wanna tell that to the cops, go ahead. It's a good twist on "the devil made me do it" or "I got the message looking at The Simpsons *TV show" or everything else every other nutcase has ever blamed it on. Go right ahead. Just make sure you enjoy the ride before the fall.*

His eyes dilated, taking in information careening toward him like a tidal wave. He was going to drown trying to process it all.

Do it. Tell Sal what you need to tell her. There are evil people in this world. Wickedly evil. Evil beyond what Sal or Fredito or anyone knows.

"Kordell … are you there … why are you in a garbage can?"

"Because I like to get down and dirty, Salina. In the mud. Like pigs. Real fucking pigs."

"Whoa. What's going on … can you hear me … Kordell?"

"The trash can is at the beach." *Look on the outside of the can. No … you already know the name. Remember it, faggot.* "El Destino. The wind at El Destino Beach is causing a shitty connection."

Sal said something that came back as garbled as the rotted, vomit-covered French fries he was staring at.

"Listen to me, Sal. The wind at this beach—El Destino Beach like it says on the trash can—is strong. I can't talk long, but I called to keep my promise."

"Did he … didn't he?" Sal begged through the weak signal. "Kordell, just tell me that. Did Mario try to … my son?"

"He did. I did. We do. And we're about to do it again." He peeked out of the can. Mario was a few steps away from the restroom. Kordell had to go. "Mario would confirm this, but he's about to enter the restroom at El Destino beach and do it again. I've got to go. I've got to catch up and help him. We're partners in crime, Sal."

Sal began blathering words that were broken up every other second.

"At least I'm being honest … Sal, are you there? Sal?"

The phone went dead. The signal lost. Kordell knew he could call her back or catch up with Mario, but not both. He chose Mario.

The closer he got to the restroom, the more he wondered: did I do this to Mario? Was it me or the people responsible for the images in my mind? I was strapped down … no, hanging from the ceiling!

There you go with that virtual brainwashing shit again. Maybe you should also tell the police that other killers talked to you from the Great Beyond. Son of Sam. Bundy. St. Jack de Ripper—

I was hanging from the ceiling, dammit—

No, you fantasized hanging from the ceiling—

I corrupted Mario. I turned him into this—

By George, I think he's got it. Again—

I corrupted Mario—

Again—
I corrupted Mario—
Again—
I corrupted—

"Ouch, that hurts!" It was a boy's voice, coming from inside the restroom. "Stop it, you big bastard ... I'm gonna tell Mom."

Kordell raced inside the little room. The two boys' shorts were down to their ankles. They were at the trough, taking a piss.

"You said 'bastard' yesterday and I didn't tell mom," claimed the boy to the right. He was an inch taller, probably the older of the two. "If I hit you again, you can't say it, then I won't tell Mom."

"Not fair," cried the younger brother.

Kordell scanned the room. Mario was crouched in the far corner, trembling with a crazed look in his eyes. When he saw Kordell, he nodded to the ceiling above him and a barely noticeable button of some sort. A camera, Kordell thought instantly. *Pizarro is taping us.*

Two consecutive thoughts raced through Kordell's mind, so fast, they were almost simultaneous:

Who the fuck is Pizarro?
Saint Evil.

Kordell turned back to the two boys. Nine? Ten? Eleven? Twelve?

Doesn't matter. You know what to do.

Kordell's hands came up in front of him. He could see his digits reaching out as he inched forward. He could see the kids' necks on the other side of his fingernails. He could see a glitch form just to the right of his right eye. He jerked his head as if trying to avoid a small insect that had flown into his line of vision. The glitch happened again.

Glitch?

What kind of nonsense you talking 'bout, crazy nigga? Get dem boys.

His hands reached farther. The boys pulled their shorts up, stepped away from the trough and brushed by Kordell, who stood there frozen.

Turn back and attack. I said turn back and attack.

"Kordell," Mario's quivering voice cried from the corner.

Kordell looked down at his hands, the hands that knew what to do.

Just like you've done over and over.

I have not done this over and over. I have never done this.

Oh, yes, you have, old man. Does the name Mario Cervantes mean anything to you?

The kids were washing their hands. There was still time.

"Boys!" Kordell uttered through his fog, then slowly turned around. The brothers looked at him with a combination of respect and fear. An adult had spoken. A black man, at that. They didn't know whether they were in trouble, in for some adult wisdom, or in need of Mommy. "It's … it's …"

The boys couldn't move, wouldn't move, were afraid to move.

"It's good that you washed your hands," Kordell forced himself to say. "Germs equal disease."

"He's right." Mario was standing next to Kordell now. "You'll stay a lot healthier that way."

The older brother nodded shyly and threw his wadded-up paper towel into the trash can. His little brother followed suit, then they both made a hasty exit.

Mario grabbed Kordell by both arms and hauled him out of the men's restroom and into the adjacent women's restroom.

"I knew it. I knew it," Mario said, releasing the pent-up energy ricocheting through his body. "Our minds are way stronger than anything they can do to us. I knew you wouldn't touch those kids and neither would I. Let's go."

"I don't want kids!" Kordell jerked away from Mario. "I don't want to touch them sexually *ever!* I'm not evil! I'm not that way!"

"I know, Kordell, but we're not safe here. This is a field test."

"What's going on, Mario, you're into little boys? You're a pedophile? I did this to you? I made you a pedophile?"

"No, Kordell, no. I'm not a pedophile, just come—"

"What the fuck?" Kordell sank to the ground and grabbed at his head.

"Kordell, you've got to get a grip. They'll be here any second."

Mario grabbed Kordell's arm and tried to stand him up.

"Get a grip?" Kordell resisted. "I just tried to molest—I saw the kids and my mind—something took over. I forgot who … what …"

"You didn't do it. That was Pizarro's bullshit talking."

"Pizarro?" Kordell scooted to the corner and coiled up in a fetal position. "Who is this guy? Who is he? What is he?"

"He's watching us and coming for us. We've got to get out of here." Mario lunged for Kordell.

"Get away from me!" Kordell jumped to his feet, his back pressed against the wall in the name of putting distance between him and Mario. "When I was … before I came in here, I was …"

"What, Kordell? Think! Feel! Whatever you have to do, but do it quick! What is it?"

"I called Sal." Kordell moved around the room, keeping his back against the wall, the only thing that seemed real. "I thought about Pizarro when I called Sal. Sal! I molested Sal, I mean, her boy. No, *you* did. No, it was Pizarro. Pizarro put something in you. He tricked you into molesting Fredito. Pizarro is evil … will stop at nothing. I have to stop him. Listen to your insides, your voices. Your real voices. I called Sal. I told her … to get the police … tell her that you and I are both evil … so she'll get police … and they'll be on their way … but Pizarro might be listening … give her the location … secretly … there's something inside me. When I saw those kids … Mario, help!"

"Kordell, listen to me." Mario made sure to keep his distance. "The molestation urge is not you; it's computer bullshit."

"What the fuck are you talking about?"

"I got it, too," said Mario, "but less than you. You made sure of that when you scratched up my goggles. It worked! I'm halfway sane, I mean, myself. But we've got to get out of here. They know we did-n't come through."

"How do we know we're not both under the same program right now?"

"You've got this EVL chip; I don't," said Mario. "I heard the whole thing in the van on the way over here."

"Van?"

"Before they put us in your car with all those child porn pics.

This is a test. I had to play along. When they caught us trying to escape last night, I fainted and started regurgitating all their predator bullshit. I played dumb. I told them I thought you were taking me away for sex and I went because I wanted sex. I made up this shit about how I was gonna pretend you were a preteen boy. Pizarro wanted to believe it, so he did, but now—"

"Now you've both disappointed me entirely." It was Pizarro, a face Kordell recognized immediately, even if he didn't remember the full extent to which he knew the man.

Mario looked around for something to grab, but stopped when Pizarro pulled a gun from his leather jacket. A short blond man entered the room, also holding a gun.

"Don't try Brother John's patience," Pizarro warned Mario.

"Right … Brother John," Kordell said, as if the name rung a bell. Pizarro and Brother John looked at each other with resignation.

"Total failure. The drugs if I had to guess." Pizarro went over to Kordell and passed a glowing wand over Kordell's neck. Before there was time to react, Kordell felt a brain freeze a hundred times worse than any frozen dessert could ever produce. His body convulsed; he collapsed to the ground and slipped into unconsciousness.

The next thing he was aware of was the aroma of smelling salts invading his nose, giving him a start. He was still on the floor of the women's restroom. Pizarro and Brother John were standing over him. Another man was in the corner, back to them, hands on his head as if under arrest. He was Latino, Kordell realized, and in the next instant, he realized it was Mario.

Kordell's vision was blurry, but his mind was very much aware of what was going on. Pizarro had deactivated the EVL chip in his body. That Kordell knew what an EVL chip was came only as a minor shock. Like coming up after fainting while crash-dieting, he was remembering more and more and increasingly able to distinguish from virtual reality and actual reality.

He was also now aware of the fact that Mario had been trying to save them both, but that Kordell had been stubborn, terrified, untrusting, all the above, and now they had been recaptured by Pizarro and Brother John, who both had guns pointed at them.

"Looks like it's all come back to him," said a seemingly bored Pizarro. "Let's round up the animals and take them back."

Kordell and Mario were loaded into the van without incident, partly because of the guns their captors discreetly brandished, but also because Kordell was praying that the plan his subconscious had conjured up would work: that Sal had summoned the police to El Destino Beach and the cops were on the lookout for a black man and a Latino, both in their thirties. Turned out, his subconscious had acted admirably and even heroically. Three squad cars pulled into the parking lot with sirens blazing and tires screeching. But it also turned out that their timing was slightly off. By the time they pulled up to the restroom, the van was cruising down the highway at 75 miles per hour.

SIXTEEN

W hen the white minivan pulled into the Facility's back parking lot, Clive was standing on the curb, arms folded, his superior smirk barely concealed. Only then did Kordell remember that a pudgy little queen was a partner in crime with Pizarro and Brother John. Kordell's memory had returned in scattered chunks on the drive from El Destino. He had all the parts of the jigsaw puzzle that was the last few days, but he still wasn't sure how to connect the pieces together so that they fit into one clear, concise picture. He also wasn't sure that it mattered now anyway.

The van pulled to a stop near Clive. Pizarro, who was in the front passenger seat, and Brother John, who had been driving, got out first. Then, with their guns, they waved Kordell and Mario out of the back.

"Not a success?" asked Clive. He also had a gun, making it three against squat.

"Up against the van, facing me," Pizarro said to Kordell and Mario, then turned to Clive. "There are many definitions of the word *success*. If by success, you mean that the EVL chip worked on the nig-

ger faggot, the answer is no. Obviously the multitude of drugs in his pathetic system screwed up everything—as you warned, I know."

"And the Mexican?" asked Clive.

"Problems there, too, most likely stemming from the nigger's interference." Pizarro walked over to his captives, coming within inches of their faces as he passed by. "But if by success, you mean eliminating the threat of these two mutants, ask me again in about one hour."

"Do I get to kill again, Victor?" asked a hopeful Brother John.

"I'm afraid not, my son."

Brother John sank with disappointment.

"But," Pizarro added, "you can assist in arranging their tragic hiking-related accident."

Brother John clasped his hands in front of him with glee and seemed on the verge of shouting, "Oh, goody!"

"There are others who know we're here," said Kordell. "Others who know about your sick doings."

"You do know your primetime cop dramas, don't you?" said Pizarro. "I'm sorry you both couldn't be of further service to society, but you must understand: the only truly good queer is a dead queer."

He grabbed Kordell's balls and squeezed them so tight, Kordell fell to his knees. Then he grabbed Mario by his neck and choked him until Mario was gasping for air.

"Everything status quo here?" Pizarro calmly asked Clive.

"Status quo," said Clive.

"We're going on a hike, boys," Pizarro announced. "You can come along willingly, or you can have your bodies sliced into pieces one by one, starting with the filthiest part of you, and I think we all know what that is."

Like a Scout troop leader, Pizarro marched toward the barren hills beyond the parking lot. Brother John pushed Mario ahead, then lifted Kordell to his feet and shoved him in the direction of the mountains.

"Who was it, Pizarro?" Kordell shouted without budging.

Pizarro kept walking and waved his gun, as if to say, "Shut up and march."

"An uncle?" yelled Kordell.

Pizarro ignored him; Mario stopped moving forward.

"A relative?" asked Kordell. "A neighbor or cousin?"

Pizarro kept going. Brother John kicked Kordell in the ass, knocking him to the ground. Kordell got up, but refused to march.

"Who hurt you when you were a child?" he yelled to Pizarro, who was getting farther and farther away. "Was it some older friend?"

"Move the prisoners," Pizarro said without turning around.

"Somebody did this to you," said Kordell. "I wanna know who. Somebody hurt the little boy Victor. Was it your father?"

Pizarro stopped dead in his tracks, but didn't turn around.

"What did he do to you, Victor?" asked Kordell. "He hurt you bad, didn't he? Bet he caused you all kinds of pain—destroyed your spirit."

Pizarro swung around so fast, Kordell thought a bullet hurtling toward him would be the next and last thing he'd ever see. But Pizarro just stood there, percolating, his lips and chin quivering with rage. Finally, he came to a boil and shouted at the top of his lungs:

"*You know nothing about my father!*"

The words echoed off the hills. For a moment there was only silence.

"I know he hurt you," Kordell said, maintaining his distance. "And you still feel that hurt. But it wasn't about you, Victor. It wasn't because you were a bad boy."

"That's what you all say." Pizarro rushed toward Kordell, not stopping until the only air between their faces was that of their hot breaths. "You filthy, lying, backstabbing, child molesting … *filth!*" He turned away, ashamed of his flare-up.

"Not all gays are child molesters," said Kordell. "And not all child molesters are gay. Statistics don't even … there's good and bad in every … your father had a problem. He had no right to—"

"Don't you dare talk about my daddy!" Pizarro swung back around and raised his gun until the end of the barrel was inches away from the space between Kordell's eyes. "I'll put a bullet in your faggot ass here and now. I did it to Dad; I swear I'll do it to you."

The revelation stunned them all, even Brother John and Clive, who stood there, not knowing how to aid their boss.

"We're not your father," Mario said, his voice full of sympathy. "I'm not my father."

"None of us are our parents' sins," said Kordell. "You don't have to pass the legacy of shame on."

"Shut up," Pizarro cried. "Both of you, shut your filthy faggot mouths! You're evil! You spread disease and filth and make people sick, then you lie about it!" His eyes were glazed over, his face covered in dirty sweat. His tone went from adult rage to scared little child. "You tell me to not tell anyone, but it hurts so bad. Hurts so much, Daddy. Please make the burning stop. I don't want no more burn, Daddy. I don't want *phifless*. Daddy, why did you give me this *phifless?*" Pizarro collapsed to the ground. "*Phifless* is bad, *phifless* hurts so much, Daddy, help me."

Kordell, Mario, Brother John and Clive stood in shock. For a moment, they were neither gay nor straight, captors or captives, enemy or foe. They were four adults, surrounding a child whose scars might never heal.

Brother John knelt and put an arm around Pizarro.

"Your father had no right to hurt you," offered Kordell.

"Just shut up or I'll kill you myself." Brother John pointed the gun at Kordell and Mario.

"Happen to you, too, Brother John?" asked Mario.

"No, you idiot; I just like to kill."

"He's in serious emotional pain," Kordell said of Pizarro. "His father abused him and that's why he's taken this … path."

"He thinks he's sick because of his father," said Mario. "I know a thing or two about that."

"You don't know a damned thing." Brother John caressed Pizarro's sweaty hair. "Don't listen to them, Victor. Your father didn't make you sick."

"What do any of you know?" said a whimpering Pizarro.

"I know we're changing the world," said Brother John.

"None of you knows anything." Pizarro stood up, turned away and muttered indecipherable words. Before long, his rage was recharged. He did a quick about-face, unzipped his pants and pulled down his black boxer shorts. "Did any of your fathers give you this?"

His penis was like nothing Kordell had ever seen. It was beet-red and engorged on one side, as if part of the head had eaten itself alive.

"This is what sick gay fathers give their kids," said Pizarro. "A dick that doesn't heal from syphilis. Syphilis you get from your filthy father and you're too scared to tell anyone because he's sworn you to secrecy."

"Why didn't you tell your mother?" asked Mario.

"Predators," said Pizarro. "You never get it, never understand, which is why I must control you, alive or dead."

"Listen to Mario, Victor," Kordell pleaded. "He's been ... he's had experience."

"Enough of this!" Pizarro fired a warning shot in the air. "There's no talking your way out of this. To the woods!"

Kordell indicated Mario. "You realize his father Giovanni is a child molester."

"Of course, I do," said Pizarro. "I rescued him years ago. That sexual deviant registry is good for many, many things. Sex offenders and outcasts make good lab rats and laborers."

"Did you know he molested his own son?" asked Kordell. "Just like your daddy?"

Pizarro glared at Mario with disbelief.

"The family never reported it," said Kordell. "Just banished him."

"Not me." Mario answered the question that was evident on Pizarro's face. "My twin, the one you killed."

"That was my handiwork," Brother John interjected. "Give credit where credit is due."

"All lies!" Pizarro shouted. "Distractions. Games. Delay tactics."

"Koji Yamamoto knows about Mr. Cervantes," said Kordell. "How could *you* not?"

Pizarro turned to Clive. "Bring them here. *Now!*"

Clive disappeared into the Facility and the parking lot fell silent. Pizarro paced around, muttering. Brother John held his gun on Kordell and Mario, the pretty boy's greedy eyes pleading with them to make one wrong move. It took less than five minutes for Clive to round up Giovanni and Koji. Giovanni was wearing a white kitchen

apron stained with gravy and tomato sauce. If Koji had any reaction to seeing Kordell and Mario, he did a good job of not showing it.

He made sure I had the cell phone, Kordell realized. Another piece of the puzzle becoming clear.

"Is it true?" Pizarro said as soon as the three men came within earshot.

"Is what true?" Giovanni asked, realizing Pizarro's curious gaze was focused on him.

"Mr. Yamamoto?" Pizarro turned to Koji. "Is it?"

Koji hesitated, then looked to Kordell, who wanted to give him an inconspicuous, affirmative nod. But Brother John put the gun up to Kordell's temple to prevent any tampering with the witness.

"You're going to have to bring me up to speed," Koji said in his deferential Asian voice.

"Giovanni," Pizarro said calmly, then yelled: "Is it true?"

"Is what true, sir?" pleaded Giovanni.

"I'll ask nicely." Pizarro rubbed the sweat from his forehead and took a deep breath in an effort to calm down. "Did you or did you not molest your other son Javier?"

"You know my past," said Giovanni.

"I know what the police record said; it mentioned nothing about family members, only two teenage boys in Lompoc." Pizarro circled Giovanni like a shark. "You weren't arrested for touching your own flesh and blood. Maybe that was a dirty little family secret kept in the dirty little closet, something which I wouldn't have known about when I pulled you from depths of the sexual offender gutter."

"You tell *me* something," said Giovanni. "Did you kill my son? And are you doing something funny with my other boy that I should know about?"

He doesn't know about the predator training, Kordell realized.

"I'll make a deal with you." Pizarro stopped in front of Giovanni. "Truth for truth—no one else speaks—do we have a deal?"

Giovanni thought about it, then said, "You first."

"Mario is in training to become a productive citizen just like you." Pizarro calmly walked away. "And no, I did not kill your other son Javier."

Relief washed over Giovanni's face. "Yes, I did molest Javy a long time ago, but—"

Pizarro promptly turned and shot him in the forehead.

"*Papi!*" Mario tried to run to him, but Brother John shifted his gun from Kordell to Mario. Mario ignored the weapon and started toward his father—who was on the ground—but Kordell held him back.

"*I* didn't kill your son," said Pizarro. "Brother John did."

Without another thought, he resumed his march to the hills.

Clive froze. Koji attended to Giovanni, but not for long. He felt Giovanni's neck, chest and wrist, then covered Giovanni's disfigured face with the apron from the cook's torso.

"Put the guns down, all three of you." Koji stood up. "No one else dies and makes this any worse."

Pizarro turned around and fired a second shot, this time at Koji, who fell so quickly, Kordell wasn't sure where the bullet hit. He tried to run to Yamo—his last hope for freedom—but Brother John kept swinging the barrel of his gun from Mario to Kordell, then back again.

"Come on," Brother John shouted with enthusiasm of a choir boy gone mad. "Gimme a reason, gimme a reason, a reason, gimme a reason."

Kordell and Mario held their ground. Clive came out of his coma and knelt down to help Koji. But Pizarro rushed over and grabbed Clive by the back of his shirt. Clive leapt up and screamed like a little girl, expecting his head to be blown off next. Pizarro ignored the outburst, his mind more consumed with instructions.

"Stay here," he told Clive. "We'll dispose of these bodies later. No one will miss Giovanni. We'll figure out Koji's story later. Brother John, let's go. Two accidents mean two less worries."

Pizarro started for the hills again, this time with the utmost confidence that nothing else would try to get in his way. As he passed a stunned and motionless Mario, he stopped and nodded to Mario's father's lifeless body. "Don't mourn that man" was all he offered, then, like a general possessed, marched on.

The way they were hiking, Kordell figured Mario's and his deaths would come from exhaustion, if nothing else. Pizarro walked in front of them with brisk determination fueled by madness and rage.

Brother John brought up the rear, no doubt waiting for Kordell or Mario to stumble on a pebble or twig, giving him reason to think they were trying something funny and needed to be put out of their misery.

They hiked through all kinds of rough terrain: grassy inclines full of ice plants and darting lizards; gravel-laden trails that wound in and out of dense forest; steep, dirt-filled upgrades that cramped their thighs. They ventured off the main trails and into thickets full of nothing but bushes, which rattled as they passed, and low hanging tree branches that scarred their skin and threatened to stab their eyes. They went up rocky slopes—the kind that looked impossible to ascend from the freeway. They teetered on narrow cliffs, cliffs that Kordell thought of jumping from to beat Pizarro to the punch. But why give him the satisfaction? And what about Mario? Maybe somehow they could fight their way out of this together. Hope of the damned.

"I guess asking for water is out of the question," Mario shouted up to Pizarro at one point.

"Keep walking," Pizarro shouted back. "All homos must die."

Kordell wasn't sure how far they'd hiked from the Facility. When they could see anything other than the mountains surrounding them, there were no signs of man or anything man-made. They did see the ocean from time to time—far off in the distance, down there, over there—the crown jewel of the paradise that was Santa Barbara, out of reach, never to be enjoyed again.

"I don't think I can go on." On one narrow cliff, Kordell stopped and grabbed the back of his thigh, hoping a hamstrung hamstring might somehow lead to a way out.

"If it's hurting," Pizarro said, "I'm sure Brother John can think of a way to kill the pain."

Both Kordell and Mario regarded Brother John, who looked all too happy to put a bullet through any of their ailments. They hiked onward. Kordell tried to think of a way to communicate to Mario, to tell him: we're not going down without a fight. He thought of the arcade games they'd played ... the punching bag!

"Boxorama?" he said softly to Mario, who was ahead of him.

"Huh?" said Mario.

"No conspiring!" Brother John yelled, killing that idea.

They walked in silence until they climbed atop a plateau half the size of a tennis court. The ridge sprung up in the center of a vast valley. Around them sprawled brown slopes and oddly shaped gorges full of rock formations and brush. Around that, farther away, undisturbed mountains and hills, sleeping like quiet, uncivilized mammoth giants. And to one side, a long horizon of blue: the Pacific, maybe twenty, thirty miles away. Had they been there for any other reason—a picnic, the culmination of a nature hike, wild sex in the great outdoors—this would have been the moment they all paused to inhale the scene before them and thank God or fate that they lived in California.

"This is where you get off." Pizarro nodded in the direction behind his captives. "And I don't mean in the dirty bathhouse way."

Kordell and Mario stood in the center of the plateau and turned around. Brother John was still armed behind them. They looked past him to ... the edge of the plateau.

"Now I suggest," Pizarro began, his tone sounding like that of a sarcastic friend, "you take a good long, running jump. That way, well, who am I kidding? I just want this to be a little dramatic, you understand, I'm sure."

Kordell and Mario eyed each other, then Kordell glanced at Pizarro, while Mario looked at Brother John.

"This isn't a John Wayne western," said Brother John. "And don't think you can get out of this by kung fu fighting."

"But this is America," Pizarro said. "So I'm going to give you a choice. If you don't want to jump, we'll shoot you in your general groin area and leave you here like that. You might die; you might bleed to death; you might heroically make it all the way back to civilization and the police and turn us bad guys in. And you may even survive without your manhood. Just maybe. Or you can take a flying leap and be done with your miserable homosexual lives right now. See, I'm a reasonable guy who's willing to compromise."

"You're so cool, Victor," said Brother John. "And compassionate."

"Why, thank you, Brother John."

Kordell mumbled to Mario. "You take Pizarro, I'll take John?"

"They're plotting!" shouted Brother John.

"Both of you, toward the edge!" Pizarro yelled. "Now! Hands in the air."

Kordell and Mario did as they were told, backing up slowly while keeping an eye out for the edge. Brother John stepped around them and joined Pizarro on the opposite side. When Kordell came to the edge, he saw nothing but huge, jagged rocks, the head-spattering kind.

"What's it gonna be, faggots?" Pizarro pointed a gun at Kordell while Brother John pointed his at Mario. "Suicide or surgery?"

Rage replaced fear inside Kordell. Four days of hell boiled in his forehead. A lifetime of ignorance burned in his chest.

"You can't do this!" he yelled.

"Fight me like a man!" yelled Mario.

"Koji is a cop!" yelled Kordell. "He's got backup! Koji will get your asses!"

"I'm not dying this way!" yelled Mario. "I'm gonna ... I'm not gonna ..."

"You're a fucking lunatic, Pizarro, both of you!" Kordell couldn't hear himself. The sky roared and rumbled. His eardrums betrayed him; he shouted anyway. "Kill me! Kill me, fucker, so they can find you and put you away!"

But no one could hear him. The plateau shook as if in an earthquake. He turned to Mario, who was literally blowing away. Kordell's own clothes made a desperate attempt to fly off his body. Mario was yelling something in Kordell's face. They were engulfed by a strong wind. A tornado. A hurricane. A helicopter. Kordell saw the spinning blades and realized Mario had already spotted it. The chopper was behind them. Seemingly inches away. As if it had ascended from the valley below. Kordell turned away from the blast of swirling air. Pizarro and Brother John were rigid with panic; this was an unwelcome, unwanted surprise to them. Kordell turned toward the copter, then to his captors. Then he realized exactly what was happening.

"Koji."

Of course, not even Kordell could hear himself say the name, but just as he uttered it, he made eye contact with Pizarro, and judging by the horrified look in Pizarro's face, the head devil himself had no problem reading Kordell's lips.

A cocky half-smile materialized on Kordell's face. Fury materialized on Pizarro's. He began shooting at the copter. Mario grabbed Kordell and threw them both to the ground. Bullets flew over their heads. Gunfire was coming from both directions. Sure, it would have been prudent to keep their faces glued to the grass, but they were human. They had to look up.

Pizarro and Brother John were in a shootout with a man in the passenger seat of the copter. Dust, metal and glass rained on Kordell and Mario as they lay on the ground. The two men in the chopper had cover, Pizarro and Brother John didn't. Brother John juked his way around the ridge, creating a moving target, but Pizarro stood there, defiantly firing at the copter until suddenly his body jerked and convulsed. He staggered backward, hit by a seemingly endless number of bullets.

Pizarro's face gave up before the rest of him. His expression went blank. Blood poured from his shoulder, chest and gut; but his legs retreated in stilted steps, as if the bullets riddling his body dictated his momentum. He didn't stop until his heels were on the edge of the plateau. Then he rocked back and forth, more back than forth. Brother John, who had been moving about, was too far away to do anything. They were all too far away to do anything. The gunfire stopped. From a kneeling position, Brother John reached out anyway, even though he was a good ten feet away. Pizarro noticed him, then his eyes rolled toward the sky and his body fell backward. In the blink of an eye, he disappeared. Brother John began sobbing and threw his gun at the chopper's window. It fell harmlessly short to the ground, landing at Kordell's side.

Kordell rolled over in the opposite direction, partially landing on Mario, who had also rolled over on his back in relief. Looking up, they both saw the man who had been in the passenger seat of the helicopter coming toward them, an angel on a ladder, descending from the sky.

The front parking lot of the Facility was swarming with a calm but steady hum of worker bee activity. Lights swirled atop idle police cars, but the sirens were muted. Yellow crime scene tape cordoned off much of the parking lot and the building itself. A tall, burly man who

looked to be in charge stood outside his SUV cop car, doling out instructions to the various law enforcement officers who approached him. Plainclothes detectives huddled in packs, pointing, discussing, then dispersing. No media were present, not just yet anyway. Several school buses had been commissioned and the now-former patients of the Facility were being herded onto them. On the opposite side of the lot, staff members were locked inside a different school bus. Clive sat near the front, head in his hands, looking as if he were sobbing. Brother John's face and hands were pressed against the window, stark disbelief etched in his sad, wide eyes. He looked like a child whose trip to the amusement park had just been canceled.

Kordell and Mario were near the front entrance, being questioned by a black plainclothes detective in his forties who had a small graying Afro. To Kordell, he looked like the actor Danny Glover. He had introduced himself, but Kordell couldn't remember his name. They'd only been down from the ridge less than two hours and life was nowhere near ready for assembly back into concise, sensible pieces. Mario was still recovering from an attack of airsickness courtesy of the helicopter ride. Kordell's legs were cramped from all the hiking. Still they tried their best to answer Detective Glover's questions, which were, after all—so he promised—just preliminary queries "so we can get grounded and know where to begin sorting out this whole mess."

"This Area 2," he was saying now. "You say you never saw any other students in there?"

"Just him." Kordell indicated Mario.

"I was in there with a whole class, but they graduated before I did," said Mario. "They're out there, doing crap."

"We'll get their names." Detective Glover made a series of notations on his PDA. "They'll be rounded up by the end of the day."

"What about Pizarro?" asked Mario.

"Still no sign of his body." Detective Glover saw the fear in Mario's eyes. "No way he survived that fall though."

"While full of bullet holes?" Kordell added. "He's not coming back, Mario. This isn't *I Know What You Did Last Summer* and he's not Jason of *Friday the 13th*."

"Search and Rescue will find his body." Detective Glover chuck-

led to himself as he penned another entry in his PDA. "And it won't have any life left in it, guaranteed."

Mario seemed unconvinced. Kordell started to say something, but a gurney rolled up from behind. A hand emerged from underneath a white sheet, instructing the Latino paramedic who was pushing the stretcher to stop. The paramedic complied and a smile washed over Kordell's face.

"Yamo!" he said, breathing a great sigh of relief. Hearing that Koji was alive and in stable condition was one thing, seeing it for himself was altogether heaven. "Thank God. And thank you."

"Ease up on my boys here," Koji told Detective Glover. "My collar, my Q&A."

"Then you'd better get your ass to ER so you can finish your job," said Detective Glover.

"Don't you worry about me," said Koji. "We've all got some stories they'll be telling the rookies for years."

Detective Glover and Koji shook hands. "Now get in your goddamn chariot." Detective Glover indicated the ambulance, then stepped away to meet a stocky plainclothesman hurrying toward him.

"I think you should follow Detective Glover's orders, Mr. FBI agent." Kordell wanted to take Koji's hand but held back.

"Funny, we call him Glover, too." Koji laughed, but his abdomen—which was where he'd been shot—didn't get the joke and sent a shot of excruciating pain through his torso. He winced and coughed, causing more pain. The Latino paramedic stepped toward him, but Koji waved him off. They all waited for a moment while Koji closed his eyes and found some kind of inner peace that calmed his body and eased the pain. When he opened his eyes again, he was smiling. "Where were we?"

"Man," said Mario. "I can't thank you enough for helping Kordell. And me. And you gotta get well and soon. I got a lot of getting down on my knees and thanking you to do."

"Mario Cervantes." Koji's expression turned wistful. "Good to finally meet you. Kordell's a lucky man. And so are you." Koji's gaze turned to Kordell. His smile faded a bit. Another kind of pain languished in his eyes. "You're both very lucky."

For Kordell, this was one of those moments where there were so many things he could have said, his brain froze like a desktop computer gone bad. How to explain in that awkward instant that Kordell and Mario weren't an item. At least not now. And maybe never. And that, yes, Kordell had thought Koji was a jerk, but that was when the man was playing the irritating cult follower.

The moment passed and Kordell said nothing. The Latino paramedic became the director of the scene. Without waiting for anyone's approval, he wheeled Koji toward the ambulance. Kordell watched until Yamo was safely loaded and locked in, then sheepishly turned to Mario, who—judging by his embarrassed expression—was also thinking of Koji's insinuation.

Again, what to say?

Before there was time for anything more than their adolescent-like shrugs, Detective Glover rejoined them, having finished his mini-conference with the stocky plainclothesman.

"We called Miss Salina Del Rio," Detective Glover informed Kordell. "I'm told she broke down in tears. Of joy. She's waiting for you back at her house."

"Thank you, officer—detective," said Kordell. "Thank you a zillion times over."

"What's gonna happen to all these people?" asked Mario as he surveyed the busload of students.

"They'll be taken in for questioning, drug testing, chip scanning," said Detective Glover. "We need to see if any crimes have been committed against them, see if *they've* committed crimes. If not, most likely they'll be released to custody of a family member and we'll monitor them for abnormal behavior."

Kordell and Mario fell silent, the sense of triumph evaporating from their faces.

"Look," said Detective Glover. "I know what you're thinking, but these men came here voluntarily. Trying to change from homosexual to heterosexual is a personal choice and helping a man do so is not a crime. You want respect for your lifestyle, you've got to respect them for theirs."

Neither Kordell nor Mario offered any rebuttal or response.

"I'll go see what's holding up the mobile drug testing unit," said Detective Glover. "I know you two want to get out of here ASAP."

After he was gone, Kordell eyed Mario. There was still so much to talk about, so many questions to ask, so many things to remember—not just from this extended weekend from hell, but childhood things and adult things related to those childhood things.

"You still wanna change your sexual leanings?" was all Kordell could ask for now.

"I never wanted to change, just *look* into it. And you won't catch me doing that again. I'll figure it out for myself." Mario shrugged and grinned. "Maybe with the help of a good friend?"

Kordell managed a fake smile. Of course, he wanted to help Mario in any way possible, but would Mario want his help once the truth about their childhood intimacy came to light? As Kordell shuddered at the thought, he heard footsteps approaching along with a very excited squeal.

"There you are!" It was Sabatino, the Latino who had begged Kordell to fuck him in the Contemplation Gardens. He came up and gave Kordell a gigantic kiss on the lips. "*Gracias* for freeing me."

Kordell wiped his lips and let out an unabashed guffaw. "Why the hell were you here to begin with?"

"My parents offered me a new car if I tried. They bribe. They filthy money." Sabatino rubbed his fingers together to indicate wealth. "I was ashamed. I'm still ashamed, but I don't care. I tell them: I can't give it up. I need dick. I need a man!" He flashed a wide-eyed smile Mario's way, then announced. "I got to go. To LA to get fucked and fucked and fucked again."

He turned toward the yellow buses, waving his hand effeminately as he did.

"Sabatino," Kordell called out, causing the fey Latino to stop and turn back around. "If you do it safely, you'll be around longer and get more dick."

Sabatino thought about it for a second, then said: "I promise I think about it." And with that, he was off.

"You sure did make a lot of friends in a little time, homie," said Mario.

Kordell laughed inwardly as they stood and watched Sabatino board the bus.

"If I were a crier, I'd cry now," said Mario. "Some out of sadness for losing my twin bro. Maybe a little for my father dying. But mostly it would be because I can finally start to put this all behind me. And be me. And grieve properly for Javy."

"Amen to that," said Kordell.

Two hours later, there were plenty of tears. From Kordell, his best friend Sal, her lover Jenna and their heavyset friend Arthur. The reunion happened on the front lawn of Sal's place. As the police car that had been Kordell and Mario's ride drove away, Sal, Jenna and Arthur came running from the house (Fredito was learning how to be a great baseball player at camp miles away). Mario stayed on the sidewalk, but Kordell ran to them and the four friends came together in a communion of hugs and apologies. Kordell couldn't count how many times he said and heard "I'm sorry" and said and heard "it's okay, it's okay."

"I didn't believe it, never believed it," Sal said of Kordell's molestation admission from El Destino Beach. "I knew it was a call for help. What kind of help, I didn't know or understand, but I knew, I knew. I knew the police were the only place I, or you, could turn."

There was a lot of sorting out to be done. There would be some emotional and physical detoxing, and not just on Kordell and Mario's part. But one thing was sure: they were all waking up from the nightmare of the last four days.

Mario watched from the sidewalk until Kordell noticed that he had been missing from the reunion. It was then that Kordell untangled himself from his longtime friends and walked over to the sidewalk. Once there, he took Mario by the shoulder and led him to the middle of Sal's front lawn.

Then Kordell introduced his friends to the real Mario Cervantes.

SEVENTEEN

"Plain or peanut?" came from Mario, who was in the next aisle over.

"Peanut, of course." Kordell opened the glass door of the refrigerated compartment and welcomed the icy breeze on his sweaty brow. "Diet or regular?"

"Regular," said Mario. "We're men. Heads up!"

"Huh—whoa!" Kordell barely had enough time to spot, then catch the large bag of M&M's catapulting over the aisle. "Dude!" he said as he seized the candy in midair. "How immature—heads up yourself."

He sent a two-liter bottle of Pepsi flying over the same aisle and heard Mario cry out "whoa," followed by a thud on the linoleum floor of the convenience store.

"You break, you pay," said the burly Turkish man at the cash register.

"He started it," both Kordell and Mario said from their respective aisles.

They were still laughing about their sophomoric behavior as they exited the store, carrying their stash of junk food.

"Maybe we should go see the latest Eddie Murphy remake of a

kooky classic," Kordell said after they calmed down and began walking down State Street, the main commercial drag in Santa Barbara. They were on their way to an afternoon showing of Alfred Hitchcock's *Spellbound,* where Ingrid Bergman plays a 1940s shrink trying to help amnesia victim Gregory Peck sort out the messy chaos inside his head, including the fear that he may have killed someone.

"No way," said Mario. "It's my choice and I ain't waffling."

"But Mario ..."

"I can handle a movie about a messed-up dude, Kordell. Geez. It's not like Peck molested children. Or thought he did."

Kordell dropped it and they walked on.

The ordeal in the Santa Ynez Mountains was behind them. Three weeks behind them to be exact. Instead of exposing twisted homophobes and being hooked up to predator programming devices, Kordell and Mario had started a new routine: after their weekly Friday visit to the hospital for various tests requested by the FBI (the EVL chip had been removed from Kordell's neck), they'd lose themselves in an afternoon matinee, taking turns choosing the movie.

Both the Facility and Project H.O.P.E. were shut down faster than a whorehouse during an election year. Of the staff members arrested, only Clive and Brother John were refused bail and remained under lock and key. Both men had hired hotshot lawyers reputed to be funded by Right Wing interests, but prosecutors had in their possession all kinds of hard drives, smart cards, virtual goggles and other assorted digital evidence.

Technology can be a very good thing.

Pizarro's body hadn't been found. Yet. The FBI was sure he was anything but alive, theorizing that coyotes, wild animals or maybe the river that snaked through the canyon below the ridge had swallowed him up after his blood-soaked, bullet-riddled corpse fell into oblivion, bouncing off jagged boulder after jagged boulder, descending toward its final destination: hell. The bureau's theories, however, didn't comfort Mario, who preferred to see Pizarro's body resting in all its gory glory in a drawer at the county morgue. But therapy was helping. Therapy was helping Kordell as well.

Mario was staying in the guest bedroom at Kordell's house.

They'd both attended Javier's memorial service (Giovanni didn't have one) and Mario spent time with his family as they supported each other through their grief. But he still wasn't prepared to go back to his own empty apartment in Ventura. Besides, he hinted on more than one occasion, maybe he had a good reason for wanting to move to Santa Barbara permanently.

The thought was both alluring and distressing for Kordell. Yes, they got along famously, liked the same things (arcade games, sports, old movies, rap music, just to name a few). And yes, the real Mario (as opposed to Mario the Android) was funny, sexy, masculine, feminine, strong, sensitive, *hot* and fun to be with. But so far, Kordell couldn't bring himself to think of Mario *that way,* to get physically intimate with Mario, to touch Mario as if it were natural, to want to see Mario naked again for the first time in over two decades. Mario, on the other hand, seemed more than open to getting to know Kordell intimately, if not sexually. Once, he had asked Kordell to sleep (really sleep) with him in the guest room. Mario had just awakened from a nightmare in which Pizarro had starred as the villain. Kordell had raced to the guest room to investigate the shriek that echoed throughout the house.

"Stay with me," Mario had pleaded. "Hold me, just as a friend. At least until I fall asleep."

That night, Kordell took comfort in being able to serve as Mario's temporary security blanket, but he was also troubled by the idea that the little boy inside Mario may have been irrevocably damaged by what happened back in Oxnard all those years ago.

So they remained just friends, which was best for now by all accounts. After all, Mario was still a virgin to gay sex and wasn't sure when and if he'd be ready, if ever. Thus it was agreed that, first and foremost, they had to become acquainted as adults, without the shroud of Pizarro's machinations, but also without knowing what the future might hold. Kind of like normal people.

Once they were planted in their seats in the old-fashioned movie house, they removed the store-bought food and drinks from their baggy pants and began to chow down while watching the seemingly endless parade of ads and trailers.

As the words "Feature Presentation" flashed across the screen,

THE DEVIL INSIDE 237

Kordell looked over at Mario, whose eyes were glazed over and unfocused.

"You know," Kordell began, taking a good guess, "even if by some crazy *Scream IV* scenario Pizarro survived, he can't hurt you anymore. Despite what he claimed, none of his methods are stronger than your own willpower. *No* computer is stronger than the human mind. At least not yet."

"Like I was still dwelling on him," Mario said with mock edginess. "Watch the movie, whydontcha."

Kordell gave him a playful shoulder-to-shoulder nudge and they settled in for the show. Ingrid Bergman was as magnificent as ever: strong, vulnerable, determined, sensual in a time when sensuality had to be subtle. The weirded-out Gregory Peck was a lot like Mario had been a couple of weeks ago: one big memory-challenged mess.

"Can't even remember his own name," Mario scoffed at one point. "What a wimp."

He kept making comments like that throughout the movie, getting a risc out of Kordell, who welcomed the comedic break, especially since the theater wasn't crowded and they had a whole section to themselves. Their running commentary went on until the screw that was the plot begin to turn tighter and tighter. As Gregory Peck's subconscious came spilling out in a Salvador Dali-esque dream, Kordell and Mario fell silent and became oblivious of each other and their surroundings. So engrossed was Kordell that he barely noticed Mario leaving for a quick trip to the restroom. In fact, it was only after a very prolonged absence by Mario that Kordell realized his friend had said "gotta take a leak" and had left long, long ago.

Call it Mario's paranoia rubbing off on Kordell. Call it Ingrid Bergman and Gregory Peck lurking about in eerie shadows. Whatever it was, Kordell got scared. He stashed his Dr. Pepper in the cup holder and leapt to his feet, only remembering that his lap contained a bag of Doritos when it fell on the floor and a couple dozen orange chips scattered in the aisle. He'd clean up the mess later, he told himself, and hurried through the darkness of the theater, using the dusty cone of light from the projector as his guide.

The lobby was ... normal. Empty except for a patron or two

and some teenage staffers. Next stop, the restroom. Kordell had to walk through an unused lobby, then down an excruciatingly long and narrow hallway that smelled of moldy carpet. Finally, he saw the sign that said MEN.

Please let there be MEN, no BOYS.

It was an old restroom to match an old theater. He opened the door, wooden and creaky. First, a foyer of sorts. Dirty yellow tiles on the floor, thousands of them, small as thumbnails. He peeked around the corner. *Sneak peek. Preview of coming attractions.* Nothing. No one. To the right, he saw the bank of sinks, a half dozen of them. He'd have to go all the way in to see the rest of the place.

No turning back. Go all the way in.

To the left, very tall wall urinals. Why so tall?

The urinal on the far left.

Oh, no, a boy. He's young. He's only … twelve at the most.

Mario, where are you?

Kordell's feet were still moving. The boy was still peeing. Kordell moved past him, toward the brown wooden stalls. Brown and yellow bathroom. Wooden stalls. Wooden. Gloryholes. He passed the first stall. In the gaps, the unmistakable shape of a body.

The unmistakable shape of Mario's body.

Kordell wasn't sure which he did—push the door open with his hands or kick it open with his foot. Either way, he forced open the door. Mario was sitting on the toilet. Mario was fully clothed. Mario was looking through a tiny hole in the stall wall. Not big enough to be a gloryhole, but certainly big enough to spy on little boys taking a wee wee.

Still crouched at the hole, Mario looked up and started to say something, most likely starting with "what."

But Kordell didn't allow him to utter a word. Kordell bum-rushed the stall, grabbed his friend and lifted him off the toilet. Then somehow, Kordell got behind him, gave him a big bear hug and literally lifted Mario off the ground. Together they came bounding out of the stall. The little boy looked more terrified and confused than Gregory Peck in black and white. Mario offered little resistance; he was probably in shock. Kordell didn't wait to find out. He carried

Mario out of the restroom and through the nearest exit, which was off the unused lobby.

They burst into daylight, squinting to get a grip on their surroundings: a parking lot, garbage dumpsters, the back of the old movie house.

"I was just looking through the hole, homie!" Mario freed himself from Kordell's grip. "The kid wasn't even there at first, then when I saw him, I wanted to see if I still had any predator shit inside me."

"And?"

Mario shook his head and looked at the ground. Was he disappointed by Kordell's lack of faith and/or trust?

"Homie, under no circumstances in this world would I—"

"Mario, there's something I gotta tell you."

"I just wanted to know: was it really possible for Pizarro to brainwash me?"

"Something we need to talk about or all of this might never go away."

"And I still can't forgive myself for my bro's death—"

"I did something to you when my sister babysat you and we've got to get it out in the open now."

"I know therapy is supposed to help, but I lost something, some part of me that I may never get back, and not just my bro."

"Mario, I had sex with you when we were kids."

Mario looked up, not at Kordell, but straight ahead.

"I'm not sure how old we were," said Kordell. "Maybe I was eleven or twelve and you were seven or eight and we were at my house and I was changing in my bedroom and made you watch and next thing you know … and it continued off and on for I don't know how long, weeks maybe, maybe months, but at some point it was you who wanted to stop, and I didn't. I probably coerced you into doing it a few times more after that. That faint memory you said you had, the moving painting … I think that was it."

"I asked if I could see your dick," Mario said, as if the memory suddenly became real.

"And I pulled it out."

"And I sucked …"

Silence. Mario refused to make eye contact.

"You remember?" asked Kordell.

"Vaguely." Mario turned and tried to take a step, but a large dumpster blocked his path. "Maybe I tried to block it out. I knew I might have done it with someone. I never remembered it was you."

"I always felt bad about it," said Kordell, "especially when I heard a rumor one time long, long ago that you might be ... well, more in touch with your feminine side."

"Huh? Why? You thought ..."

"That maybe I had something to do with it, that maybe I was the reason you were gay or bi or just confused."

More silence. Still no eye contact.

"I feel like I molested you," said Kordell.

"I asked to see your dick."

"But ..."

"It was a man's dick compared to mine." Mario paused. "I wasn't gay or straight at that age. I was just a kid. I was just sexual."

"Me, too," Kordell said hopefully. "You know, I played doctor with a female cousin back then. We used to call it *Saturday in the Park*."

Mario let out a half-hearted chuckle, then fell silent, processing.

"What's your reaction to this?" Kordell's voice cracked.

"The moving picture in my mind makes a little more sense now, but it's not like I remember everything we might have done." Mario turned so that his profile was facing Kordell. "I don't know how I feel. Maybe relieved in a way."

"Relieved?" Kordell asked.

"Not glad," Mario insisted. "I guess now I have to face the fact that it happened, that it's not just ... not like the virtual programming. It happened. The whole reason I was looking into H.O.P.E. and thinking about my sexuality because I know I need to understand who I am. We all need to understand who we are. So maybe I'm feeling part understanding and relief, I don't know."

"Can you help me understand something?" asked Kordell. "Why'd you stop wanting to play around back then?"

Mario looked at him. Thank God Mario could still look at him.

"Dunno," Mario said, then stared at his feet. "Maybe I heard

something, some comment my family made. I don't remember exactly—and it's not a Pizarro memory thing." He let out a groan and arranged himself so that his back was against the theater's white brick wall. "You know how you were saying children are sexual? I guess this is a prime example. Did what we did make me gay or bi? I don't know. This is your memory, not mine. At least up until right now. I mean, I believe you; I don't think you're lying, but is the moving picture completely clear in my mind? Hell, no."

"How would you feel if you decide that what we did as kids influenced your sexuality?"

"That it could have been the reason I might end up bi or gay? Angry, I guess." Mario turned away, his shoulder leaning on the wall. "Like maybe I didn't have a choice. Maybe I would have just liked girls and been fine with that and not even be thinking about homosexuality. Life might have been just fine not dealing with this."

"You say that like homosexuality is bad." Kordell shifted uncomfortably.

"No way," said Mario. "How so?"

"You say you're okay with gays, right?"

"Completely," said Mario. "I've never been prejudice, even when I wasn't questioning. I went out of my way to say wassup to gay kids in school, just so they knew I was cool with them."

"How can you be angry for something making you gay unless you think gay is bad? If being gay was okay, why be angry?"

Mario paused. "I can't answer that."

"Can't or won't?"

"Neither."

Kordell recoiled a bit, feeling the familiar sting of homophobia, however slight and unintended. "I'm gay. Am I okay in your eyes?"

"Of course you are, homie. Damn."

"So being gay is okay," said Kordell, "just not for Mario Cervantes?"

"Isn't it obvious that I'm still figuring that out?" said Mario. "I can't answer that now, not at the moment. Especially not now."

"Because you just found out about us as kids?" asked Kordell.

"Because of everything." Mario stood rigid against the wall, his

fists tightened at his side. Suddenly, he exhaled. His head dropped
back until he was looking at the cloudless sky. "In the moving painting, I always pictured it being a black guy. I don't know why I blocked
your—the face out."

"I have moving paintings, too." Kordell thought of Jamaal—the
older kid who may have been his dad's out-of-wedlock son—and the
humping that young Kordell took to be horsing around but the adult
Kordell recognized as teenage Jamaal getting his rocks off at the
expense of a prepubescent Kordell. Had Jamaal passed down to
Kordell what Kordell passed down to Mario?

"Do you think they had an impact on you?" asked Mario.

"One way or another." Kordell leaned against the dumpster,
clean clothes be damned. "I'm not sure how and how much."

"Then you see where I'm coming from."

Check, Kordell thought, as if this were a game of chess.

"So what now?" he asked.

Mario stared at the marquis at the parking lot's edge. Next
week's feature: *Double Indemnity.*

"Isn't what we've been through in last few weeks way more
important than what we went through as kids?" asked Kordell.

"You saved me." Mario turned to him, looked him in the eye.
"There's no doubt about that." Then he turned away. "But maybe I
wouldn't have needed saving if what happened as a child hadn't happened—"

"Thought I wasn't the only moving painting."

"I was just about to say that. I'm not blaming you or that experience for my whole life." Mario cracked a smile. "You ain't getting
that much credit."

Kordell managed a token smile.

"More importantly," Mario focused on the marquis, "and I'm
just being honest: I'm also thinking about Javy. Maybe Javier would
still be alive if things were different. I know that's one huge 'if' right
now, but still ..."

Kordell could have stood there for the next ten years and not
come up with an appropriate response. They were at an impasse and
this was no thirty minute TV sitcom. There'd be no neat little bows

tied around this conflict, wrapping things up before the credits rolled and the network began promoting the next program.

If only we'd done this at the beach like I envisioned, Kordell thought. A picnic in the sand. At sunset. Someday when we were both emotionally prepared.

"I think I'm ready to move home now," Mario said, taking Kordell by surprise.

"Because we might … because of any awkwardness?"

"No," Mario said hastily, then confessed: "Well, maybe a little."

"You should know I haven't been trying to, I mean, I find you attractive, yes, very attractive, but I don't know if I could ever act on, I mean, as an adult, I don't know how comfortable I'd feel being physical with you unless we got past … know what I mean?"

"That's why you jump out of your skin whenever I touch you," Mario said, half-joking, half-serious.

"Not true," Kordell said with equal parts truth and humor. "But you're welcome to stay. Regardless."

"It's all right, really."

"As long as you like."

"I'm cool."

Kordell's mind mobilized with all the reasons they should continue as temporary roomies and how they could work through their issues with open, honest communication and maybe even mutual therapy sessions. Typical Kordell Christie. Ready, aim, fire. Only this time, as all his ammo was marching from his brain to his vocal cords, he did something different: he shut the hell up.

The man is an adult, Kordell thought. Didn't I do enough coercing him as a child?

"Hey batter batter, hey batter batter," Sal shouted from the aluminum bleachers.

"You're supposed to cheer *for* your son, not against him." Jenna tapped her lover's head with mock scorn.

"The kid needs to learn to play with distractions," Sal said, then shouted to Fredito, who was inside the batting cage: "Come on, sweetie, show Mama what you learned at camp. Show me how you're

gonna make more money than Alex Rodriguez and buy Mama a brand new mansion up in the hills."

"*Chile*, you're shameless," said Jenna.

"Can I live in the guest house?" Arthur asked. He was laying on his back on the top bleacher, soaking up the sun.

"I'm gonna buy Mommy *six* mansions," Fredito said as he choked up on the bat and swatted another ball into the outer reaches of the cage. Kordell, who was sitting next to Arthur's horizontal body, nodded to the white adobe building behind them and said:

"All I want is an autographed photo for the arcade."

"Hell," said Sal. "I want Batter Up renamed for my son."

Another ball came whizzing out of the pitching machine. Fredito swung with all his might. He made contact, but the ball didn't set sail as expected. Instead, it died a humble, naked death a few feet in front of the plate. Fredito's cut had ripped the cover right off the ball.

"Call up the big leagues and fast!" Arthur cried out.

"What's the age minimum for a Dodger rookie?" Sal asked with mock panic.

"I'm gonna be like Jeter," Fredito said just before laying into another pitch. "Not A-Rod."

"You go boy!" Arthur turned to Kordell. "Now there's a sandwich I'd kill or die to be in the middle of: Derek Jeter and Alex Rodriguez. Yum, yum. They can pull a double play on me anytime."

"I'll still take the Rock over any man alive," said Kordell. "Wrestling rules."

"Don't you mean *wrestlers* rule?" asked Arthur.

"Guys, guys," Sal said in a low voice to the men behind her. "Give it a rest, *aiight*? Yes, under normal circumstances, I want Freddy to hear all points of view so he can see that girls or guys talking about girls *or* guys is normal, but … we ain't reached 'normal circumstances' quite yet—agreed?"

"Agreed," said Kordell, Arthur and Jenna.

Sure they had plenty of reasons for this celebration picnic—Fredito's return from baseball camp, tomorrow's re-opening of Batter Up, the fact that their lives and friendships were mending—but they had only just passed the one month anniversary of the fall

of Pizarro and Company and the wounds and scars were still there. Healing, but there.

"Would you take the Rock over that man?" Arthur asked, nudging Kordell with his foot and nodding toward the tall fence that separated Batter Up from the street.

Kordell turned expectantly and grinned when he saw who was standing on the other side of the gate.

"He's baaack," Arthur said ominously.

"Speaking of being in the middle of a sandwich," whispered Sal.

Kordell shushed them, hopped down from the bleachers and headed for the gate.

"Thanks for coming," he said when he reached the end of the driveway, not bothering to hide his smile. "I'm glad you're here. Good to see you."

"I couldn't not be part of a celebration that I caused to begin with." Mario was also smiling. "I mean, one I put the wheels in motion for, I mean … sorry, kinda nervous."

"I feel ya." Kordell took in the sight of Mario's anxious face, which was checkered with thin shadows from the chain-link fence. "So how have you been?"

"Working hard deejaying," said Mario. "Making up for lost time and money."

"Heard that," Kordell said, realizing that since *Spellbound interruptus*, seemingly every conversation between them began with the same stilted awkwardness.

Their time spent together had diminished considerably, but the space and distance turned out to be what they both needed to reclaim their respective lives and digest all that had happened. They still had their weekly hospital visits and subsequent matinee movie, but other than a few late night, "can't sleep" phone calls, they hadn't seen much of one another.

"So," Mario said, kicking up dirt with his sneakers. "Your friends ready for me?"

"Are you ready for them?" asked Kordell.

Mario squinted, sizing up Kordell's pals from afar. "What do they know?"

"Everything," said Kordell. "Well, but … well …"

"Yeah, *that*. Good." Mario exhaled his relief. "What about the grandma?"

"Down in LA visiting other relatives before heading back to San Salvador. Everything's right in her world now that Freddy's fine. And he is."

"Cool, cool," Mario said absently.

"Are you ashamed of it?"

"No, no." Mario knew Kordell meant their childhood experience.

"Hard to stop being hard on myself," Kordell said sheepishly.

"I'm here, aren't I?" Mario held onto the fence above his head with both hands, a casual pose: homie hanging. "We still go to the movies on Fridays, don't we?"

"And I'm glad for that," said Kordell, "especially the part about you being here today."

"Cool." Mario fell silent, seemingly unsure what to say next.

"Mario, I can't change the past. I can only apologize for any negative effect it had on your life. And if it did, it doesn't matter if I was a kid or a ninety year-old man: I'm sorry. I'm truly, truly sorry."

"It's cool, homie." Mario said without looking up. "I accept your apology."

"And I promise to be a better friend to you and to learn from my past experiences, all of them, including what we just went through. And I'm not gonna just dwell on the negative parts of the gay world. I'm gonna take the good with the bad. And do what I can as a strong, out and proud black gay man to encourage the good and deal with the not-so-good. In a healthy way. Lord knows, we don't need no more Pizarros or Brother Johns."

Mario looked him in the eye. "You given this a lot of thought, haven't you?"

Kordell nodded and they shared a warm, friendly smile.

"I appreciate that," said Mario. "I really do. And I don't know where we go from here, but ..." He trailed off, his attention commandeered by something in the distance over Kordell's shoulder. Kordell turned and saw what Mario saw: Koji Yamamoto, looking quite healthy and tanned in a white tank top and khaki shorts. He was walking from the arcade to the bleachers, carrying a large cool-

er on one of his bare shoulders, looking like an Asian Hercules.

"What's he doing here?" Mario blurted.

Kordell shrugged. "He's recovered from his wounds and back to his old self. Or, I guess I should say, his real self."

That didn't answer Mario's question and both Kordell and Mario knew it.

"We made a connection during everything," said Kordell. "He's an interesting guy. We've had dinner a couple of times."

"You're dating him?" Mario let go of the fence and took a barely perceptible step backward.

"No ... no ... we haven't ... no, just dinners. And stuff. He's into video games, too."

"But you're dating him," Mario said, a statement more than a question.

"I'm not dating anybody, Mario. But I do want to get to know him. To what extent I have no idea."

Mario looked away. Was that hurt in his eyes? Hard to tell with the shadows from the fence on his face.

"Yamo's a nice guy," Kordell said. "And so are you. I want you both in my life. And for something good to come out of—"

"So our friendship isn't a good thing to come out of all this? Helping me isn't a good thing?"

"Of course it is—"

"I mean, he shoved a phone up your ass!" said Mario. "You guys have been practically intimate."

"To help us. *Hello?* And it was in Saran Wrap, you know. And just in my butt cheeks." Kordell stopped, unsure what to say next.

"I'm sorry." Mario shifted uneasily, then said sheepishly: "This is ... listen to me ... I have no right ... my bad."

"It's okay, Mario, really."

"I got no problem with you living your life," Mario said, his tone truly repentant. "I just mean, like, well, do you still find me ... is there still ... are we ... you know ..."

"Are you saying you're ready to think about ..."

"That's not what I'm saying at all," insisted Mario. "I mean, you're not ... are you?"

"Ready to … you?" asked Kordell. "No. Not ready. Not ready at all."

"Ditto," said Mario.

"And may never be," said Kordell.

"Big time ditto," said Mario. "Or who knows?"

"Or who knows?" repeated Kordell. Both men paused, then broke out in laughter. If you're gonna have issues, it pays to have friends in the same boat, more or less.

Kordell opened the gate and, for the second time ever, Mario entered the grounds of Batter Up.

"There is one thing I'm ready for," Mario said as they walked.

"Yeah, what's that?"

"To open up a can of whoop ass on you in the arcade."

"Oh, you think so, huh?" Kordell said with a cocky smile and a good dose of rough bravado. "I know you are not challenging the owner of this establishment at *his* own games."

"Oh, it ain't got to be no challenge," Mario said, sounding all bad-ass. "It's just a fact. Yo' ass is going down. In Boxorama. In Daytona Dash. In air hockey. In foosball."

"Man, you better check yourself before you wreck yourself," said Kordell. "Either that or put some money down to back it up …"

Fredito was busy hammering homeruns in the batting cage and Sal and Jenna were in the bleachers capturing their boy on tape. Kordell and Mario were still jawing and woofing about who was going to do what to whom when they joined Arthur and Koji at the picnic table behind the backstop.

"What's got you two talking like two ghetto thug wannabes?" Arthur asked upon hearing the commotion.

Kordell indicated Mario. "Homeboy here thinks he's better than me at *my* video games."

"I don't think," said Mario. "I been there and done that."

"Watch out, Mario." Arthur put his arms around Kordell. "Miss Thang here is a Video Game Queen."

From the other side of the picnic table, Koji threw Mario a soda. Mario caught it, nodded "thanks," and both men understood that they had just said hello. Was there already some sort of unspoken rivalry between them for Kordell's affection? True or not, Kordell

allowed himself a brief moment to become giddy with the notion.

"Watch this one, Uncle Kord," Fredito called out from the batting cage.

"Watching," said Kordell.

"You better both be warned," Koji said to Kordell and Mario. "I got baseball *and* video games in my blood. The Japanese perfected both, you know."

"The Japanese perfected baseball?" Kordell asked incredulously.

"Asians in general," said Koji, "if you wanna get technical."

"Latinos dominate baseball, homie." Mario began counting with his fingers: "Pedro, Nomar, Luis Gonzales."

Koji began counting with his fingers: "Ichiro, Nomo, Sasaki."

"Don't forget about the bruthas." Kordell began counting with his fingers: "Bonds, Henderson, Williams."

"Hold on," said Arthur. "Let me represent with some white baseball boys—Sal, Jenna, gimme some jock names!"

"You'd think they were straight the way they're thumping their chests," Jenna said as she joined the men standing around the table. Right away, she greeted Mario with a hug, commenting that he looked much better than the last time she'd seen him, the day he was freed from the Facility. As Mario thanked her, Kordell saw Sal approaching. She too had not seen Mario since that day. Kordell tensed up as mother and former alleged molester came together, a groundbreaking ceremony of sorts.

"Welcome, Mario." Sal extended her hand. They shook.

"Thanks," said Mario. "Big time. I mean it."

"*De nada.*" Sal waved her hand as if it were nothing, then grabbed a paper plate and called out to her son in the batting cage. "Fredito, come meet—"

"I know Mario." Fredito hit one last pitch, turned off the pitching machine by pushing a remote box on the fence and joined the party at the picnic table.

"Good to see you again, Fredito," Mario said when they stood face-to-face.

Kordell, Sal, Jenna, Arthur and Koji collectively froze. If Sal and Mario shaking hands was a groundbreaking ceremony, Fredito and

Mario breathing the same air was an experiment of epic proportions.

"I just got back from baseball camp," Fredito told Mario very matter-of-factly. "Did you ever play ball?"

"In school I played big time."

Mario began recounting his glory days as a high school athlete, but Kordell, Sal, Jenna, Arthur and Koji didn't hear a word of it. They were too busy appreciating the relief that was evident in each of their eyes as they glanced around at one another. As had been the case that fateful morning after Gay Pride, Fredito possessed only positive energy toward Mario. The young boy had always maintained that he did not think he was on the receiving end of Bad Touch from Mario. And thanks to Uncle Kord, who put his life on the line to find out the truth, some very bad, homophobic men were put out of business, Mario's temporary illness had been cured and summer was going to be all about baseball and Monkey Warriors.

"… but the three no-hitters is what I'm proud of most," Mario said in summation of his own career on the diamond.

"Jenna," —Sal put an arm around her lover's shoulders— "let's show these males what the sisters can do with a bat and ball."

"You go right ahead," Jenna told Sal. "I'll film it and send it into one of those blooper shows for some prize money."

"Now batting," Sal announced as she headed for the cage, "Superwoman!"

Fredito laughed. "She doesn't even know how to hold the bat."

"Then don't make fun of me, *mijo*, show me." Sal picked up a bat, tapped it in the dirt and grabbed her crotch like a man in over-dramatic fashion.

"I've got to record this." Jenna hurried to the bleachers and the camera.

"Mom, let me show you what to do." Eager to be the one in the know, Fredito joined Sal in the batting cage. As he began the daunting task of turning his mom into a baseball player, the men ate and watched in amusement and Jenna captured mother and child on tape from the stands.

"Who would have thought the summer would turn out so good?" Arthur said to Kordell at one point. They were sitting on top

of the picnic table, polishing off their sandwiches.

"Friends who stick together can make it through anything." Kordell let out a deep appreciative breath. They hugged while sitting and when they untangled themselves, they realized that Mario and Koji had moved over to a spot between the bleachers and the building that housed the arcade. Koji had a bat in his hands and, from their motions, they appeared to be talking baseball, perhaps giving each other the *SportsCenter* version of their individual career highlights.

"Is this gonna be a day all about testosterone?" asked Arthur. "Because if it is, I'll need to rent a porn movie on the way home. I'm feeling like a little—or should I say, a lot of—Bobby Blake tonight. Brutha got it goin' on front *and* back."

"Arthur, please." Kordell stood up, crossed his legs and winced ever so slightly.

"That steel contraption from the Facility still ruining your sex drive?" asked Arthur.

Kordell readjusted his pants to provide more comfort and space. "I get hard now and it doesn't hurt. I just can't get *too* hard *too* often or—let's just say it doesn't feel pretty."

Arthur nodded in the direction of Koji and Mario. "So I guess sex with either of your beaus is outta the question."

"And how."

"When do the doctors think you'll be a full-fledged, raging homosexual again?"

"Soon, soon," Kordell said hopefully, never taking his eyes off Yamo and Mario, who were still engrossed in sports talk, seemingly trying to one-up each other. "Trust me. My reproductive organs will be just fine much sooner than later."

"And when that happens, watch out world!" Arthur held up his hands as if to shine a spotlight on the new, improved and recovered version of his friend.

"I'm getting there." Kordell laughed and smiled, still eying the new men in his life. "Believe me when I say: I am definitely getting there."

RANDY BOYD has been a professional writer all his adult life. His first novel, *Uprising,* was nominated for two Lambda Literary Awards: Best Men's Mystery and Best Small Press Title. His second novel, *Bridge Across the Ocean,* was a Lambda Literary Award nominee for Best Small Press Title. Randy's words have appeared in numerous other publications and anthologies, including *Frontiers* magazine, *Flesh and the Word 2, Buttmen 2, Friends and Lovers: Gay Men Write About the Families They Create* and *Best Gay Erotica 2001.* Currently, Randy divides his time between Indiana and California and lives with his dog Boomer, who is named after the Indiana Pacers mascot, and who is also known as The Boo, Phat Dog and many other monikers.

ACKNOWLEDGEMENTS

Thanks to Alan Bell for his tireless work and dedication to all my projects. Plus, thanks to the following individuals who contributed their unique perspective and expertise to various subjects relating to this suspense thriller: Newlyn Kozan, Emerson Mancia, Robert Gaylord, and Joshua De Mers. Special love and thanks for my family and friends, who are like angels to me. Big thanks to Max for bringing such boundless joy into my life and that of my family's. And last, but in no way least, thanks to all who have bought a novel by Randy Boyd and passed on a kind word, thought or recommendation to a friend. Your support is greatly appreciated.

west beach books ● more about the devil inside ●
coming up next ● in the author's own words ●
● submission info ● contact west beach books ●
the book ● other west beach books ● more about
tact the author ● coming up next ● in the
reviews ● author photos ● submission info ●
ty butt challenge ● behind the book ● other west
buttmenfunzone.com ● contact the author ●
write your own review ● reviews ● author photos
ebook info ● celebrity butt challenge ● behind
the devil inside ● buttmenfunzone.com ● in the
ing up next ● write your own review ● reviews ●
beach books ● ebook info ●

celebrity butt **surf's up** challenge ●

behind the book ● more about the devil inside ●
● contact the author ● coming up next ● in the
reviews ● author photos ● submission info ●
ty butt challenge ● behind the book ● other west
buttmenfunzone.com ● contact the author ●
write your own review ● reviews ● author photos
ebook info ● celebrity butt challenge ● behind
the devil inside ● buttmenfunzone.com ● in the
ing up next ● write your own review ● reviews ●
beach books ● ebook info ● behind the book ●
inside ● buttmenfunzone.com ● celebrity butt
● in the author's own words ● write your own
info ● contact west beach books ● ebook info ●

buttmenfunzone.com • contact the author • write your own review • reviews • author photos ebook info • celebrity butt challenge • behind the devil inside • buttmenfunzone.com • con- author's own words • write your own review • contact west beach books • ebook info • celebri- beach books • more about the devil inside • coming up next • in the author's own words • • submission info • contact west beach books • the book • other west beach books • more about author's own words • contact the author • com- author photos • submission info • contact west

www.westbeachbooks.com

buttmenfunzone.com • other west beach books author's own words • write your own review • contact west beach books • ebook info • celebri- beach books • more about the devil inside • coming up next • in the author's own words • • submission info • contact west beach books • the book • other west beach books • more about author's own words • contact the author • com- author photos • submission info • contact west other west beach books • more about the devil challenge • contact the author • coming up next review • reviews • author photos • submission celebrity butt challenge • behind the book •

Also from Randy Boyd

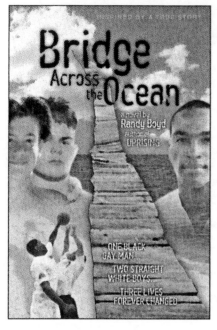

"A funny, sexy and very poignant summertime novel."
Gay & Lesbian Times

"Sincere and suspenseful, *Bridge Across the Ocean* is a great escape and a very important piece of writing, something Randy Boyd should be very proud of."
XY Magazine

"An intimate novel with raw emotion. The sexual attraction and the conflict it poses are beautifully handled. Ultimately, this is a powerful, emotional novel that cannot help but move the reader. The book works on every level, and Randy Boyd is definitely a writer to reckon with."
Lambda Book Report

ONE BLACK GAY MAN
TWO STRAIGHT WHITE BOYS
THREE LIVES FOREVER CHANGED

Bridge Across the Ocean by Randy Boyd

A Lambda Literary Award Finalist

**Available at bookstores and on the net
In traditional print and eBook formats**

www.westbeachbooks.com

Also from Randy Boyd

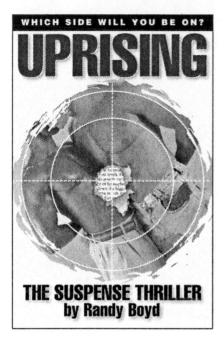

WHICH SIDE WILL YOU BE ON?

UPRISING

THE SUSPENSE THRILLER
by Randy Boyd

"*Uprising* offers a surprise at every turn."
Kick Magazine

"A striking, exciting and thought-provoking thriller."
Zenger's Magazine

"A provocative, compelling tome that is decidedly not politically correct. The story—part thriller, part love story—adds up to a morality tale that basically asks the reader: is violence ever justified?"
IN Los Angeles

"Not only is *Uprising* thoroughly entertaining as a suspense thriller, [it] deals frankly and directly with some of the most important issues of our age."
The Blade Newsmagazine

**Three closeted celebrities
One homophobic US Senator
A deadly plan of assassination
A straight FBI agent out to stop it**

Which side will you be on?

UPRISING by Randy Boyd

Nominated for two Lambda Literary Awards
Best Men's Mystery and Best Small Press Title

**Available at bookstores and on the net
In traditional print and eBook formats**

www.westbeachbooks.com

Printed in the United States
1187800001B/412